De𝚊

(A Li𝚗 ...𝚜𝚑i𝚛e Murder Mystery)

Spit v.
be the spit (or the dead spit)
of
look exactly like

by

Cary Smith

ISBN: 978-1-291-41484-4

PROLOGUE

November 12th 2011

The long agonizing wait was finally over as shivering emotion wrapped its long arms to smother an embrace of hideous fear. The figure at the front door had run through the procedure dozens of times. Even practiced parts of it to ensure it was exactly right. Absolutely no room for error.

The letter box was rattled hard with a black gloved hand which was then pulled off and stuffed into a trouser pocket. Big black coat flung open wide, stomach grasped, face screwed up in pretence of agony as movement was just perceived behind the spy hole.

Help was requested close to the door, in the fraught hope Caron Gorich would hear, but prayed the neighbours would not. The door opened and then jammed as the chain clunked and held firm. A further frantic plea through the gap, and the young woman was told there'd been a stabbing. Door closed, the rattle and scrape of chain and the green door opened, as nerves engulfed mind and body. A wretched appeal for aid was made again as young Gorich in grey and pink jogging suit looked down at the mess of blood oozing through the white shirt and fingers. For a second as emotions close to terror overcame all else there was a desperate need to run. The plea for her help was repeated and the bloodied figure stepped forward as the door opened wide and with a sway the hooded visitor staggered down the hall, stomach clenched to stem the flow. Heart beating fit to burst. No going back now.

Gorich ushered her unexpected arrival through to the kitchen as the front door slammed shut behind. She was all questions about what had happened, how and where it had happened as the young woman's hands acted as a guide down the hall. They turned right at the end into the kitchen and the caller slumped against a small table. Fear by now had utter control.

1

Gorich was asked for a cloth as a shaking gloved hand was stuffed into a coat pocket. Heart racing, body in acute turmoil, mind working overtime. Never ever had agitation close to this been experienced before.

Young Caron offered to phone for an ambulance and grabbed for a black mobile on the table. She was told in no uncertain terms a cloth to stem the blood was more urgent as the phone was dropped and a dirty tea towel pulled from the metal draining board. With heart beat wildly out of control when Gorich turned the figure looked into the blonde's dark ringed eyes and motioned her down to the bloodied stomach. As she crouched down the hand came out of the pocket and the short handled hammer slammed violently into her head and she sagged down into a heap on the floor.

A push away from the table in a flash, stuffing the hammer back, brain on automatic pilot took this caller through the well rehearsed system. A packet from an inside pocket was next, a syringe slid out and held up. Great difficulty stuffing the packet out of sight before bending down to find the point in the pale neck.

'Just a prick,' was followed by a snigger and the dank pony tail had to be brushed aside as the intruder struggled to stop hands shaking and the needle was slid into the victim and then slowly the plunger was pushed down.

This violent grockle stood up and checked the floor all around. Next was a hand wash in the sink as part of the planned process, with second black cycling glove off. Water swilled and washing-up liquid used to wash hands quickly, wipe the sink and tap thoroughly with a dirty dish cloth that was then stuffed into a coat pocket. Nitrile gloves pulled from a shirt pocket were pulled on furiously and it was time to walk back into the hall to put the chain back and slip the sneck down on the front door. With heart still beating wildly it was necessary to creep slowly but silently up the threadbare carpeted stairs to peer into one room dominated by an unmade bed strewn with clothes and a hair dryer, out and into a second. A small body was spied fast asleep in a single bed. Child safety gate on the landing was closed quietly. Time taken to stop for a second to listen, and then trot quietly back down the stairs. The intruder took the trouble

2

to bend down close to her body to check Caron Gorich was dead or engulfed in a stroke that would lead to the inevitable.

Muddied footprints on the floor were quickly scuffed with a foot, gloves quickly exchanged, all pockets double checked. Hammer, synthetic gloves, cloth, spare hat, empty packet, syringe. All mentally ticked off on the check list. Top bolt slid open, key turned, backdoor opened, light turned off. The dark figure stepped out and closed the door silently. Quick check all around, woolly hat pulled down, hood up, checked left and right in the dark and walked to the back gate. Opened and closed without a sound, turned left into the passage between the houses and started on the long roundabout route home. Escape had always been a priority.

The trespasser had gone a fair way before the heart rate was anything like normal, the sweat had eased, and anxiety levels had dropped to a level one could cope with. Fear was still holding hands very tightly as hats were changed again and hood lowered. A damp cold bleak November evening was perfect in that it kept the nosey parkers indoors. The killer had bought a street map to devise a route out, a confusing roundabout route to anybody trying to retrace in the hours and days to come.

Two young lads astride bikes were passed halfway down Hemswell Avenue as the stranger strode briskly down a walkway to Uffington Avenue and headed for the close at the end. Opposite the Evangelical Church building it was a turning into a passageway and the red and white woolly hat was swapped for the black version, coat turned inside out and glasses stuffed into a zipped top pocket. From there it was quickly out onto Skellingthorpe Road opposite the Lincoln Academy. Pretence of a limp across the level crossing and beyond until Tritton Road was crossed at the lights.

The plan was recalled in detail when the next step was a quick nip into St Helens Avenue to drop the glasses into a drain and the coat turned inside out again. The limp forgotten as the stride increased all the way to St Peter and Paul's. There was something rather reassuring about reaching the church.

In Boultham Park Road there was the pre-planned pretence to tie a shoelace to enable the syringe to be plopped into a drain, then it was just a few steps into the entrance to allotments. The pay-as-you-

3

go mobile bought off a stall in Leicester Market was pulled out. 999 was pressed and when they answered it was time to turn on the tiny tape machine, hanging on a lanyard around the neck.

'A child is on its own at eight Rushams Close see' said a voice with a sort of Welsh accent. Phone switched off. 999 pressed carefully again: *'A bairn is on its oon at eight Rushams Close'* said a voice this time with a very bad attempt at Scottish. Next it was the syringe packet that had to be stamped on and heeled into the muddy ground. Back on the road into town, it was not long before Dixon Street was reached where the SIM card from the mobile was dropped over the wall and into the river. Now it was an easy stroll down to High Street and home, despite a never ending stream of attacks by a perplexing range of emotions.

Once back home and indoors all clothes were quickly removed, jogging bottoms and an old pullover thrown on. Mother was then woken enough to give her an injection as was mandatory three times a day. When that fat nurse first suggested this carer learn to deal with all of mother's demands, it seemed a good idea. That was almost a year ago. When was the last time the cow had visited at weekends? You can bet your life the bitch still claimed to have been there doing the caring, and got paid for it.

Sat at the kitchen table for half an hour with a mug of drinking chocolate and three biscuits, all thoughts were of what had happened, what had been achieved. Time to hope the child had been found safe and well.

Then it was time to clean the hammer head with wire wool, wash it and place it on top of the coat, gloves, Lincoln City bobble hat and stained white shirt on the floor. Remnants of false blood from the jar was swilled down the sink and empty jar tossed in the bin. Insoles were removed from the shoes, cleaned, polished and the now black shiny pair added to the pile. This was not the time to make a botch-up.

Upstairs for a relaxing long soak and thorough wash in a hot bath. The rampaging fear had left now, but was still within touching distance.

Very early on Sunday morning with the hammer wrapped in a carrier bag, the dirty tea towel, dish cloth and gloves had all been washed in turpentine along with the dirty shirt. All stuffed into a black dustbin bag and slipped under the load tray in the back of the old Peugeot. Tea and toast made for mother, her pills administered together with another injection and she was left comfortable with the Sunday paper. A quick note scribbled for the neighbour who promised to make regular checks, coat thrown onto the back seat and it was time to set off for Mablethorpe.

On the way, taking great care to watch the speed, wear the seat belt and drive perfectly this violator took a short diversion down a lane and into a small wood. The hammer was wrapped in another old black bin bag hid amongst the trees deep under a mass of thick bushes. The turps soaked shirt, tea towel, gloves, bobble hat and dish cloth were set fire to and the blackened charred remnants trampled into the dirt.

At Market Rasen a charity bin was located and those shiny shoes tossed inside when nobody was about before heading for the seaside.

In Mablethorpe with the car parked near the bus station close to a drain it was easy to drop the mobile in and then set off in search of a café off the High Street for a full English. It was probably nerves that made this assassin eat every last scrap. The big white platter was cleaned with a slice of bread and butter and followed down by a black coffee and two sugars. Next stop had to be the public toilets. The coat bought from a charity shop in Worksop, that had worked perfectly the previous evening was hung on the hook on the back of the cubicle door and left there once pockets had been checked for the umpteenth time. Hands washed with pink liquid soap it was time for a bit of sea breeze.

There was a real feeling of satisfaction sat on a bench on the seafront looking out into the North Sea. Real pleasure gained from thoughts of a job well done, linked with slight worries about errors made that had yet to come to mind. The sun was strong for the time of year and for an hour or more there was real enjoyment in reading a Sunday paper and taking in the views.

This had been a once in a lifetime chance to grab a place in history. One day soon a name would go down in the annals of violent crime to remain there forever, but that was for the future. First another was in line of sight. The next to pay the price.

1

MARCH 2012

Dressed in his Sunday casuals, grey cotton jacket, stone washed jeans and trainers, Detective Inspector Brian Daniels opened proceedings. There were nine detectives and three support staff sat on chairs or at work stations. The cream walls had whiteboards on two sides. Three of them had been wiped clean, obviously in haste with odd words and bits of blue writing still visible. One board had three photographs of the strangled girl, one close up of her head and shoulders showed the damage done to her neck. Written above them in red were the words KIRSTY MARIE PETCHEY.

'Thanks for that Brian,' said DCI Craig Darke, as DI Daniels moved away to sip coffee and sit in a chair on the far right hand side.

Darke didn't rush to get on with it. He looked around at his team. Some were drinking black coffee from white plastic cups provided. Others had a variety of to-go containers they'd picked up as they'd rushed to get in. Some were chewing gum, one was stuffing the remnants of a sandwich in his mouth. They were talking in groups in muted tones, aware that at any moment their boss would start. He took time to nod at those he instantly recognized. Others had been pulled in at short notice to swell the teams he was creating. Darke suddenly tapped one of the photos of Petchey with his knuckle.

'This is our victim Kirsty Petchey, and I am Detective Chief Inspector Craig Darke. I'm your Senior Investigating Officer.' He turned to his right. 'This is my deputy Detective Inspector Brian Daniels. In my investigations everybody contributes. No matter how stupid your idea may seem, no matter how trivial, I want to know about it. I'll decide what's good and what's bad. Right now Raza Latif and Ross Walker two Detective Sergeants from this force are collecting as much data as they can about her from her family and from neighbours and friends. We've got a team out there going door-to-door. SOCO and Forensics are still in the property and in the back yard where it happened. According to the doc last night she was strangled, which as you can see by the pics is pretty bloody obvious, and we'll know more after the PM. She's separated from her ex-boyfriend.' He glanced down at the pad in his hand. 'Hank Harding, but he's not been located so far. We've got two lads out checking into that aspect at a couple of addresses we've been given, and we've put out an APB on his car so with a bit of luck he'll be crossing our radar pretty soon.'

Brian Daniels put down his cup and stood up. 'Ten o'clock last night the next door neighbour Helen Mackay was in her spare bedroom. Thought she saw flashing lights. Opened the curtains, and then opened the window. Some silly bugger's setting off fireworks across the way. While she's watching she happens to look down and sees somebody sprawled out on the patio next door. We got the call at ten seventeen, after she'd gone downstairs, nipped round and found Kirsty Petchey dead.' He looked at and nodded to DS Ian 'Tigger' Woods who got to his feet and faced the audience, while slim Daniels went back to his coffee.

'From what we've been able to gather so far,' said Woods. 'Intel says Kirsty got herself pregnant by this Hank Harding and got a gimme council flat on the Ermine. Since the bust up, we don't know as yet where Harding's been living, but what we do know is that Jonah White aka Jonah P.Chrome has been shacked up…' brought moans from the audience.

'Hold on there,' said DCI Darke. 'Jonah White aka Jonah P. Chrome. What's that all about?'

'Rap boss. He's a DJ and…'

'Amongst other things!'

'He's a DJ,' the short and well built Tigger Woods continued.

'This Jonah. He a Rasta knob? All baggy jeans and pseudo Jamaican gangsta bitch talk he got off a rap album?' Woods nodded. 'And while we're at it. Is his name really Hank Harding?'

'As far as we know.'

An exasperated Darke turned back in his seat. 'Carry on.'

'Short for Henry, sir.'

'Think it's Dutch. Could be worse,' mumbled Daniels. 'Some poor sod's called Audio Science and another's Moon Unit.' He

7

realized all eyes were on him. 'It's true. Daisy Boo and Harper Seven may be crap but there's a lot worse.'

'That must be child abuse surely,' added a chuckling Darke. 'Carry on.'

'Jonah White's been shacked up with the dead girl. Little man thinks he's big man, fingers in a lot of pies. Into all this rap and hip-hop shit, right. So if you like we have two names in the frame. And we don't know where either of them are.' As he said that Detective Inspector Warren wrote HANK HARDING and JONAH WHITE/JONAH P.CHROME on the whiteboard. Billy Warren then walked to centre stage. Hair cut short emphasized his thick neck and broad jowls.

'You can ask about in the case of our Jonah; plenty know him. Harding's not so easy. Got nothing on him, nothing on PMC not even a parking ticket. Anybody heard of him?' There was no response. 'Get some forensics and we could get lucky and pin it on one of them.' He looked across at Darke, who rose to his feet, placed his plastic cup on a small table and propped himself up against it.

'Caron Gorich from last November is still very much on our radar, but as you all know we've so far drawn a blank.' Darke glanced at the door. 'Some people upstairs are asking questions. Young woman smacked over the head in her own kitchen by some bastard good with a syringe. Every line of enquiry needs exhausting. With her, even looking at bloody doctors, nurses and paramedics brought us to a dead end, to coin a phrase. Nothing stolen, no sex, no DNA, no nothing except for what Forensics think was home made false blood.'

'They were selling false blood in the supermarket at Halloween,' DS Goodwin contributed.

Darke went on. 'Always remember, if you talk to enough people in the end something will drop.' He pushed himself off from the table and walked the few paces to the white board and tapped the picture of Kirsty Petchey. 'Natalie Scoley and Sammy Lloyd will be joining the team. Sammy will be going through the Caron Gorich files and creating a database of matching facts.' He put a hand up. 'I know there isn't much to go on with Gorich, but how about her toddler?' He tapped Kirsty Petchey's picture. 'She's also got a small

8

kid. I know it's not much but it's a start. Did Caron Gorich catch the shit that killed her, messing with her lad? And.' He stopped to emphasize what he was saying. 'Did Kirsty Petchey catch the same bastard messing with her little girl? If this is a bloody paedo, I want him fast. Sammy will create this database of similarities. I know it's not the same MO, but we've got two women in their twenties, separated from their blokes, both with young kids. I want Sammy to put the salient points on those two boards so we can all see them. Twenty two year old on one board, twenty one year old on the other. Two year old kid on one, three year old on the other. Both killed in the evening and so on.' He turned to pick up his plastic cup, downed what was left of his coffee and licked his lips. 'Also,' he said to his attentive audience. 'I want you to put your heads together about what Forensics thought might be fake blood. You go to smack her over the head and pump air into her system. Why would you take blood? Maybe it wasn't his blood. Had Caron Gorich been to a fancy dress do recently? It was November. Bit late for Halloween, but always possible those two or three droplets Forensics found were still there from then.'

'I'll let you know about the next briefing when we see what we get today,' said DI Brian Daniels. 'With a bit of luck Forensics might have come up with something. So for now we'll say eight sharp every morning. No excuses.' He walked the few paces to the whiteboard at the end listing all the teams. 'Billy,' he said to DI Warren. 'You're heading the Comms team. Need her phone calls soonest, and can you put someone onto the nearest CCTV as fast as you can.' Next it was Jake Goodwin's turn. 'Jake, as a priority can you look up the local paedos who like very young girls and boys. PM scheduled for Monday morning. Thank you.'

'Wait a sec,' said Darke loud enough to stop them all in their tracks. 'Think on this. Did Kirsty Petchey know Caron Gorich's husband? Did Gorich know Hank Harding or that rap prat Jonah whatever? That'll be enough to keep you going,' he said. He waved them all away. 'Thank you.'

Willowy Brian Daniels waited until the room cleared except for Natalie Scoley and fair haired Sammy Lloyd. 'You think we're talking serial killer?' he asked his boss.

9

'Serial possibly but not a signature killer'' replied Darke. 'They sometimes start off as peeping toms with a slice of what they fancy, and then they go a step further, and then finish up eating the whole damn cake! With them everything's the same. Not what we've got here. Signature killers tend to have low self esteem. Lot of people like that go to gyms. Go to build a better body to cover their inadequacies. I hope I'm wrong, but I see the kid as a clue in each case. Could be he's molested...I say he, but these days who knows? For all we know our man has molested a lot more, but in these two cases he's been caught by the mothers.'

'Why carry a syringe, sir?' Sammy threw in.

Darke shrugged. 'That blows a big hole in my theory, but we'll stick with it for now. Always possible a druggie had one on him and used it. God knows what goes through the minds of these morons.'

'Make life easier if we did.'

'You taking me back to the crime scene?'

'Yes boss,' said Brian Daniels.

Craig Darke had a life where half was on the way up and the other half just stagnated. He was achieving what he had set out to with his career. He had managed to develop a good team around him and he had in the main been very successful.

His personal life was an altogether different ball game. He had been dealt a bad hand from which he had never seemed to recover.

Born and brought up in the south of the county. From university he had joined the Staffordshire Constabulary as a graduate entry. In his mid-twenties he had met and married a physiotherapist from a local hospital and they were buying their first home together.

. One cold, dark and wet winter's evening he and another detective sergeant were out investigating a series of assaults when a call came over the radio. There'd been an extremely bad road traffic accident, half a mile in front of them. As they were so close the pair went to see if they could offer any assistance.

When they got down to the dual carriageway, there were ambulances, a fire engine and other police cars. The occupant of one of the cars had been driving home in the pouring rain after work behind a big lorry. The lorry stopped suddenly, she stopped but a

10

juggernaut behind didn't. Ploughed into her and pushed her and her car right under the rear of the lorry in front.

As if that wasn't enough the ambulance took her from the horrific crash scene back to the Accident and Emergency Department at the very hospital the dead woman had just left. Driver got two years for dangerous driving and lost his licence for three. Craig Darke had lost his young wife.

Insurance paid off the mortgage, he shared her life insurance payout with her parents, but after a year knew he had to find pastures new, to move away from the constant stream of memories that seemed to clog his every waking hour. Places he visited, the people he met, the sights he saw all reminded him of her. Especially that stretch of dual carriageway just out of town. So, he moved back to Lincolnshire where he had originated. It was an attempt to put all those sad memories behind him. Not to forget Katherine entirely, that he would never do. Just push the constant reminders to the back of his mind for a while

For years he had just put his head down and got on with his career, but as the promotions came his way he found rank moved him further and further away from the only friends he had, within the force.

There had been a few women in his life, but relationships all seemed so fleeting. Craig knew his memories had an effect on how he treated women. Aware that he could not help but think about what may lie ahead in life. He was also very sure that one or two sensed they were playing the role of a substitute.

2

Craig Darke had been kept up to the minute on progress or lack of it with the Kirsty Petchey case. When he arrived at the briefing, he knew the eager looks were about to get trampled on, and he was pleased that Detective Superintendent Alan Greenhalgh wanted to handle the press. Darke was sure some clever dick from the local paper or radio would ask about Caron Gorich. Some local reporter looking for Brownie points would try to link the two, write a load of tosh and sell it to the tabloids, if they could find space amongst the celebrity garbage.

Thirteen people in the room with ten about to get the bad news.

'Ligature strangulation,' said DI Brian Daniels reading from the post mortem report. A thin almost imperceptible stripe in the cloth of his jacket made him appear taller than he was. A receding hairline had a few grey hairs at each temple. 'Probably using an industrial plastic tie or two tied together. Sort you can get from any DIY store. Over her head and yanked on it. According to the pathologist it broke the skin almost all the way round and damn near broke her neck. No syringe this time.'

'Doc reckons,' said Darke holding his hands up to form a circle as if he had a lasso. 'Came up behind her, dropped it over her head, pulled hard, knee in the back and she's on the floor.' He continued to demonstrate with thin air. 'Foot in the small of her back and he pulled up like shit. Didn't stand a chance. People next door never heard a thing, but they did have the tele on, watching some rubbish. Daughter was listening to crap music on big earphones that probably cost an arm and a leg.'

Daniels dropped the file onto a desk beside him and picked up another. 'Jonah P. Chrome was doing a gig at the Zouk Club in Nottingham. I hope I've got this right. Did three sets of bachata mixed rap, rhythmic and mainstream urban.' He turned a page. 'Hank Harding.' He looked up. 'Yes that is his real name. His old man's into cowboy films apparently,' he sniggered. 'Anyway,' he said returning to his file. 'Our Hank is shagging some tart in Newark these days. Was in a pub with his mates and this female and two others till late, and then went back to her place.' He looked up. 'He's got a problem now. He's got to look after young Amelie unless the poor kid gets taken into care. But according to Jake who interviewed him.' Daniels looked across at him. 'Seems Harding's a decent sort of bloke, reckons his new woman'll take the kid on. So one bit of good news.' He looked at his crime scene co-ordinator DS Ian Woods. 'All yours Tigger.'

DS Woods stood up and let the silence reign. A bull of a man who was their link with Forensics. 'That's it,' and went to move away. Grinning as he did so. 'Nothing. Forensics have got sweet bugger all. Not a bloody tickle about anything. Haven't even got fake blood we had back in November. No tissue in the samples taken from her fingernails, except hers. Must have been clawing at her own neck. Kirsty Petchey and our Jonah took her daughter over to her mother's place mid afternoon.' He checked his notes. 'Jonah went off to Nottingham around seven, shortly after a friend called round and as far as we can gather this friend,' he glanced at his notes again. 'April Matthews was the last person to see her alive. She says she left Petchey on her own around twenty past seven. Didn't see anybody hanging about. She lives two streets away and her partner says she got back around half sevenish.'

'That's the good news about the bad news,' said Darke as he got to his feet. 'Kirsty Petchey now and Caron Gorich last year both no DNA, no nothing. That's telling me it's the same person. This is planned, but our big question is why? Our Jonah P.Chrome has only heard of Caron Gorich because her name was in the paper and on radio when she was killed. He might be a complete Rasta toss pot who thinks he's a music maestro but I don't think he's got the bloody gumption to plan this or carry it out. Anyway, doubt if he can do sod all without a bass and drum beat,' brought a few chuckles. 'Our lonesome cowboy Hank doesn't know Caron Gorich, only knows our Rasta by reputation and neither of them know Caron's Man U supporter husband Lovan Gorich. That's according to them and a whole bunch of folk we've interviewed.'

'Know what this looks like, boss?' Darke looked at his deputy. 'Our troubles have doubled.' He just nodded slowly.

13

'Have we looked at Facebook, boss?' tall DS Ross Walker asked. 'Do both women have the same Friends?'

'Good thinking Ross. Job for you Billy.' Darke looked around the room. 'Where is there an obvious blank on the board? There's not much that matches from one woman to the other, but what one is shouting at you?'

'Both brown hair,' was on suggestion.

'I said blank. What is glaring at you from the Gorich list but is blank for Petchey?'

'Blunt instrument and syringe,' said DS Goodwin. 'But only one method for Petchey.'

'Blank.'

'Phone call.'

'Well done Raz. We got that phone call about Gorich's son being alone, but we didn't get one about Petchey.'

'Kid wasn't there, boss,' said Daniels beside him.

'How did he know?' Darke posed, but didn't wait for an answer. 'He didn't phone about the kid being on its own because he knew it wasn't.' He went on. 'There is absolutely no evidence, forensics, DNA or snot to show our man put a foot inside the house. So how did he know there was no kid indoors, or upstairs in bed?' He waited a moment. 'He must have known her, knew her daughter wasn't there. Now we do know it's not random.'

'With Gorich,' said Ross Walker. 'We don't know how he got from Hartsholme where he killed her to where he made his famous phone call. Orange say the call went through their base station at the back of the YMCA on Tritton Road. What does that tell us? Where…'

'The future's orange. That cuts it down!'

'As I was saying,' Walker went on. 'Where was he by then? Did he walk, bike, drive?'

'Big time difference with those methods,' Jake Goodwin suggested. 'Could have gone any way.'

'How d'you mean?'

'Phone company says a call was made in that area. Cheap jack pay-as-you-go can't be more specific. By car, even on a bike he could be heading into town or went down Tritton Road, Dixon Street and then back along. Or did Skellingthorpe Road down to the church. Then right after the call he's gone off to Hykeham, any bloody where.'

'He's bloody gone whichever way you look at it!'

'No sightings of the yellow coat after Tritton Road, so that one's not on foot round there,' said Walker.

'Back to the Petchey house,' said a frustrated Darke. 'He knew Petchey enough to know the kid was staying overnight with her mother. So he does know them, or in this case at least knew what she was doing.' Darke pointed to the picture of Kirsty Petchey. 'Off out for the night. One of those one shoulder on, one off things. How easy did she make it for him to bloody strangle her?' He walked a pace or two and pointed to CLOTHING written on the comparison board. 'Grey and pink jogging suit for one, but bare neck for the other. Didn't have to piss about with a syringe. Over her head in the dark, quick tug and bingo we've got a cadaver.'

'Got to be bloody close boss to know what she's going to wear.'

'Knew her enough to know she'd go out all tarted up,' said their DCI looking very pleased with himself. 'Bare neck, bare arms, and yards of cleavage on display. Stupid shoes so she'd be unstable. Easy peasy. You can't fight off some bastard with a cable tie round your throat when you can't keep your balance. Get desperate, break your ankle and you're in all sorts of trouble.' He slapped his hands together. 'Knew her enough, to know that.' He smiled. 'Two days ago we knew bugger all, now we're getting somewhere. Our man knew her enough to know she was a sea of flesh, unsightly badly drawn slag tags and a cheap dress two sizes too small. Am I right?' he asked Sammy who nodded. He rested himself on the edge of a table. 'Billy.'

'Yes.'

'Facebook. You find any friends that match; I want their names on my desk.'

'Will do.'

'And if you don't find any, I want to know that too.'

'What about Twitter and YouTube?' Raza asked.

'Have a word with IT please Billy,' said Brian Daniels. 'Tell them what we're looking for; ask their opinion on how we tackle it.'

15

'Boss,' said Tigger. 'Have these two women ever worked, do we know? Could that be a link? Somebody they both knew through work?'

'Add that to your lists. Thanks Tig.'

'Another line of enquiry is his route away. We all know what witnesses have told us about men between Hartsholme, Tritton Road and down to the church. Think about him going the opposite way, through Hartsholme Park into Doddington Park, or even out onto Fulmar Road and Doddington Road. Difficult I know in the dark, but it is possible. Then down to Newark Road and into town.' Darke changed his stance. 'Brian. How many routes are there out of Ermine and into town? I say into town because we have to assume his final destination is linked to Boultham Park Road where the Gorich phone call was made from.' He sighed. 'I'll leave it with you.'

'You head for Burton Road or Riseholme Road after that you can zigzag your way down dozens of streets from Yarborough right across to Nettleham and God knows how many in between.'

'Why didn't this Jonah go home on Sunday morning?' Darke asked his right hand man.

'According to his statement,' said Brian Daniels. 'Kirsty got jittery on her own and locked up. So when he does these gigs he crashes at a mate's house.'

'Not buying that. She went out on the piss with hardly any clothes on in the dark. We find anything?' He mimed smoking. 'Weed maybe?'

'Bits and pieces, that's all. New smart phone still in its box in the bedroom. No prints. Nothing we can pin on him.'

'Just a thought, but…he comes bowling back from Nottingham, sees us crawling all over the place. Thinks we're trying to do him for coke or weed or whatever. Nicking phones conceivably. Bunks off to his mate's place.'

'You can prove that?' Darke shook his head as he grinned.

'Jake,' he said across the room for Jacques Goodwin to look his way. 'Job for you,' and ushered him across. Craig Darke had a lot of time for DS Jake Goodwin and looked for opportunities to stretch him and also test him. This would be one of those times. 'On the night Petchey was killed, Jonah White Chrome or whatever it is

16

today didn't go home. Tells us he kipped at a mate's house. I'd like you to check that out. Not by going back to interview him but I'd like you to find out somehow when he's doing another late gig somewhere. Nottingham preferably and wait for him coming home.'

'Boss,' said Daniels to stop him. 'Says he didn't go home…'

'Bollocks Brian! She strutted her stuff in the dark enough to get bloody throttled. Planning to go on the piss with her mates then come home to an empty house, so don't tell me she was scared of being on her own.' He looked back at Jake. 'Use your own car; don't want anything he might recognise.' That was another tick in the box for Jake. Saturday night, Sunday morning on his own on some boring stakeout and not a word of complaint. No shrug, no sighing, puffing and panting he'd get if he'd asked most of the others, including Brian.

'Good weekend, boss?' DI Brian Daniels asked as his DCI plonked himself down on the corner of his desk.

'Weekends come, weekends go, same as usual' was for this lonely man the truth. Often he took work home. Very much against the rules he secreted documents in his brief case on a regular basis he should never have done, just to give himself something to do, to fill his time before Monday morning.

'We've got to sort out a woman for you. That would brighten your weekend.' Craig Darke wanted to comment but refrained. 'Jane's got a mate.' A shake of the head stopped him. 'You seen that new one in dispatch?' Brian got a look that told him to stop.

'We any further forward?' Darke asked, getting back to business. Work was where he came alive, what he thrived on.

'Anybody we could put in the frame has got an alibi. Forensics has come up with nothing from any samples they took away. It's like whoever did this floated in on the wind and escaped the same way.' He picked up a brown envelope. 'Got the bloods here. Bit odd.' Darke looked at Daniels, slipped open the envelope and pulled out the papers.

'Paracetamol?'

'And lots of it, if you read the second page.' Darke flipped over to read, and looked up.

'Paracetamol. She got a problem?' Daniels shrugged.

'Headaches, period pains, toothache. Possibly all at once.'

'We got precisely nothing from that April Matthews woman. Gave Ross a list of people Petchey might have met in town. Been through them all. Not a bite. She never said Petchey swallowed painkillers like bloody Smarties. Like all the rest she said there was never anything definite arranged. When she didn't turn up at the Ritz they didn't really take any notice. Had a couple of drinks and moved on.'

'Did Matthews go to the Ritz?'

'No.'

'You still think the two women are connected?' Daniels queried, but knew the answer.

'It's something we can keep warm, but there was nothing in Gorich's bloods like this. Not a priority. Sammy came up with not much more than being separated from their blokes, both having a young kid, being in their early twenties and copped for it in the evening. That accounts for the majority these days it seems to me. Relationships don't last a fortnight, they get pregnant – how you can fall for a kid you don't want in this day and age beats me, and they're twenty whatever. Unfortunately there are millions like them.'

'If you were the killer would you plan for a smack on the head and syringe, then go for throttling? Wouldn't you stick with the tried and tested?'

'Haven't you got to be inside or hidden somewhere for the smack on the head and a syringe? You can't do that in broad daylight. That takes a few minutes. How long to throttle. Minute maybe. Done and gone, too easy in that dress.'

'It wasn't daylight, and why the syringe at all? Why not give her another bashing?' Darke shrugged his reply.

'Did Sammy try to find suspects near the scene that were similar?'

'Not a hope. Different as chalk and cheese. Things like Lincoln City woolly hat and yellow jacket first time.'

'Hold up a minute. Hat could be Lincoln United who wear white and red, as against Lincoln City who wear red and white.'

'When they're not wearing green and white for some peculiar reason.'

'With Petchey, best we can do if you disregard teenagers, couples, women, drunks and kids, is some old bloke with a beard wearing a cap. Three on bikes, one old geezer walking his dog, a man in a black puffer jacket and one in a lumberjack shirt, tatty jeans and a fag in his mouth.' He blew out a noisy frustrated breath. 'It's Saturday night, and they're all indoors watching some reality crap on the tele. Britain's got no bloody talent or some such shit.'

'To be honest, for Caron Gorich we haven't really got a sniff. If you planned something as cool as walking into her kitchen, whether she knew him or not, smacking her over the head, and getting an injection absolutely right, and getting out again without leaving so much as a bit of spit, you wouldn't then walk around in a soddin' red and white bobble hat or a bloody yellow jacket that screams, *it's me, it's me!* So my guess is, we have sod all.'

'She must have known him,' said Daniels. 'That's today's priority. Need to know a lot more about her life. We're tracking down anybody and everybody she ever knew. We've done friends, boyfriends' mates, ex husband's mates. Gorich never worked, just claimed benefits like they do, so there's nothing there. Who would she open the door to? Long lost friend, neighbour who fancied it or a boyfriend we don't know about. Somebody nobody knew about.' He clicked his fingers. 'Something somewhere will go pop, but it won't be a stranger.'

'What makes you say that?'

'At Gorich's place, front door was locked and the chain was on, but the backdoor was unlocked. People you don't know knock at the front door. If you're a stranger you don't know who's in the kitchen with her. Would you knock on somebody's back door out of the blue at night and risk coming face to face with some big sod with a dog?'

Daniels shook his head. 'I notice we haven't got anybody in a yellow coat or Imps bobble hat.'

'Did you seriously think we would?'

'If this was a police thing on the tele, that's how they'd play it. Make it easy as pie.'

'Real world's not like that I'm afraid.'

19

'IT had a trawl through bits and pieces but nothing so far,' Daniels told him.

Craig Darke slipped off the desk. 'Keep me up to speed, and tomorrow have the coffee on.' They both grinned as Darke headed off for his office, and more paperwork.

The arrival of coffee on his desk was not Jake Goodwin trying to ingratiate himself. It was just the good honest way he behaved. Darke looked up to see Jake pull up a chair, as if what he had to say was for his ears only.

'Heard enough dub step shit to last a lifetime,' he started. Darke said nothing as anything he attempted would only show his ignorance. 'Jonah and two mates got back from Sheffield at half four Sunday morning and went to this address off Monks Road,' he slipped a piece of paper across the desk. 'Let themselves in. Then from a bit after six there was a steady stream of callers. No idea who the other two with him were, but they were all about. My…'

'But this…' Darke stopped. 'Go on.'

'My guess is, Jonah's dealing or acting as the courier from these gigs. He goes back to this place. The entire local scallywag population pops round before the streets up and about, buy all the gear, so when we called there was nothing left.'

'But this is not,' said Darke as he lifted the paper. 'Where we checked before.'

'Could be, where we went before is home to the other one. Take it in turns maybe if it's only those three.'

'All these cars just turn…'

'No,' stopped him. 'They all arrive on foot. My guess is they park a few streets away, probably all different places and just stroll there. No cars coming and going, no traffic, no noise.'

'Did they stop anywhere else on the way back?'

'Nowhere. Club to there,' he said pointing at the paper.

'Night out for the drug boys.'

'He's back at the Zouk in Nottingham, week on Friday.'

'Gotcha, my little beauty. Can't see how it's linked to Petchey, but it's a good side salad. Well done.'

3

'Off to Hykeham,' said Detective Sergeant Jake Goodwin half an hour later, as he passed Reception.

'Do me a favour will you, Jake.' suggested Detective Inspector Rachel Pickard from behind him. He turned to face Pickard with a young blonde elfin of a female beside her. 'Give Tamaryn a lift to Brant Road.'

'You're joking!' made DS Goodwin look at the blonde. 'What the hell's wrong with you?' she shouted, as Jake Goodwin glanced at Pickard and back.

'Enough of that! The Sergeant's going your way and...'

'No bloody chance,' said this thin Tamaryn as she turned and dropped herself down onto the blue bench seat against the far wall.

She was either dressed in a mish-mash of styles for effect or had put her clothes on in the dark. Pretty pink flowered blouse hidden by a black heavy woollen waistcoat was bad enough. But then she had introduced very short denim shorts held up by a huge brown belt, and the whole array ended with dark green leggings and black heeled booties. Had she not got the message every fashionista would scream at her? *Leggings are not trousers.* What a mess.

'I'll take that as a no,' said Goodwin and went to move away.

'Hang on. This is ridiculous,' said brunette Pickard and brushed her obvious pregnancy with her right hand. 'We're not running a taxi service, and in any case HR say I can't drive.' She turned to the young woman sitting legs crossed, arms folded, hunched into herself. 'Your friend hasn't turned up, so either the Sergeant takes you or you get a taxi. Or dare I suggest you catch a bus or go to work even.' The young woman sighed.

'Well, I'm not going wiv 'im. Don't care what you say,' she spat. 'Bastard stole my purse in case you've forgotten. So what do I use for friggin money?'

Goodwin was taken aback. 'Excuse me,' he said firmly. 'I haven't stolen anyone's purse.'

21

He turned his gaze to the Inspector for guidance. He didn't need this. Had no breakfast to speak of after an early shout and still had people to see.

'D'you know Tamaryn?' Pickard asked him.

'Never seen her before in my life,' he was irritated. She swung back to the female.

'D'you know him?' she barked at this Tamaryn.

'What's that got to do with anythin'?' she tossed back quickly. Ungainly wisps of blonde hair hanging down her face. 'Didn't know that bastard this morning, so what's th' diff'rence?'

'The difference is, this is a Detective Sergeant who will ensure you come to no harm. We're not running a taxi service young lady. I just thought it's better than the bus. I'm trying to do you a favour.'

'Am I allowed to ask…?' was all Jake Goodwin managed.

'Nother perv!' her voice high with anxiety.

'Think I'm outta here.' Jake gave her an injured look and went to move, as the automatic front doors slid open and this breathless brunette scurried in.

'Sorry Tammy,' she managed as she gasped in air. 'Damn car broke down. Been running.' They all waited as she gathered her breath. 'Have to be the bus,' the woman said to this Tamaryn as she scampered over to her. 'Douggie thinks it's the alternator. Why now I ask myself.'

'I take it I'm not needed,' said Jake.

'You all fixed now?' DI Pickard asked Tamaryn Bamber.

'Better'n goin' wiv 'im!'

'Wish to God I knew what I'd done,' said Jake, as the second woman looked at him.

'My sergeant offered Miss Bamber a lift,' Pickard offered as a form of explanation.

'Offer still on?' the woman asked as her head turned back to Jake.

'Your friend says I'm bad news.' The woman held out her hand.

'Sally Conway,' she said and Jake moved to shake her hand. 'Brant Road?' Jake nodded. 'Right young lady, we got ourselves a lift.' If looks could have killed this Sally Conway would now be a cadaver. 'Let's be having you. On your feet. Come on.'

Reluctantly the blonde struggled to her feet and trudged to the door, in ill fitting booties. Jake followed the two women, one smartly dressed in a long sleeved grey cardigan and matching trousers.

Jake Goodwin was trying to remember where he'd seen this brunette before, as Tamaryn Bamber said not one word all the way to the car park and all the way to Brant Road. Just sat pouting in the back of Jake Goodwin's pool Ford Escort, texting non-stop.

Sally Conway was exactly the opposite. This sparkling effervescent woman told Jake how her own car was in being serviced, and she had arranged for her cousin to give her a lift from her home in Washingborough into Lincoln. That was all just fine until he pulled up at traffic lights and then the old Peugeot refused to budge. They'd managed to push it into a side road and she had then set off on foot for the Police Station.

When they arrived in Brant Road, young Tamaryn didn't even have the decency to thank him. Sally Conway did enthusiastically and even waved to him as he drove off in the direction of North Hykeham and a chat with Gerald Mackenzie, still trying to fathom where he had seen her before.

Later that day, both back at Nettleham, Jake Goodwin made a point of checking with DI Pickard about the incident earlier.

'What were you doing down town?' he asked.

'Being punted from pillar to post,' she circled the palm of her hand around her obvious pregnancy bump. 'Second one we've had,' she explained. 'Opportunist theft. This creep gets a female on her own and she thinks it's a sexual attack. Worries too much about this creepy bastard getting a hand full of boob, and while she's worrying about him having a quick feel he's rifling her handbag with the other one. Took her purse, cash, credit cards, the works, and legged it.' Rachel lifted her arms and blew out a breath. 'Stupid high heels just going to work in a shop, gave no chance of chasing him. Women,' she sighed. 'Bag open, stilletos. Will they ever learn?' she asked nobody in an exasperated tone.

'And where did I come into this?'

'Thinks all men are sexual predators. Kept going on about what his left hand was doing while I'm trying to get a description from

23

her. Her obsession clouded her judgement. I kept telling her it's like watching a magician, all eyes on his left hand, while the right hand is doing all the work.'

'Stupid bitch thought I'd get her alone in my car...'

'About the size of it,' Rachel Pickard chuckled.

'Thanks for that boss.'

'No problems taking her home I take it?'

'Stuck her in the back. Her mate was a complete contrast. Full of life.' Had she been on her own he might have tapped her for a bit of sponsor money.

Raising money for the Japanese Tsunami Appeal was really not going well. Jake knew exactly how he had got involved and why he had said yes. One of those awkward moments in life, when you really do want to say no, to make an excuse. Alas the wording of the suggestion just makes it impossible.

He and Steve Rodgers had known each other on and off for years and he knew Jake had run the Lincoln 10K five years earlier. In fact as the last of the big spenders he had sponsored him for a couple of quid.

Steve's girlfriend of a year or two had somehow struck up a relationship on the internet with this woman in Japan. She had become so besotted with all things Japanese, the way of life, their culture and social discipline she had decided to fly halfway round the world to pay this Japanese female a visit. She had been in Otsuchi for just three days when the merciless earthquake and tsunami tore the town apart.

Despite extensive and rigorous efforts by both the Japanese authorities and the British Embassy, nothing had ever been heard of her again. No sightings, no rumours, no body, no nothing. Just washed out to sea no doubt like a piece of flotsam carried on currents to goodness knows where.

Steve as part of his mourning process had started his own private disaster appeal fund, and that's where he roped Jake into running for him. When this guy asks you to run the Lincoln 10K to raise funds for the appeal set up in the name of his dead girlfriend what can you say? Jake had hardly trained, but guessed as long as he finished, then monies would be raised.

With a month to go, it had slowly dawned on Jake that it was all down to him. Not only was he expected to do the running, he was also expected to raise the sponsor money as well. Pretty well all on his own.

Always possible Steve had found out. Could be in a bar one night after a few bevies somebody had told him the truth. Equally possible Steve knew all along, and his anguish added to his loss and mourning had taken him away from the fund raising. Possible he could simply no longer face the thought of her betrayal. Lucy Welland had gone all the way to Japan to visit a girlfriend she had met on line. Awaiting her in Otsuchi was someone a bit more interesting. Akiko Yamamoto's older brother Tetsushi.

Both murders were a complete mystery to Craig, but one aspect still concerned him more than any other. Why did Caron Gorich open the door to a complete stranger?

Billy Warren's Comms team had gone through Facebook in an attempt to find a link between both young women. Not one person on there was a 'Friend' to both, but by sheer chance when he fortunately mentioned the large bust on a woman Caron Gorich had listed, it rang a bell. Jake Goodwin happened to be sat at the next station, took a peep at Ross's screen and knew of Adjoa Kwaku. Daughter of a Nigerian musician, but more importantly shacked up with Lee Benson, for some reason best known to her. A PNC check brought him up as a regular on the naughty boys list, but nothing for over a year. Local hoodlum, with a Beckhamesque constantly changing stupid hairstyle. Squinty nose and according to the photo that popped up, in need of a shave. Word had it he had hard man pretensions, but not the guile or strength to back up the claim. He had a couple of TWOCs against his name in his youth. Handling stolen goods, got six months suspended for nicking lead from a church. In the main he'd been a lucky boy. Magistrates in their infinite wisdom had tended to pat him on the head and hand him punishment worth next to nothing that he no doubt laughed about on the streets. Bit of shoplifting, breaking and entering, possession of a bit of weed and being too handy with his fists on more than one occasion.

Craig Darke decided to go pro-active, rather than sit around waiting for Mr Who to take the piss and wipe out another young mother.

He dispatched Raza Latif and Ross Walker to pay Lee a visit. In case the low life had managed to beef himself up a bit or had got friends in, he gave them rugby playing built like an outside lavvy PC Dean Green as back up.

DC Natalie Scoley being new to the squad lacked a degree of confidence in the presence of more senior colleagues. Tall and slim, she was if nothing else very enthusiastic. Darke had recognized her as somebody, given the time, he would like to mentor. To build her confidence, to give her a freedom he sensed she needed but was unwilling to display. He was always aware how an attractive young woman could be side tracked by her peers. Pulled this way and that by the pressure all young people face in this day and age. She, like so many of her age needed time. Time the world was unwilling to give.

The Caron Gorich question offered an opportunity to not only place freedom of thought and voice in her path, but to provide him with another thought process. A young woman's viewpoint.

Asking her to pick him up on Saturday evening in a pool car was all part of that process. He guessed she would be annoyed and feel uncomfortable to a degree. Knew she was probably a bit miffed at having to spend her Saturday evening *'with the bloody DCI'*. Knew she would miss going out with her mates to a club, miss having to shout above the excuse for music from a DJ high on some pills he'd popped in the bog. Miss out on one of her alcohol nights. Driving the Ford down the bypass in the drizzle was probably not her idea of fun.

To keep his mother happy Craig had agreed to attend a Spring Fayre at the church where she was an eager member in Stamford, down the A1. Visiting his parents was always a blast from the past. To return to the town where he had been brought up, the very church where he had been christened and attended Sunday school.

When he got there the Church Hall at the rear hardly appeared to have changed, save for a fresh coat of cream paint in the three years since he was last there. There was an array of at least a dozen trestle tables. A whole assortment: tombola, second hand clothes, fresh cakes large and small, one covered in fresh produce, some of which still with the dirt on. A table of knitted dolls that were toilet roll covers, an assortment of hand made birthday cards and one full of second hand books.

He was just looking through the books when there was a tap on his shoulder.

'Craig my dear. I've brought an old friend to meet you,' was the distinctively deep voice of the shockingly bossy Mrs deCosta-Jones. The tall, white haired, well-preserved and elegantly dressed woman was probably as old as the church itself. Craig spun round, book in hand.

The bright eyes, that cascading red hair. Dressed in a coral jersey cardigan over her t-shirt, True Religion jeans and Kurt Geiger sneakers, a stunning woman faced him, one he had known.

'Craig?' he was asked as his brain whirled back the years. Back to Sunday school in that very hall in nineteen...

'Oh my word,' was all he managed.

'Hello stranger.' Craig's mind was at the seaside on the Sunday school outing. He was on the coach coming back from the pantomime.

'Knickerbocker Glory and a long spoon.' Neither of them heard de Costa-Jones say "I'll leave you to it."

'Sandcastles and...' Jillie Lombard hesitated. 'Gold, Frankinsense and...mire?' Craig had to chuckle as he recalled her misreading of the Nativity Play. Wanted to pick her up in his arms and give her a big hug. Those were the days. Those great days of his youth when the sun always shone, when life was so good. Sunday school teacher and his group of seven girls. He looked left and right.

'Coffee?'

'What's wrong with warm orange squash?' she smiled at those dark eyes and mop of hair now far less unruly than she remembered. First man ever to make an impression on her she had never ever admitted to anyone.

27

'Costa just down the road.'

'Lead on,' and an emotional and nervous Craig Darke ushered her towards the door.

Craig had been going over those first few moments in his mind all the way back from Stamford. He had also been kicking himself for as ever always putting the job first. He was sure Jillie had hinted over coffee as they reminisced that she'd love to see him again. In response to her enquiries he had explained he was a civil servant dealing with legal issues, without saying what he actually did, which he nowadays avoided when he met women.

They'd spent all their time together reliving the good old days, and suddenly here he was back at work. This evening wasn't that important. He could have phoned young Natalie to cancel their meet, and he was sure she would have been overjoyed.

His mother had never been one to lie and the detective in him quickly got a confession before he headed back up to Lincoln. Mrs deCosta-Jones, the bombastic organizer of all things church had mentioned Jillie's return to the town and had suggested how lovely it would be if the two could meet up again for old times sake. Three times Craig realized his mother had cajoled him into going to the Spring Fayre.

4

Sunday 25 March 2012

Jake would be the first to admit the Lincoln 10k had been a struggle, but at least he was on the homeward stretch when it happened. Blue sky and sunshine, with just a slight chill in the air. No more than half a mile to go, when out of nowhere this stupid kid on a bike dropped off the pavement and burst across in front of him and the bloke he was running with. Two runners rolling around in the road, bike wheel spinning, bloody kid shouted abuse as if it were their fault, dragged the bike away, jumped back on and rode off. Blood on his hands told Jake this was not just a collision with a bike he could pick himself up from and carry on.

He'd thanked the people who came to his aid, and once St John Ambulance had delivered him by car to A&E at the County Hospital, he was left to his own devices. Fortunately he'd slipped his mobile into the pocket of his leggings, which he used to call his brother. Jake had parked his car outside City Hall, and all he had with him were his running clothes, the mobile, car keys and a hankie now covered in blood.

Jake Goodwin registered and waited. Went through triage, where he tried to explain what happened, and this young nurse told him they'd had "plenty of you in", most with bad blisters. Brother Eddie and his wife turned up with Marty their morose lad, and they set off to collect his car and park it at the Hospital. They were away when he was called.

Stitches in two places was the verdict and the rest was just cuts and bruises. He was laid back on this trolley surrounded by equipment he was sure he didn't need, hands behind his head, still just wearing a London 2012 t-shirt and pants. His navy blue Adidas bottoms, slung over a chair had a hole at the knee and were dirty and scuffed. There and then dying of thirst and as hungry as hell Jake

29

decided his running days were over. Next time he'd join those sticking their hands in their pockets rather than being the plonker who stuck his feet in his trainers for charity. Another nurse walked by, stopped and walked into the cubicle.

'It is you,' she said with a smile. 'Remember me?' Sally Conway asked. Sunday morning had suddenly come alive.

'Hi.'

She picked up a clipboard and looked down ruefully at his leg. 'What have you been up to?'

'10k. Some idiot on a bike slammed into me.'

'Seemed a good idea at the time.'

'Not really,' he couldn't admit he'd been backed into a corner with all the tsunami charity spiel. 'Did it for charity. Or rather I was doing it for charity.'

'Jacques is unusual.'

'Jake,' he said quickly. 'My mother's French. Her idea.'

'Raise much?' she queried as she put down the clipboard.

'God knows. Just the excuse some of them need. Me not finishing. Wont even get a medal or a t-shirt.'

'Can I contact anybody for you?' Sally took hold of his wrist and looked at her watch. Free from make-up her skin was flawless, her eyes big and bright. 'Your wife know what you've been up to?' She prayed as she counted.

'I should be so lucky. Phoned my brother. He's gone to get my car. Probably waiting out there by now. Seems a bit busy.'

'Few sprained ankles and blisters, but at least they're not drunk.' She put down his arm. 'Strong steady pulse, that's good,' she said, and didn't comment on his strong jaw and those full lips. 'I'll leave you to it,' she said as she stepped away. 'Got a few in dire need I'm afraid. Shouldn't be long now,' she told him and was gone.

He was laid there while this young nurse eventually went about her business of putting five stitches down his shin and three just above his knee cap, and then covered it all with dressings.

'Thank you Nurse Matthews,' said Sally Conway in her blue uniform who appeared just as the nurse went to leave. 'Cubicle five next.'

'Yes Sister.'

30

'You can go,' she told Jake.

'Yes Sister,' he said with a notion of sarcasm.

'Senior Sister,' she said to get her own back and he grimaced. 'I was going to offer you a coffee hotline number, that's if the girlfriend won't object. You all right putting your socks and trainers on?'

'No problem,' said Jake as he moved to sit on the side of the bed. 'This coffee...' He was handed a small white card with a number on it.

'Day off in the week,' she put her hand out almost daring him to hand the card back. 'But if you're spoken for.' Jake wrapped his hand around the card. 'Busy shift, better get on.' Jake coughed slightly.

'Sorry. Forgotten your name.'

'Sally.'

'I'll call,' made her eyes twinkle and the corner of her mouth twitched slightly. Sally walked away and Jake watched her go, before he turned to put on his war torn leggings, slip his trainers back on and set off to find Eddie, Louise and moody Marty.

Life in the Sally and Tess Conway household had become more than a bit tedious of late. Sally knew things were bad, when her mother went off to play Scrabble with friends and she took to looking at Facebook. Sally always knew she was in trouble when she flipped through the people she had encountered in her past when the gossip began to annoy. She wanted to scream at them, give them a lecture but knew that would only make her as bad as them.

Salacious and nefarious remarks annoyed her and the perpetual anti-man stance some of her so-called 'Friends' took, really annoyed her. Sally had had her fill of men for a while, but there was no need for their idiotic and pathetic gossip. She wanted to lecture them about washing their dirty linen in public and tell them all men are *not* the same.

Sally often felt she was looking at life from a different window.

She knew to her own cost that there are some real bastards out there. One or two she had met were in need of a mother. Others would benefit from a lesson in love and caring and many were just not up to much.

Sally Conway knew only too well that out there somewhere was a really nice, considerate fella. All she had to do was find him.

Could be all she had to do was walk into the Police Station again and ask to speak to Jacques Goodwin. When she came across *lmao* and couldn't decide whether that meant *lick my ass off* or *lick me all over*, she knew it was time to log off.

That in itself was a step forward. It was only a matter of months since she had been in such a state over men that she had stalked past loves on Facebook. Told herself she was just checking in case one of these old romantics had seen the light and got in touch.

Sally Conway was not the only one on line. Craig had spent all morning and most of the afternoon at work. Going over reports. Going through interviews time and again, checking the work of his readers. Scanning through everything there was. Just in case. Just in case somebody somewhere had missed something. That clue they needed to the identity of his Mr Who or at least point them in the right direction.

Chicken Tikka and Basmati Rice was his meal of choice he had slung into the microwave before he poured a can of cold lager and turned on his laptop.

Twenty four emails in his Inbox it said and he knew the delete button would get good use. How many more surveys would people punt his way he wondered as he deleted them one by one.

Jillian Lombard HONESTY IS THE BEST POLICY caught his eye long before he got to it. It was a somewhat abrupt Jillie apologizing for getting his email from his mother and then apologizing again by saying that if he really did not want them to communicate then she would prefer if he was totally honest and said so.

The policeman in him wanted to ask where she had suddenly appeared from, and why? He behaved as he would with any enquiry. He phoned his best contact, his mother and she suggested he give

Lavinia deCosta-Jones a call. "But not until after evensong, son." was her advice.

He had the patience to wait, to call his 'snout' in her big house with the long drive he had been to for lavish Garden Parties in his teens. That had been a much bigger affair than the modest Spring Fayre and in the evening he recalled there had been Olde Tyme Dancing on the lawns.

Thoughts of dancing the Boston Two Step, Veleta and Quickstep in his youth brought a chuckle.

His chat that evening with Mrs deCosta-Jones had revealed that Jillie Lombard had been working near Canary Wharf for a merchant bank. But. And it was a big but. Apparently she had suddenly upped sticks and turned up at her parents home in Stamford just after Christmas, and had since taken up a temporary post at one of those 'fitness places' on the outskirts of town.

Interesting.

5

When Caron Gorich was killed Craig Darke had personally interviewed her ex-husband. Under caution as well if he remembered correctly. He had a waterproof alibi, travelling back from Old Trafford after their Saturday tea time kick off, with his pals.

On a personal level Lovan Gorich had not been very forthcoming, but had admitted that his relationship with the brunette had slowly gone downhill since the birth of young Toby. In the end he moved out when he guessed he was being cheated on. Had actually missed a United match against Blackburn, to spy on comings and goings at the house. Now had a new girlfriend, although according to him they didn't share his two room bed sit.

Darke looked down at DI Billy Warren. 'You were in on the interview with Hank Harding. What did you dig up about his relationship with Petchey?' Warren grimaced.

'Very little. Not sure that was a priority at that time. We were more interested in where he'd been and with whom at what time. Know he's now shacked up with some female in Newark. Got her name somewhere.'

'Georgia Tillyard.'

'That's her. Why?'

'Think I might just give somebody a tug.'

'Want me to...?'

'No thanks,' said Darke as he walked away. 'Natalie,' he said across the incident room as he got to his office. 'A word.' He sat on the front edge of his desk and folded his arms, to wait the arrival of the young DC. 'Doing anything that can't wait?' she shook her head. 'Get a car, meet you outside in fifteen.'

Inside the Petchey house, it was like thousands of others up and down the country. An obsession with carpets. Most of the world could not understand. Wallpaper that may have looked good in the store, but was God awful on a long wall. Furniture was a step up from the flat pack norm, looked like IKEA and the light grey three piece suite was fairly new but already stained. Downside was Jane Petchey's sister.

A half empty bottle of cheap vodka and two glasses she probably bought at a pound shop on a long coffee table in front of them was a dead giveaway. He'd have a look at that bottle. It didn't look pucker.

Darke and young Natalie Scoley plonked themselves down in separate grey armchairs, as Petchey's eyes flicked between the two women.

'You fuckin' locked 'im up yet?'

'Who should I lock up?'

'That fuckin' bastard Harding,' said her sister, but Darke didn't take his eyes off Petchey. Her eyes were bloodshot with weeping and worrying, and the hankie in her fist was probably sodden.

'Mind your language,' was ignored.

'Who else is there?' Petchey asked.

'That's why we've come to see you,' Darke responded. 'Who knew she was going out that night? Who knew she used the back door? Who knew the area?'

'That wanker Harding!' was ignored with some difficulty. Darke could not abide unnecessary swearing. His team knew that. And he knew it was usually the dregs of society who resorted to it at every corner.

'Did she have a friend we've not been told about?' he continued.

'What you suggestin'?' Petchey queried and motioned to her sister for more drink. Her dank hair was in need of a good wash and brush.

'I'm suggesting,' said Darke calmly. 'That there must be someone else she knew, we've not been told about.'

'You think we're fuckin' hidin' somethin'?'

'What's Hardin' say?' thin gaunt Sandy Reynolds asked as she poured more vodka for them both. The sort of woman who could do with a good meal. Hooked on dieting probably or struggling with anorexia or somesuchthing. Nylon navy blue jumper and matching trousers in need of a wash. One of those who quite often didn't bother to put her teeth in.

35

'He doesn't have to say anything,' said Darke firmly. 'He was in a pub in Newark all evening, and he has several witnesses and the landlord to vouch for him.'

'Oh yeh.'

'We have witness statements, and everything he's told us checks out. He couldn't have been on the Ermine and in Newark at the same time. End of.' He turned back to Petchey as she downed more than a double measure of vodka. 'Forget Harding, he's not in the frame and...'

'Best thing what she ever did,' said this scowling Reynolds. Sort of excuse for a woman you find screaming obscenities at prison vans outside the court.

'Why?' Scoley asked.

'Nasty shit,' was Reynolds very pleasant and useful contribution.

'In what way?'

'Didn't care 'bout Kirsty. Best thing she ever did getting' 'im fuckin' banned. Don't need 'is sort round 'ere.'

'Banned?' said Scoley just beating Darke to it.

'Not allowed t'see Amelie. Finished with 'im like, didn't need 'im calling round any time he fuckin' liked. Probably trying to get a poke while he's there, like.' Nice woman.

'She's his daughter,' said Darke.

'More's the fuckin' pity.'

'That's enough!' said Darke as he got to his feet. 'I don't want to have to warn you again about your language.'

Petchey looked at Natalie Scoley as she stood up.

'Was the matter wiv her, she fuckin' precious?'

'One more and I'll arrest you for a public order offence for swearing in public.'

Petchey sniggered. 'Yeh?'

'Try me,' said Darke. 'And we'll finish this conversation down at the station. Without your vodka. Reckon you can last thirty six hours without a sniff?' He waited for a reaction that never came. 'And you're happy with this Jonah White character?'

'At least he cared for our Kirsty. Been a real father to Amelie. Not like that sod Harding. Don't know how she got mixed up wiv 'im.'

'Can we please forget Harding,' said Craig sternly. 'That road leads nowhere. It's the unknown we need to know about. Any other men Kirsty might have been seeing?'

'How dare you!' screamed Jane Petchey. 'Get out!'

'Mrs Petchey. I'm trying to establish who might have killed your daughter. So far we've drawn a blank. Anybody and everybody we've been told about has got an alibi. Shut up!' he shouted at Reynolds, as she went to speak. 'I hope for your sake you're not hiding somebody.'

'Such as bloody what?' was a slight improvement.

'That is exactly what we are trying to establish. Somebody somewhere knew what Kirsty was doing that evening, and somebody has to give us a clue. Forget Harding; forget Jonah and all her friends. We know where they were and what they were doing.'

'Thought you were clever buggers who could tell who it is wiv this DNA business.'

'To do that,' said Darke to Reynolds. 'We need DNA. We have none. Nothing at all. That is why we need a name or names. Somebody she once knew, somebody she upset.' He looked at Petchey and back at Reynolds. Nothing. If they knew they most certainly would not say, and maybe it was somebody these two upset.

'Do you see Amelie now Harding's got her?' Natalie asked.

Both Petchey and Reynolds chuckled. 'You're joking.'

'Why?'

'Not going kowtowin' t'him.'

'You're her grandmother. Surely you want to see her.'

'Not through 'im I'm not.'

'Why are you playing games with Amelie?' Darke wanted to know. 'What's she done to deserve this?'

'You wouldn't understand,' Reynolds told him.

He turned to June Petchey. 'And you?' she looked at him through red watery eyes. 'Don't you want to see your granddaughter?'

'Not going cap in 'and to the likes o'them' Darke looked at young Scoley who shrugged.

'Did Kirsty have any problems before she died? Like toothache, bad back?' Both women looked at him. 'Anything she might take

37

painkillers for?' He might as well have spoken to the wall, the way Petchey looked at him.

'How the fuck would she know that?' Reynolds threw at them. 'She didn' live 'ere.' Stopping the bad language was a full time job. A world in which they and many others like them were forced to operate.

Craig Darke and Natalie Scoley let themselves out, and then he remembered he'd wanted to have a close look at the bottle of vodka in case it was illicit. Too late now.

'Find out about this ban,' he said to Scoley in the car on the way back. 'Is it official, and on what grounds?'

'Restraining order, boss,' said Natalie Scoley at Craig Darke's office door. 'Officially he was banned from visiting Petchey because he was a pain in the arse and caused problems at the house.'

'Did we know about this?'

'My guess is, they didn't want the police involved,' said Scoley as she moved to perch on a chair. 'Talking to Harding. He'd arrange to visit Amelie and take her out for the afternoon. When he turned up, she wasn't well, or she'd gone to her gran's or Petchey was taking her out or some other excuse, like he'd got the wrong day. Then when he turned up Jonah White got involved. In the end they went to court to get an injunction, said he was making their lives a misery. According to Harding he didn't see Amelie for over eight months.'

'No wonder he was pissed off.'

'Actually asked him if there was anybody else, but he said he had so little contact for the past four months since the ban he didn't know much at all. Said she just told a bunch of lies in court, had all her family and friends to back her up. Accused him of all sorts. Her word against his.'

'Thanks Natalie.'

'And says he's sent a condolence card to her parents and put in it they can see Amelie any time. But he's heard nothing. That's not all…'

'Sit down,' said Darke and leant back in his chair.

Natalie moved to the chair by the door, sat down and crossed her legs. 'Day she kicked him out she's straight onto the Child Support Agency and together they've been stinging him for a small fortune.' She shook her head. 'Sorry sir, that can't be right. He got the divorce on adultery so he's the innocent party, how come he pays?'

'It's his child.'

'So the innocent Harding pays and the guilty rap man doesn't. That can't be right. She was in the wrong. Surely it's the guilty should pay.'

'I agree with your sentiments, but I doubt whether you'll find the average woman agreeing with you.'

'I'm not your average bed hopping woman.'

'I've got a friend who lectures on women's issues and will talk all night about the evil that lurks in certain women.'

'The ones who screw the system and any man who passes by, and sod the good guys.'

'The very ones.' He smiled at her. 'All you've got to do is find the good guy.' She really had come on.

'Could be easier trying to win the Lottery.'

Evening meal over, strong coffee, laptop and having made all his decisions in his mind about Jillie during the day he was ready to take the next step.

On at least four occasions he knew of, females had ended a relationship with him once they knew what he did for a living. One was concerned about how her friends would react with him being the 'enemy'.

Craig Darke kept his email reply very formal. He'd written and re-written it five times during the day, but made sure she was under no illusion about his honesty. Yes he would very much like to retain contact.

The response he got within twenty minutes made him smile.

Between the lines he sensed she was criticizing him for being so formal. Second paragraph talked about when and where they would meet, and paragraph three caught him off guard.

I expect you're used to taking down a lady's particulars told him to relax. Chances are she had used the same snout in Stamford and the long arm of the law didn't seem to be putting her off.

When he offered her an empty diary to choose from and a venue of her choice he was able to sit back with his coffee and chuckle to himself. He felt strange in an almost sexual way. He had a date with his pupil. He was seeing a gorgeous redhead he last had a meal with – if you can call a McDonald's burger in a cardboard box, a meal - when she had just turned thirteen.

Jillie chose the following Friday evening, picked a restaurant, offered to book and then as an aside just let him know that she knew he was a widower, and he might care to know that she had never married and was not in a relationship.

It had been a very long time since Detective Chief Inspector Craig Darke had been that excited.

6

Craig Darke walked into the Incident Room to find Brian Daniels in the middle of a meeting.

'I'll come back.'

'Join us, boss. We can do with all the help we can get. We're running back through the Petchey crime scene, in case we missed something.' The DCI walked across to the coffee perculator.

'This for anybody?' he asked as he poured black coffee into a pale blue mug. Brian Daniels and Raza exchanged glances.

'Er...yes boss.'

'Who wants this for the swindle?' he said and held up a ten pound note. More glances were exchanged. Craig always had to be reminded to contribute to the coffee fund.

'Everything all right boss?' was a 'Tigger' enquiry. He couldn't remember him offering money before. He always paid up, contributed above the odds usually but had to be reminded constantly.

'Will be when we find someone for this little nonsense.' He put the note on the table, and pulled up a chair. It was the tried and tested system. Go through everything with a fine tooth comb, and when you've done that go back through it again.

'The house is a complete blank and the patio produced exhibits but no leads,' said 'Tigger' 'We reckon the kitchen is a waste of time. Chances are he never went in there. He was waiting outside in the dark. Knew she always went out the back door.'

'Hold it there one minute,' said Craig Darke. 'She always went out the back door. How did he know that? Do you know what door your neighbours always use?' He looked around the room for a reaction. 'Be serious for a minute chaps. Think about your neighbour say six doors down from you. Which door do they use?' They looked at each other. 'That's my point. Carry on,' he said when all they could manage was little more than a mumble.

'Plenty of DNA on stuff from the kitchen,' said Daniels as he thought about what his boss had said. 'Those we haven't matched could be anybody.'

'If our man did as the pathologist suggests and slipped the plastic tie over her head, pulled hard, knee in the back, on the floor, foot on and yanked hard, what will we find?'

'Bruising to her back,' said 'Tigger' Woods.

'Exactly,' said Darke. 'That's in the PM. Shoes with a heel. Not trainers with flat bottoms.' He glanced across at Raza Latif. 'Put yourself in his shoes, Raz. You've done it; she's dead as a dodo on the bit of a patio outside the backdoor. Cut the tie and off you go. What do you touch?'

'Nothing. You don't need to touch anything.' Darke smiled as he nodded. 'He's like Cassius Clay. Floats like a butterfly and stings like a bee.' He waited a second, but nobody said a word. 'All he's done is hold the plastic tie, probably with gloves on and stood on her back. What the hell will we ever get from that? Forensics, DNA ? Don't make me laugh. He's taking the piss, that's what annoys me.'

'Only two worries,' said Brian Daniels. 'What to do with the tie that's now got blood on it, and will he be seen?'

'Plenty of routes, boss,' said Billy Warren. 'Remember it's quiet. We've already established that the average dork around there is watching crap tele or on line. Farting about with Xbox or pissing about on their phones. If this isn't a spur of the moment thing, you can bet your bottom dollar he's surveyed the area. He knows the quiet route to take. Even a roundabout route, not the obvious one.'

'North, south, east and west. If he's going into town how many routes are there? Take your bloody pick.'

'He didn't catch a bus; we've checked CCTV with Stagecoach. Did he have a car parked?'

'That's risky. You park a car up for an hour; chances are somebody will see it. People are bloody nosey. Hello what's that white Honda doing there? When we did house-to-house some clever dick would have wanted the limelight. Saw a white Honda parked up mister policeman.'

'I'll admit something now,' said Darke. 'With the Gorich case. Two weeks after, when all the fuss had died down. Forensics had finished and the areas were back to normal, I went for a walk.' He put his hand up. 'Sad git, yes I know. I went for a wander around there on a Saturday night about half eight. You could hear a bloody pin drop, only saw two people, and I'm damn sure neither of them saw me. When I got home, I walked around the roads near me. Same thing. Nothing. Our man could have walked away from Petchey's back garden knowing the chances are he'd not bump into anybody. When Natalie and I went to watch the Gorich place, it was like a morgue.'

'I think he walked,' said Billy Warren. 'Cars can be seen, you've got to wait for a bus, especially at that time on a Saturday night, and they've got CCTV. You're more likely to remember somebody on a bike than just some fella out for a stroll.'

'Let's move on then,' said DI Daniels. 'Relationships. Members of both families have given alibis we've checked. Most of them were said to be indoors watching tele, desperate to phone up to vote for their favourite dope singer and put more money in Cowell's pocket. That's her parents and her younger sister. Close friends were either doing exactly the same thing according to statements or already in town. We have Hank Harding in Newark with his new woman and a few mates. Harding's parents are separated. Intel says his old man lives in Leeds now and his mother was at home on her own. His brother's in the army and his sister's a nurse at Grantham. Jonah White was trying to be a DJ in Nottingham and his family is all in west London as far as we can gather.'

'DNA matches?'

'Most have been swabbed once the ACC agreed the samples would be destroyed if they were clear. Which they were except for her mother who had been there earlier in the day, our Jonah and that April.'

'This has gone cold,' said Darke. 'It must be getting on for six months since the Gorich case, and we've not had a sniff. I think if we try to ask questions now about her case we'll be wasting our time.'

'Boss,' said Tigger. 'Like you did with the Gorich case, why don't we go back to the Petchey scene? Why don't we get out there at around the time and look for movement. Just a couple at a time. Is there somebody delivering something.'

43

'Pizza,' sounded good to DS Latif.

'All checked,' brought that to an abrupt end. 'And taxis.'

'Tesco!' Raza Latif almost shouted. 'Sainsbury's, Asda.' Everybody looked at him. 'They deliver. Was there a delivery in that area that night? If there was did the driver see anybody? We've got one or two sightings; can we get another one the same?'

'Thanks Raz,' said Daniels. 'You've got yourself a job,' brought a few chuckles. Raza always looked as though he needed a shave, but never did. Asian parentage had given him that look.

'Not sure they deliver that late,' from Tigger brought Raza back down to earth. 'They don't come in. Just plop the trays down with the bags in, so it wasn't one of them did it. Still, worth a try.'

'Delivery driver wanted for Tesco, must have syringe experience? I don't think so.' Daniels hesitated a moment. 'Check it. Check who it was. I know it's clutching at straws, but what else we got?'

'And they'd all deliver to the front door, not the back.'

'Have we really dug deep into Petchey's relationships?' Raza asked. 'She was shagging that Jonah when she was with her Hank bloke. Who's to say she remained faithful with our music maestro? How did she actually break up with Hank? Did he find out and dump her, did she kick him out or had he got somebody on the side already?'

'Knew she was screwing around,' brought that to an end.

44

7

All the back-up, the door-to-door probationers, all the Forensics team and SOCO had moved on. Craig Darke was once again left with his basic teams, like he had when the Gorich case ran itself down. The white boards had remained unchanged for days. There were now regular meetings every other day rather than an early morning briefing and an afternoon de-brief. Phone calls had dried up, paperwork volumes had returned to normal.

Serious questions were being asked of him. Why still no progress on the Caron Gorich case, and now nothing much with the demise of Kirsty Marie Petchey? Lots of questions. Notebooks full to bursting with interviews, lots of theories, but no answers.

He was excited at the prospect of a meal with Jillie, but doubts were always there. Would this be just another occasion when he would be left to eat alone in a restaurant? Once again as had happened a couple times in the past be the lone male saddo all the customers would whisper about sat in the corner of the country pub.

Craig Darke knew he was good at his job, knew he was a good cop, but had doubts about himself as a person. The man inside. Did he just have too much baggage trailing behind him? Was he really the sort of male who could form a full-on relationship with one of the most beautiful women he had ever set eyes on? And damn clever with it.

Had his life experiences made him too over-protective towards women? Did he sub-consciously see them as a Katherine substitute?

He was convinced that before Friday he would get an excuse from Jillie. A quick email, and this relationship would all go for a ball of chalk before it had started. Young ginger Jillie from the old days. The one now with the figure as perfect as he could ever imagine. The woman with the top job, and no doubt top dollar to go with it. Or in her case probably top Euro. The one who no doubt would if she turned up, be in a brand spanking new top of the range Porche or Maserati.

Jake was pretty sure Sally wouldn't turn up. The phone call to that nurse had been annoying as well as being packed full of confusion:

'Sally?'

'Yeh.'

'It's me, Jake.'

'Jake?'

'I made a good impression then.'

'You from Paediatrics?'

Jake kept his amusement to himself.

'You gave me your number.'

'I did what?'

'Gave me your coffee hotline number.'

'And?'

'Phoning to arrange day, time.'

'Busy.'

'Every day?'

'By the look of it.'

'Wednesday?'

'Working.'

'Saturday?'

'Going out.'

'Morning?'

'Probably,' she said when suddenly out of the blue that Jacques and his leg on Sunday came to mind.

'After lunch, no how…'

'Wednesday '

'Next Wednesday?'

'No this Wednesday.'

'I thought you said…'

'Never mind what I said. Wednesday ten thirty.' Told him the café and click.

It had all given him the distinct feeling it was not what she wanted. Handing out her phone number to a patient had probably been very much against the rules and an action she now regretted, just as he had wished to God he'd never agreed to run. There was always the possibility she handed cards out willy nilly, just to see how many pillocks like him fell for it.

How he wished women could just step into a man's boots for one day, just to see how confusing women were! Most of the time what they did and said made no rhyme or reason. Far too busy being distracted by multi tasking obsession to do just one job properly.

Sitting in the cafe at the outer edge of a shopping complex no more than a decade and a half old, Sally told the waitress she was waiting for somebody as she looked around. Knew she was older than most, but it was not far from the university and this was probably what amounted to studying. Destitute students who could afford to pay for a quality coffee most days. Told their friends it had to be Brazilian Rainforest Fairtrade when in truth it was usually a cappuccino with marshmallows, whipped cream and chocolate sprinkles. All paid for with a credit card. Females in the main, all dressed alike mostly. Individuality an absolute no no. One girl with pink hair was sitting on her own reading a thick book.

As he walked away from his car Jake had managed to squeeze in near Burger King that Wednesday, he did wonder if the card was a nurse scam he'd fallen for. Had this Sally already reported back to her pals that another randy sucker had phoned up expecting a meet for coffee? He made his way with a step that was unhurried.

A waving hand at a table in the window on the right hand side motioned him over, and he had lost the bet with himself.

'What'll it be?' he asked down to her.

'Latte...please,' said Sally. 'They take your order,' she advised pointing to a young female hovering behind him with a menu he ignored. 'Latte and Americano with cold milk, please,' he told the girl and sat himself down.

'How's the leg?' Sally asked and he shrugged.

'No gangrene yet,' made her smile nervously. 'Your friend get over her attack?' Sally blew out her breath.

Were her eyes brown or black, he couldn't decide. Wearing a navy and white stitch sweater and slimming royal blue drawstring trousers. Nobody in the café was better dressed.

'Why do people do that? Just because I'm a nurse they think I'm the fourth emergency service. Quite sure if their house was on fire

47

some friends would call me first. Had to get a taxi home in the end, her bloke wouldn't get off his fat arse and give me a lift. Where was he when she needed him? Some of my workmates would tell me that's men all over.'

'We could have done with a better description,' he offered as he considered what she had said. 'Think she was too preoccupied with being violated.'

'Probably the first time she's complained,' was a surprise remark. Said in such a way, that after a couple of words you know the speaker wishes she had kept her mouth shut. 'Sorry,' she offered and looked past him to the front door, as if in need of help. She shrugged when she looked back. 'Big mouth,' she muttered but could not resist a soft laugh.

Sally had wrapped the thin turquoise scarf around her neck as an after thought. Arranging and re-arranging it until she thought it was just right. Conversion was a bit first date hesitancy and they discussed the pluses and minuses of the establishment almost for something to say.

'Anyway,' she said with a breath to change the subject. 'How much did you raise? People should have given you double after what you went through.'

'Four hundred and fifty odd if they all pay up. Probably did better than if I'd finished. Some of my colleagues actually felt sorry for me.' High cheekbones and a near perfect mouth.

'Who were you raising money for?'

Jake explained the whole sorry saga, as Sally looked at him. About Steve Rodgers girlfriend and her internet friend, the tsunami and destruction of Otsuchi. He was wearing a thick grey jumper. One of those that have been knitted inside out.

'And you think he now knows?' Sally queried.

'That's my guess.'

'Suppose he finished up in a difficult position. Raising money for something he now really doesn't want reminding of.' Jake noticed how Sally's head had gone down. 'Probably found it difficult to admit it to you.' Conversation stopped when their drinks were delivered. This Sally pointed to her eye and it took Jake a moment or two to understand. When he looked at the waitress with unnecessary extravagant eye make up he got the message. It was good to see his companion smile.

'Haven't heard from him for a month,' he went on.

'Be embarrassed,' she said into her mug as if she was talking to herself. 'Never easy, admitting you've been conned. All the things you thought were special have probably been banded about to others as a joke.' She scraped her bottom lip through her teeth. 'You've become the subject of derision.' Where had that bubbly talkative woman gone, where was the organised and efficient Senior Sister? Jake was unsure how to react as her mood had gone downhill so fast. When she lifted her head, there were tears in her eyes. 'Sorry,' she mumbled, looked forlorn and desperate not to be there, wiped her eye with a finger and went to get to her feet. She just looked at him as a tear rolled slowly down her cheek. A tissue to both eyes, a shake of her head and a sniff. 'I really am sorry. Shouldn't have come. In fact shouldn't have given you my number.'

She stood up, bent down to grab her bag from the floor, but faced Jake stood in front of her. He went to cup her shoulders with his hands, but left those inches from her.

'Stay and chat to me,' was so quiet she had to be the only person to hear, although he sensed others were desperate to know. To stare, to look, to snigger. 'What harm will it do? I'm a good listener.' Sally looked at him, as if seeking an assurance. 'Would you say no to a muffin?' brought a big lump to her throat but at least made her sit back down.

This really was too much of a flash back. This was where she and Derek had often stopped off for refreshment. He'd have his black coffee...and all the time he was...Sally screwed her eyes shut. She really wanted to start all over again. Go to Starbucks or Café Nero, in fact anywhere but there. Sally wanted to order a Cappuccino. Even a Macchiato if she knew what it was.

'Mind if I didn't right now?' she asked, as her reputation for nervous talk took a back seat...

'You haven't touched your drink,' was true. 'No good? Want something else?' He saw the hesitancy in her face as he rose to his feet. 'You name it.'

'What's a Macchiato?' she dared up to him.

'Think that's an espresso with a bit of milk. Hang on.' Jake walked back to the door and picked up a menu and returned to sit opposite Sally. 'What about Mocha Choca?' she looked bemused. 'Half coffee, half chocolate with cream and a flake,' made her smile. 'Go on, be a devil.'

'Go on then,' and Jake was gone. Staff seemed confused that he should go to the counter, but accepted his order.

. 'Tell me about your job,' he said the moment he returned.

'What's to tell?' she asked, and had to clear her throat.

'Every day must be different. You must have a lot of responsibilities.'

'Sometimes it gets boring with just all the usual nonsense, particularly at weekends with the drunks.' Those smashed out of their skulls annoyed her more than anything. Made her so angry. 'You wish something different would turn up, would just pile through the doors. But no. All we get are more halfwits stoned out of their brains. Spewing up all over us, offering us sex we'll never forget.' She stopped. 'Sorry. It's just; a change would be nice sometimes.'

'Like some idiot knocked down by a kid on a bike,' brought the first hint of a smile.

'Senior Sister oversees the whole department. Being in charge is a buzz. It can be stressful, one day it's good, and then it's bad. Think my problem is I don't have someone to talk to at the end of the day. My mum's lovely, but is not really interested. Too pre-occupied with her own career. Bit of a high-flyer.'

Did this guy need a lecture from her on drunks and drink driving? How weekend shifts in A&E were an absolute nightmare almost every week? The binge drinkers who saw their habit as something to celebrate. Why could successive governments not recognise a symptom of societal decline happening nationwide week in, week out? Turn high streets into absolute war zones. Was it simply because the drink trade had such a powerful lobby? Didn't MPs have enough common sense without giving in so easily to outside pressures to realise it was causing real destruction of society? That this abhorrent behaviour was making the nation a laughing stock world wide?

'This is quite nice,' she said when this Mocha Choca arrived. 'Think I'm a bit staid. Always have latte or cappuccino, because I don't really know what the others are.'

'That better?' She nodded her response.

'Patients being stressed doesn't help,' she said suddenly. They were back to her job, talking in that fast way she did when nervous. 'They are in an alien environment. All these people they don't know, and all most of them can do is look at the ceiling. Machines, wires, drips. People sticking needles in the most intimate parts, covered only by an ill fitting gown. The good ones are obviously terrified by things they simply do not understand. Worried sick a lot of them. Specially the ones who act all brave and carefree. They're the worst.'

'And the idiot with the cut leg thinks his problems are as important as the woman having a heart attack.'

'You didn't moan so I'm told.'

'Been checking up on me?'

'Just asked. I have to ensure patients are moving through the system; make sure they've been seen by a Doctor. We can have six in resus – now that's a whole different ball game. Queue building up, and then it can be a bit much.' She was by then dipping her flake into her drink. 'I need to know who the awkward ones are. Who looks likely to cause trouble? Sometimes I jump the queue with them, just to get rid of them.'

Just something about him. His good manners, his politeness, the dark looks and kindness in those chocolate button eyes. Something had caught her attention when she sat beside him in the car with Tamaryn and then saw his from afar in A&E. She'd had that old man with what she diagnosed in her mind as a triple A, and the doc then confirmed as abdominal aortic aneurism. Once she had him shunted into a cubicle it was the broken femur and a dog bite before she'd got a real look at this Jacques Goodwin in cubicle three.

Sally told herself she daren't let things get out of control. One step at a time, not a step too far.

This was just a mid-morning coffee with a nice guy, a single nice guy, but she had to know why. If she never ever found out anything more about him, she had to know why this man was in the shop window. Why a sold ticket was nowhere to be seen.

51

'Tell me about your job,' was a way to get him off the subject and for her to probe.

If she was expecting an insight into the latest robbery, rape or scandal, she was disappointed. Jake took care to keep all his chat to little more than she could get from local radio.

'Seem to spend half my life chasing moonbeams,' he said.

Twice Jake managed to mention that he had no pressing engagements, but she just never took the bait. No matter what he tried, she steered him back to a copper's life. The cases, the shifts, a few anecdotes and before he could turn round he had paid and they were outside not knowing what to do. Shake hands, give her a peck or...

'You've got the number,' said Sally before she turned on her heels and walked off into the shoppers on the High Street. After a hundred yards Sally stopped dead in her tracks, dared to look back over her shoulder. Cursed at her stupidity. He was gone, lost in the crowds of uninterested nobodies. That lovely man had somehow moved her from her melancholy state and she had just let him go.

Derek had proved to be devious and traitorist and Eddie had just been a secretive thug. What then would she discover about this Jake if she saw him again? Were all men painted with the same brush? If not the same brush, the same oils and pigment. Or should that be pig men?

Jake wandered away, plonked himself down on a metal bench near Debenhams and thought about the experience. Controlled, talkative, bubbly and efficient in one guise. Subdued, confusing and somewhat nervous in another.

As he sat there, long haired scruffy students in their Idresslikeaprat uniforms scuffed along. Pretty young girls from stores were out window shopping in their lunch hour. In tight black skirts and high heels they clicked their way past like clones. Comfort blanket mobiles in one hand they just had to keep peering at. Half empty bottle of water in the other. A lot of kids from academies with their shirts hanging out at the back and ties in huge knots acting just as if they were schoolchildren. What were they doing out? Women with their mandatory name badges pinned to their bosoms or hung

52

round their necks scampering to do a quick shop before they grabbed a Prawn Mayo and Mocha to go.

One option he considered sitting there watching visions of many an attractive and appealing young woman walk by, was to visit his mother. It was probably her age, but Sabine Goodwin had become broody. Not for herself he guessed at fifty four, but for her children. His sister's marriage had lasted no time at all, and now Marianne was flat sharing with a woman she worked with. Correction. A woman she worked for, which Jake found somewhat strange. How can you not carry work into your home life? How can workplace discipline not be an issue, particularly after your boss has had to pull you up on something, cause you concern or been a downright bitch?

Running off home to mummy was not an option. She'd remind him a nephew or niece had a birthday coming up and he should send a card. Then in the same breath mention his lack of a 'young lady' for the umpteenth time. Tell him in no uncertain terms how he needed somebody in his life. Trouble was, she was probably right.

Anyway experience told him the wrong conversation threads with his mother could make him maudlin. He was not going to pine after a woman he hardly knew, who probably saw him as no more than a coffee date, and was now off to pastures new. To meet her pals for lunch, and then some charismatic hunk in the pub tonight. Still, he did think about her.

Sally was quite obviously a problem, or rather it appeared she had problems, but at least it was a step on the ladder. A bright lady with that "I'm vulnerable, please look after me", look. Confused over coffee was a first step only, but unbeknown to his mother it was real progress.

At home Sally would not mention how she had enjoyed coffee with a new man. Leaving her mother unaware of this new development.

Peter had been dead fourteen years, yet annually Tessa Conway's mind replayed the video of that very kind policeman stood on her doorstep that cold wet January evening as a vivid reminder.

A need to get home in a hurry to his young wife after a late Christmas works 'do' was how drunk as a skunk businessman

53

Randolph Brookes Fielding had described his reason for driving his Lancia at well over the speed limit.

Deep inside Tess felt that she and Peter were still writing their love story. Until that dreadful day, when that hideous man just spun the pencil upside down and erased her love from her life.

Some things had never left her. That man in a green tunic, blue rubber shoes, nitrile gloves and a ridiculous green and purple bandana. Stubby nose and big eyebrows had stayed with her, as he pulled back a white sheet to reveal her dead Peter. The awful wet weather at the funeral, the huge car and the flowers. Silly cucumber sandwiches after with the crusts cut off, and week old sausage rolls

Fielding had been left with a broken arm, dislocated shoulder, a degree of whiplash and a few cuts and bruises.

Tess Conway had been left alone with a daughter, engulfed in puberty and exams on the horizon.

At the time Tess had felt guilty about her inability as a parent to mollycoddle her only child, to allow through circumstance the freedoms to roam that other mothers were so against, had been beneficial. With the loss of her father it had made Sally far more streetwise than her peers, more able to cope in the big wide world as she grew up.

As a couple the Conway's had started out with a set of simple dreams. An enchanting home, careers they could enthuse over, a family of two or three and early retirement to allow them to enjoy the fruits of their labours. Peter had been studying law when they first met, and when he was killed had been a partner with Monkton, Flavell and Hotchkiss for just eighteen months. Tess had been manoeuvred into an all encompassing career in local government by her father. A career that at times gave the impression she was self centred and driven. When her family unit had been suddenly reduced by a third she was thankful for their support.

Now she was head of adult services. This meant that half the people her staff had to deal with were in need of care, help, advice and guidance. The remainder just needed their arses kicking! Tess Conway had never seen non-interventionalism as a way of life. At the forefront of a new breed with radical more determined ideas.

Two careers had put an increase in family on the back burner, they had moved into their dream home but had somehow never got round to adding to their family but now Tess could afford to retire whenever she liked.

On the downside Peter's death had in an instant removed the role model from Sally's life that all daughters need. This had now manifested itself in a succession of wrong male choices. She had no standard by which to compare these jack-the-lads with. No template by which to pluck the wrong uns from the bunch.

Tess was aware her daughter suffered from an element of fear and insecurity. The one man in her life she really truly loved was gone for ever.

She knew Peter, like so many fathers, wanted his daughter to follow in his footsteps, so he could continue to watch over her. Within months it was as if his demise had seen that idea come crashing down. Nursing was her sudden choice, as if she had an engulfing need to care for those desperate for respite from the bad times.

Just as she had once wanted somebody to take away her pain.

When his phone rang, for just a second or two Jake did wonder whether this would be Sally. Then when he looked at the screen and it told him it was a priority text from work, he knew a surprise call from Sally was the sort of thing you only see in cheap movies.

8

'Settle down,' said Craig Darke, and everybody obeyed. Eventually. 'We've identified the victim. In her thirties, Eilish Mona Kavanagh. She's the joint managing director of TwinPrint. For those who don't know, it's located on one of the industrial estates off Doddington Road.' He leant his backside on the edge of a desk. 'The other joint managing director is her twin sister Eimear. When I say twin, I mean twin. These are identical. Dead spit of each other. They live next door to each other in identical houses on the outskirts of Saxilby. It's the sister who identified the body. I was there. It was like she was looking in a mirror. Bloody creepy.'

The door opened and in walked pregnant DI Rachel Pickard. 'Talk amongst yourselves,' Craig Darke said loudly, ushered Pickard back out into the corridor and closed the door.

'Been told you want to see me.'

'Got a job for you if you fancy it.'

'Such as?' the brunette queried and smiled.

'Co-ordinate this Kavanagh murder for me. I've already got Caron Gorich and Kirsty Petchey. Now this.' Her look asked the question. 'Big cheese from a local printers found dead this morning. I'm a bit pissed off with this if I'm honest.'

'Connected?'

'Can't imagine so. But anything's possible.'

'How can I help?'

'Be my eyes and ears, come and go as you please. Little bird tells me you're fed up with being...' He hesitated and put his head on one side. 'Incapacitated.'

'Being a filing clerk is not me.'

'What I thought. Give you a DC for the mundane and it will free up d'Andrea they've given me.' He moved in close. 'One rule. Baby comes first. That can never be compromised. Little lady, then you, then the force. Understood?' Rachel nodded and smiled.

'Thank God for that. Something to get my teeth into.'

56

What a great guy he was. Hard as nails, bright as a button heading for the heights, but still respectful, kind, considerate and oh so charming. And to top it all, a great mate.

Craig Darke opened the door to the Briefing Room. 'Natalie!''' he called out and was quickly joined in the corridor by young blonde trim DC Natalie Scoley. 'DI Pickard is co-ordinating this all for me,' he told the youngster. 'Advantage of pregnancy. I get a higher rank and you young lady get the chance to learn from a bloody good copper. You're her assistant, her gofer, you do any damn thing she wants and if need be you boil the kettle and call the midwife.' The two women sniggered. Craig Darke opened the door to the Briefing Room and ushered them back in. 'Listen up! DI Pickard is my coordinator on this one, every last snippet goes through her. Understood? Natalie's her right hand woman, but they are not a dumping ground. Is everybody happy?' nobody responded. 'Tough shit if you're not. We've got extra hands coming our way, but in the meantime we need to know about friends, families and associates. I want positional statements filed and cross checked with the ladies here. You know the procedure. It's down to the minutiae at this point, and I'm not ruling out anything. I'm not even ruling out a link between this Kavanagh woman and either Petchey or Gorich. Jake,' he looked across at the Detective Sergeant. 'We've picked up the victim's partner an IC1 male aged about forty. Downstairs now. We'll start preliminary interviews after this.'

Brian Daniels was not happy. Why her? Why did bloody Rachel get the coordinator job? Probably because she's female, and the grapevine said there was 'history' there. That how you get on is it? Shag your boss.

Craig Darke was not happy. The last thing he needed was a full blown murder when he had a date on Friday. Always possible it wouldn't be Jillie who would cancel first, probably have to be him. Whichever way it went, looked like it was doomed before it had begun.

'Understand this,' said Brian Daniels. Dark receding hair with a hint of white and grey flecks beside each eye. 'This is all very bloody odd. First person on the scene was one of their drivers. He was waiting at the house where he found the body, when we turned up.

Said he hadn't been in the other house. It's at that point we discover the sisters live in identical houses. SOCO found us a set of keys to next door.'

'Bollocks!' was Darke.

'Sorry, sir?'

'Nothing, nothing,' Craig said and shook his head. He'd spoken out loud when it was a private matter between his two lives. Work and play. He would go on that date, as long as she didn't cancel, even if it meant a very early start or coming back in after to catch up. Friday evening was going to be for him. Just for once in his life.

'They're absolutely identical,' Daniels went on. 'Both houses are off limits while Forensics goes through them both of course. The sister's shouting her mouth off at the Chief Constable about access to her belongings. Tough shit! She can muddle through, but she's not getting access.'

'Nor is the dead woman's partner.' Darke looked across at two detectives, sat together arms folded legs crossed. 'Toni. Get onto telecoms. No mobile found so far, according to SOCO. Get me a list of all her calls. I'll get her number off this Quinn I'm seeing. And Toni. Credit Cards while you're at it. What has she been spending money on? Who's using them now? They've gone missing. While I have a word in the shell like of this Quinn character.' He rested his arm against the doorpost. 'Nobby.' DC Hatchard looked up. 'Is CCTV on your list for this one?' Hatchard nodded. 'What chance CCTV in the village? See what you can dig up. Billy, get a staff list pronto see if any names from Gorich and Petchey cases pop up. Long shot, but you never know.'

'Are you sure there isn't something you want to tell us Mr Quinn?'

'I have already told you all that I know.' Craig Darke pulled Jake Goodwin's notepad from in front of him.

'You last spoke to your partner first thing yesterday. You went off to do your painting at around....'

'And photo...graphing,' Quinn said in such a precise manner it was as if photo and graphing were separate words. His face was very round and broken veins on his cheeks told their own ale story. His eyes very blue and his blondish hair looked like somebody had plonked a mop on his head.

'Photographing and painting just after five. Your partner should have left for work yesterday morning around half past seven.' Sebastian Quinn nodded. 'You then received a phone call out at Bassingham at one fifteen.' Quinn didn't acknowledge. 'Why do you need photographs when you're there painting?'

'I need the early morning haze that lasts only for a short period. I photograph it, and then I have it with me as I paint the scene,' he said in his deliberate way of speaking

Sebastian Quinn gave the impression he was trying very hard to be 'arty' without doing it naturally. The patchwork cap on his head he had removed and was now being fiddled with at his lap, the dull brown and cream check shirt, mustard coloured trousers, bright yellow woollen socks that screamed at the trousers and brown boots.

'And when did you last speak to your partner's sister?' Darke asked. 'Was that the previous evening?'

'Yes.'

'You check on her every evening?'

'No.'

'Why not? You're on the edge of the village but your two houses are pretty isolated.' Quinn just shrugged. 'And we understand you don't socialise in the village very much at all. Why is that?'

'The girls prefer not to.'

'Therefore you live a pretty remote sort of life. Tell me if I'm wrong Mr Quinn but my guess is you spend all day painting outdoors or in your studio at the back of your house, and in the evenings and weekends you don't socialise.' Quinn just shrugged.

'Tell me,' said Jake Goodwin. 'Do the Miss Kavanagh's have to socialise through their business?'

'They have people to deal with that.'

'How do you mean?' Darke asked before Jake could get the words out.

'Harry Coates and Kenny Jones deal with that sort of thing.' Jake pulled the pad towards him and flicked back two pages.

59

'Harry Coates the Production Manager and Kenny Jones Sales Manager?' Quinn nodded. 'And the sisters. What do they do?' Darke asked.

'Joint Managing Directors.'

'We know that Mr Quinn. But what do they actually do? Would they get involved in anything that might create enemies?'

'Enemies?' Quinn threw back, and then scratched the couple of days beard growth on his chin. 'I cannot imagine they would have enemies.' Was the suggestion of a beard there on purpose, or under the circumstances had he just forgotten to shave?

'I'm sorry Mr Quinn, but you don't build up a business as big and successful as TwinPrint without making a few enemies along the way.'

'I do not get involved in such matters, thank you.'

'What else do you do apart from paint?' Quinn screwed up his face in reaction to Darke's question. 'Is painting financially viable?' Quinn just looked at him. 'If you didn't have a fairly wealthy wife, how would you fare?'

'That sir, I would suggest is hardly any concern of yours.'

'It most certainly is my concern Mr Quinn,' said Darke firmly. 'Your partner has been found dead in her kitchen without any obvious signs of what might have caused that. You claim you were sitting in the middle of a copse painting and your wife's identical sister was at work.'

'I can assure you I most certainly was and if she says she was, she was. Let there be no mistake.'

'But can you prove that Mr Quinn?' he was asked. 'We only have your word for the fact that you left home,' he pulled the pad back and checked. 'Around five yesterday morning, your partner's sister claims she left two and a half hours later. Her staff at TwinPrint say she arrived just after eight, and CCTV recorded her arriving. But you Mr Quinn, what have you got?'

'I want my solicitor.'

'Solicitors are for people who have been charged with an offence, Mr Quinn. You are simply here, helping us with our enquiries. Helping us piece together the sequence of events for

60

people who for reasons best known to themselves really do not like meeting and talking to other people.'

'It is the way we are, thank you.' Quinn folded his arms and looked completely disinterested.

'Why Mr Quinn? They must communicate at work with people, but it seems the moment the two sisters leave the building they become invisible. And you Mr Quinn, you're invisible all the time.' Darke had realised Quinn never contracted two words. No "aren't" or "it's" in his speech.

'People.' He said, while Darke and Goodwin across the grey table waited. 'People for some reason see them as living curiosities.'

'Because they're twins?' Quinn nodded a response to Darke. 'There are plenty of twins about.'

'Because they always dress the same. Have the same interests, enjoy the same things. It has to be an element of their genes.'

'That's your excuse for them. Being seen as the local freaks. What about you? What do your neighbours think of you? Why don't you play in the Anglers' darts team?'

'Please.' Darke looked at him for more. 'Freak is not a term I appreciate in reference to my...' He hesitated. 'Eilish and her dear sister. I support the girls,' made Craig sigh.

'When our crime scene guys have finished at the house, we will need you to tell us if anything is missing. Was this a robbery gone wrong?' Darke knew there had been no sign of disturbance at the property already.

'We do not have personal possessions like that.'

'Like what?'

'Jewellery and items of adornment that make women look cheap. Bling is it, they call it?'

'Tell me Mr Quinn, man to man,' said Darke holding back a snigger. 'Were you happy with Eilish dressing the same as her sister? Didn't you ever want her to dress the way you prefer, didn't you think she should be dressing to please you and not her elder sister?'

'Dressing to please me?' he mumbled something to himself. 'How full of last century sexism is that? If Eilish is happy, I am happy.'

'Mr Quinn, we're going to leave it at that...'

61

'When can I get in the house?'

'When we've finished.'

'But I need…'

'When Forensics gives the all clear,' said Darke with more than a hint of disinterest in his predicament. 'You'll be the first to know. But I must warn you, it won't be anytime soon.' He flipped over a page of Jake's notebook. 'I would ask that you have a good think about two things. First, is there anybody who can give you an alibi for any part of yesterday before you returned home, and is there anybody who might well have had a reason to cause Eilish Kavanagh harm.' Craig Darke stood up and walked to the door. 'Give your present address to my sergeant if you would be so kind. And I want you to report back here at eleven tomorrow morning with your answers.' and without another word Darke ambled out. Quinn had left him with an awkward and uncoordinated impression.

Back in his office Darke was waiting for Goodwin. 'Get onto Intel and get a proper profile. I want to know everything there is to know about that tosser, his background and the dead woman. Let's start to build a case against him.' Jake slid a piece of paper onto the desk. Darke picked it up. 'And see what you can find out about…Austin Myers.'

9

'Two issues,' said Craig Darke firmly next morning before Sebastian Quinn had hardly sat down. 'Need an alibi for your movements, and tell us about your partner's enemies.'

'I do not have an alibi, Inspector.'

Craig Darke let the rank error go. 'Seven hours in Bassingham and you saw nobody. Is that what you're telling us?'

'I saw people. Nobody I know. I do not know folk around there.'

'What about the local shops? D'you nip in for a paper? Buy a packet of crisps, can of something? Or d'you take it all with you?'

'I am not at all sure what you are talking about.'

'What you survived on. A pack up, snap, lunch. Food,' Darke raised his hands. 'Whatever. Bag of chips from the chippie? Bottle of water?' Quinn let his head shake.

'Not something I would do,' he said as if it were a most unsavoury suggestion. 'I would never drink from a bottle, Inspector. What do you take me for?' He chuckled. 'Eating in the street?' He grimaced. 'How disgusting.'

'You telling me. You sat there all that time without as much as a drink.'

'Probably.'

'Eilish not make you a pack up?' Darke asked and Quinn looked aghast, struggled for words and folded his arms.

'Do you mean sandwiches and…that sort of thing? That what you are suggesting?'

'Yeh,' said Darke as if it was obvious. 'Roll, sarnies, wrap, packet of crisps, banana, yoghurt…'

'Really, really Inspector,' Quinn's chortle turned into a laugh.

'Detective Chief Inspector.'

'You mean like a picnic? Like a hamper?'

'No need to go over the top. Tupperware box will do.' Darke sighed noisily. 'So you didn't take anything with you and you didn't go to the local shops for anything.'

'No,' was part of a chuckle.

'Do you ever?'

'No,' was said in a way that suggested the idea was absurd.

Darke switched. 'Your partner's enemies,' had Quinn looking even more confused.

'I cannot imagine she would have, and in any case Inspector how on earth would I know?'

'Because she was your partner.'

'Social partner, not business partner.'

'Even so. Didn't you talk? Didn't she talk about people she had problems with? Customers, staff whatever.'

'No,' once again had a don't be ridiculous laugh with it.

'And if I asked you to write out a list of the five people most likely to kill your partner, who would top the list?'

'There would be no list.'

'I sincerely hope Mr Quinn; we are not getting into the realms of refusing to help the police, or obstruction of our duties.' Quinn just looked at him. 'That'll be all,' said Darke.

'All the way in here for that?'

'What do you mean?' Darke asked as he rose to his feet.

'I have come here to answer two nonsensical questions. For why?'

'Helping the Police with their enquiries, and I had hoped providing yourself with an alibi. To be honest Mr Quinn, I don't believe you. You happen to know nothing about your partners' business dealings; I'll accept that for now.' He pointed at Quinn. 'But nobody spends six or seven hours without food or drink. Without taking a pack up with them or calling in the local shop.'

'Inspector,' said Quinn as he moved to stand up. 'I was painting. I was not having a picnic. It was not a Sunday school outing. I am not a child. I do not go around buying packets of those crisp things and bottles of fizzy pop.'

'That may be so. But at some point you have to come up with proof that you were in Bassingham that day. Goodbye Mr Quinn. For now.'

Craig Darke remained seated and watched Quinn out of the top of his eyes just wander out.It has been unusually warm and sunny for the best part of a week. And Darke decided to go for a stroll. Enjoy the sunshine, clear his head and think this through.

'You seeing that Sally Conway Sarge?' young DC Harry Botting asked, as he scoffed down Spag Bol as if there was no tomorrow. Sauce all round his mouth.

'No,' Jake Goodwin snorted.

'Saw you talking to her,' came before another forked load.

'And?' stopped him stuffing his mouth full.

'Man hater like that. Thought shit, that's a lot for Sarge to tackle,' and he was off ramming food down his throat again.

'Man hater?'

'Yeh, don't you know,' he spat out along with droplets of tomato sauce.

'Know what?'

He had to wait for most of the pasta to be swallowed, but the young man still spoke with his mouth busy. Sauce had dribbled down his chin, where wisps of adolescent hair clung to life.

'Bout her. With that Derek Morgan prick.' Jake's mind searched his personal database for a sighting of Derek Morgan. The name rang a bell somewhere. 'Big headed bastard, thinks he's God's gift to women,' brought him into view. Black sports car, top down, tinted windows, sunglasses, illegal number plates, huge exhaust. Yes he knew him by reputation. It had been sunny all week. He could picture the prat now in shorts, vest and flip-flops.

'What about him?'

'He was givin' that Sally one, but all the time he was cheating on her. Big time I think. Mate knows all the gory detail.'

'Ask your mate will you?'

'Hey! You are giving her one!'

'No Harry I am not. She was the nurse when I went to A&E, just bumped into her in town.' He lied. 'Just curious.' Jake leant across the table. 'In case you hadn't noticed I'm a detective. I like to know these things.' He sat back, drank his tea, and felt raw inside

65

10

'Thank you for seeing us Miss Kavanagh,' said Craig Darke, sat beside DI Brian Daniels on black real leather chairs in her big office. Eimear Kavanagh had her fingers on both hands splayed, with tips touching at chin level. A sharp black business suit and crisp white blouse had no doubt cost a small fortune. Certainly not something she'd plucked off a rail in Primark or Matalan.

'You took your time.'

'We have a number of routes of enquiry Miss Kavanagh,' Craig Darke responded. 'I spoke to you if you recall when you identified your sister. And I have to say we already knew your whereabouts.'

'If you say so.'

'We just need to go over a few things, if you don't mind. We'll be as unobtrusive as we can. Just need to establish the facts.' Darke cleared his throat. 'Would you care to take us through events as you saw them with regard to your dear sister?'

Eimear Kavanagh thought for a moment without looking at either man. Very black hair looked fixed by something she'd sprayed liberally. The office was oblong with one long wall of three windows at right angles to her desk. As they walked in both officers had sneaked a look down onto the factory floor. Four black leather chairs were set in a semi circle in front of her, with a long low black ash table. On this were what looked like brochures. The main wall to Eimear's right was adorned with what were obviously framed examples of TwinPrint work. Everything from paperbacks they both recognised to posters, magazines and catalogues.

'Sebastian would have gone off around six. He can probably be more precise.' Craig Darke knew it was in fact five. 'Half seven I followed.'

'Answer me this if you would?' said Darke. 'Was Sebastian Quinn likely to take a pack up with him? Something your sister had prepared for him possibly?'

'Like a skivvy would you mean?' Craig Darke wanted to look at Brian after such a strange response.

'No. Like a partner. Like one half of a relationship, for a man about to spend six hours alone in the countryside.'

'I shouldn't imagine so. This is not nineteen fifty.'

'D'you think spending all that time without food and drink is normal?'

Eimear Kavanagh tapped an empty cup on her desk with her nail.

'Ten o'clock coffee. Do you find that strange Mr Darke? Tea at three. Do you have a problem with that?'

'Such as the fact that he wouldn't have coffee at ten or tea at three.'

'If you say so.'

'And lunch?'

'I don't. An hour eating unnecessarily, is an hour of business wasted.' Answered two questions. Why she was so painfully thin and probably why poor old Quinn didn't get a pack up. 'To be honest with you Mr Darke, I wish we'd thought of that. Putting the idea of...grabbing a sandwich as they say, and a...to go drink into people's minds is a great business idea. Perfect business, sell people something they really have no need of. Obesity springs to mind. That really is out of the box.'

'You've never done that,' Daniels suggested.

'Eaten in the street?' she looked aghast at the suggestion. 'Certainly not!' was a response akin to Quinn's. Craig Darke would also never eat in the street but it was still interesting to note her reaction.

'Your sister,' Darke said. 'Did you see anything of her?'

'Sorry?' she said slowly as she tried to catch up.

'That morning.'

'No.'

'But you'd both be heading here presumably.'

'We might be twins but we don't synchronise front door locking and ride on a tandem.' Darke sensed talking about her dead sister may be difficult for her, but she was very composed. 'Nine o'clock I buzzed through to Maureen to ask if she'd seen Eilish. Then I asked her if she had any appointments. She told me she had a meeting with our marketing team at ten, and a little before that Maureen phoned to ask if I would see them.'

'Maureen is...?'

'Our secretary.'

'Didn't this seem strange? No Eilish.'

'We're not answerable to each other,' was abrupt. 'Possible she needed to see the doctor, or had broken a tooth and headed for the dentist. These things happen.'

'And you saw the marketing people?' Brian checked.

'Of course.'

'Does that mean you have specific roles,' her frown meant clarify. 'She deals with marketing, you deal with auditors and accounts say.'

'No,' she said firmly and looked at him as if his suggestion was ridiculous. 'I saw them. They're busy people.'

'What happened next?' Darke continued, to move her away.

'Once I'd dealt with them I asked Maureen to phone her...'

'Why?' stopped the woman.

'Why did I ask her to phone?'

'No,' insisted Darke. 'Why didn't you phone her?' Eimear looked confused and glanced at both policemen, in a way that said she was searching for a reply.

'I was busy, I'd just wasted my time dealing with the marketing guys I had no business with at that time. Anyway that's why we employ Maureen.' Brian looked at his boss out of the corner of his eye, and sensed a look of interest. 'There was no reply. Well, answerphone.'

'For both?' Craig Darke knew it was both. He'd played back the messages on the landline in the house and Eilish's smart phone.

'Of course.'

'When you left the house. Did you see anyone hanging about?' Darke wanted to know.

'How do you mean?'

'Car parked. Someone loitering in the road maybe.'

'No.'

'Your route? To work.'

'Down through the village, A57, by-pass, turn off at Damons,' she said quickly as if it was obvious.

'Just now you suggested that having particular areas of business you each dealt with was not the way you operated. Yet, you also said you had to deal with marketing people you had no business with.'

Daniels loved these. The way his DCI suddenly changed tack or in this case, went back to move the subject out of their comfort zone. He was fascinated by her stiff black hair, like a newsreader on *Sky*. It never moved, looked uncomfortable as if it was false or plastered down. It took Eimear a moment or two to backtrack.

'Eilish had marketing business to deal with, not me.' She looked out of the window and down to the car park, and then twisted her big chair back. 'Do I need to explain everything?' Darke nodded. 'Priority listing. We have a list of priorities. We deal with them one by one in a pre-determined order. Good business practice.'

'Then what?'

'We had a van going out of town. Asked the driver to take a detour, see if there were any signs of life at the house.'

'You weren't too concerned?'

'Only that I needed answers.'

'You weren't concerned enough about your own sister's well being or whereabouts to pop home,' had Eimear grimacing for comprehension.

'I'd sent somebody. Why would I want to go too?'

'Not as well as,' said Daniels firmly. 'Instead of.'

'That's why we employ people,' she said slowly with just a hint of a nervous chuckle and deliberately as if Daniels was a complete fool.

'How many marketing people did you say there were?' took Eimear four seconds to twirl her mind back to deal with.

'I didn't. But three.'

'And when he phoned you?'

'Who?'

'Your driver.' Daniels was close to smiling at how confused she looked.

69

'I er…made arrangements with our secretary.' She closed her eyes to compose her thoughts. 'Called senior members of staff in to discuss what we were going to do, and make plans…'

'What sort of plans?'

'We had an important meeting in London. We had seats booked on a train from Newark. I had that to sort out.'

'How long?' Darke asked bruskely. 'How long was it from receiving the news of your sister's death before you went home?'

She sucked in a breath and sighed. She looked at the pair of them waiting.

'Maybe an hour…maybe more,' was very unsure.

'It was your sister Miss Kavanagh,' said Darke..

'Yes.'

'And you were so interested in her well being; you messed about at work for an hour.'

'I did not mess about!' was firmly delivered without raising her voice. 'Listen here Mr Darke. My sister had been reported dead. Ken the driver said he would phone for an ambulance and the police. So what good was it me going there? What was I going to do? Perform a miracle? Raise the dead?'

'I would certainly show more concern for my sister,' she was told. Her look was there for all to see. 'You phoned Mr Quinn, out painting.' Was an annoyed Craig Darke curve ball to put an end to the politics, said without even a glance in her direction. He was looking at a paperback in a frame on the wall. To some extent he hoped not paying her any attention would annoy her and also an opportunity to remind himself it was one he wanted to read. There was a moment's silence.

'Yes'

'Why?'

'Why what?' she threw back at Darke.

'Why did you phone Mr Quinn?'

'He's my sister's partner!' was loud.

'And?' was Darke throwing everything at her.

'No wonder you're not in business Mr Darke,' she blew out a sigh and shook her head. Absolute insolence in her eyes.

'What's that got to do with anything?'

'Your comprehension of situations is abysmal.' She had no need to raise her voice, despite her flat unemphatic delivery.

'I intend to carry out this investigation in a robust manner.' Darke knew he had to be careful as it was obvious she would assault him with a carefully constructed riposte given an opportunity. 'Therefore, I ask again. Why?' he tossed at her with a hint of a snigger.

'She is my sister, he is her partner.'

'But you didn't bother to go to the house.'

'What's that go to do with anything?' Eimear asked. 'Are you just being particularly obstinate or is this all part of your training Mr Darke? You work for us, not the other way round. I think you need to remind yourself of that.'

'Can we just deal with the matter in hand?' Darke was annoyed but did his level best not to show it.

'You spray paint your own front window with your disrespectful attitude to the populus, Mr Darke. And you wonder why the public see you in the way they do.' Darke knew when she spoke, people listened. This time it was two police officers used to being on the other side of the fence.

'When your driver phoned you, what did he say?' Daniels tossed in before his boss could get into a war of words, he might later regret.

'Ken had had a good look round, tried the front door. It was unlocked, so he went in and found her in the kitchen.'

'Did he say if he'd seen anybody in the vicinity?' Daniels then asked. Darke knew he hadn't, they'd interviewed him and gone over his statement very carefully.

'No.' She looked down at the one sheet of white paper in front of her.

'I notice you refer to your staff by their first names. Maureen, Ken.'

Eimear sighed loudly for effect. 'Those are their names, they are people I work with, day in day out. No lord and lady this cobblers here. No eighty year old Major Generals, in berets, dirty blazers they've dribbled down, festooned with old medals you can probably buy on the internet or get free with cornflakes.' She looked down at

71

the paper. 'House. When can I get in the house? And car. How long is that going to be locked in the garage? We've got a business to run.'

Eimear Kavanagh knew at some point she would have to return to her house. A house she was so proud of had been invaded by police and no doubt a garden trampled over during a 'fingertip' search. Big boot search was more likely, none of them would be on their hands and knees.

'You've got a car,' Craig Darke reminded her. Parked outside. A red Lexus RX.

'No Mister Darke I do not own a car. The company owns all our vehicles. I do not crave personal possessions.'

'Does that mean you drive any vehicle?' Brian Daniels wanted to know.

'Generally just one of the Lexus.'

'So you or your sister will drive either car?'

'Yes. They're identical.'

'Tell me,' said Darke. 'Just out of interest. How do twins decide which cars they will buy? Do you both like the same cars, the same make, same model, and the same colour. Is that all part of twins DNA?'

'Whatever is best for TwinPrint. If a dirty jeep would provide the image we are trying to portray then so be it. Our personal preferences have no place in our lives.' Darke looked around.

'And that go for everything?'

'Yes,' she said firmly. 'What image does this office portray to potential clients, what message does it give out? Not, I prefer pink cushions on the chairs and Eilish likes green, or I'd rather have a red carpet. That is of no consequence in our business.'

Ten more minutes the pair of them were there, and Miss Kavanagh didn't even bother to see them out. She had agreed reluctantly to allow a team in to take everyone's fingerprints. 'To eliminate you all from our enquiries'.

'What a cold bitch! And what's all that Mr Darke business?' Daniels scoffed. 'Silly cow!'

72

'Casual attitude to staff, but they haven't gone the whole hog. Nobody wearing shorts, their pyjamas and no shoes which they tell me is business trendy.'

'Her way of dealing with her loss, possibly?'

'I don't think she gives a toss.'

'I get the feeling both women were like that,' said Brian as he slipped into the driver's seat. 'We've not really interviewed staff, but I think we should boss.'

'I think you're right. We really need to get the feel for these two,' Craig said as he put on his seat belt. 'People talk about them being freaks. Looks like it's their attitude that's freaky. That's why they have no social life. She'd be the life and soul of the party, that one.'

'If her sister was the same, no wonder nobody wanted to know them.'

'And why our Sebastian sat in the woods for hour on end.' He started the car. 'Imagine having to shag that when you get home.'

'Rather you than me!'

Back in the squad room the pair were handed a report that read like a car auction sales list. According to DC Jimmy Hatchard's diligent work he had discovered CCTV at the petrol station a quarter of a mile from the Kavanagh's house. They had two cameras. One concentrating on the forecourt and another looking out onto the road to capture any bilking. The early birds were two Toyotas, a light blue Corolla and a blue Yaris. They were followed by a silver Seat Leon, a Mazda 6 diesel and two Fords – a Fusion and an old Fiesta. Then Kavanagh appeared in her bright red Lexus followed by a metallic grey Suzuki Splash with false number plates. They had been removed from a car parked in someone's drive in Chesterfield. Just a minute later there was a white Fiat 500, a red Astra hatchback, then a 2 litre Peugeot 407, and a Rover 45 on its last legs. There were two vans, four people on bikes including a newspaper boy. Heading in the opposite direction towards the Kavanaghs' and heading for Sturton by Stow were just three in the half hour before she appeared. Then it was a Peugeot, a Corsa and two Escorts. Eight other cars including a white Daihatsu, a green Ford, a black and a grey Honda all of which had been traced and checked through PMC and DVLA.

One poor fool got done for having no insurance for his Fiesta, and trying to trace the Suzuki they discovered only three Silky Silver Metallic models had been sold in the county since the colour launch. All traced, all checked out.

11

'Looks like murder, then' said Tess Conway as she and her daughter Sally settled down to steamed Haddock, baked potatoes and broad beans.

Just the two of them as there was every day of the week. Yet there was a procedure. There was a cotton table cloth spread on the kitchen table. Matching serviettes. A relic of her mother's mother. But gran had silver napkin rings as well, that had somehow been discarded over time. Quality cutlery, place mats and condiments neither woman touched. Salt had been a no go area for some time, but it was still on the table for every meal.

'What does?'

'That woman they found,' said Tess reading from the weekly paper. Sally reached across and lifted the page.

Table cloth and napkins, yet the paper was spread out beside her. A real mixture of cultures, but at least they never sat with processed food on their knees watching television.

A 40-year-old man has been arrested and is helping police with their enquiries after the body of the 37-year-old boss of TwinPrint in the city was found in her kitchen.

Paramedics were called to Saxilby village where Eilish Kavanagh was pronounced dead at the scene.

A Home office pathologist is due to carry out a post mortem examination.

Lincolnshire Police have confirmed that a 40-year-old man is helping with their enquiries and is being interviewed at Police headquarters.

Police are carrying out house-to-house enquiries in the areas as detectives try to establish what happened.

'It was on the radio,' said Sally and placed the pages back carefully where her mother had been reading.

'That would do you.'

'Being murdered?' she chuckled a response as she went back to her meal.

'No. A policeman.' Sally's heart skipped a beat.

'I'd have to get arrested first, and I don't fancy that.'

'They're solid and dependable.'

'You don't know that. They're just people. There's nothing special about them'

'Well, there a lot more special than some of the rubbish you've thrown yourself at.'

'Thank you mother.'

'Well I'm right.' Sally put down her knife and fork, and held her hands up.

'Enough now. I'm not in the mood to go through all that again.'

'That Eddie Knight. I just don't know how you couldn't see that a mile off.'

'Enough!'

'Is he out yet?'

'Must be. Only got six months. Only do half with good behaviour.'

'No, no. Eddie Knight and good behaviour don't go together. You seen him?'

'Don't be ridiculous!'

'You need to get a move on. Not fair on your kids for them to have to explain at their graduation that the grey haired old soul in the wheelchair is their mother.'

'What on earth are you on about?' Sally threw at her.

'You and starting a family.'

'For God's sake, I'm only twenty nine.'

'Nearly in your thirties and you haven't even found anybody yet. Ever thought about a doctor?'

'Going to?'

'No going with.'

'No thanks. Too many fantasies about uniform and exploring intimate parts for my liking.'

'So you do it in uniform, what's the problem?'

'Mother!'

'See Lincoln City won.'

'That's different.'

'Red Alert everyone,' said DCI Craig Darke as he walked into the world of scribbled whiteboards and scrawled flip chart in the corner. 'Settle down, settle down.' He waved a folder, as everyone sat down and he plonked himself on the edge of a table. 'Eilish Kavanagh Post Mortem. Pink lividity, smell of bitter almonds was the give away, no puncture marks so it was digested. Only other things in her stomach were muesli and coffee. Cyanide killed her. Where did she get it from, or more likely who gave it to her? The doc told me her suspicions very early on, but now it's confirmed. So unless I'm very much mistaken we certainly do have a murder on our hands gentlemen. You know the form, let's get to it.'

'And a name in the frame?' DI Brian Daniels asked as he stood up in front of Darke.

'Bloody Rembrandt!' Craig Darke closed his eyes and threw out a breath. 'Why can't he be normal? Why can't Quinn be like anybody else? No. He sits for bloody hours in a wood on his own with nothing. He doesn't take a bottle, or a flask. No pack up, and more importantly for us, he says he didn't call at the local shop for a Snickers, packet of fags or to buy the bloody *Sun*.' He spun to look at Rachel Pickard. 'Am I being a male chauvinist?' he asked her. 'Am I expecting every wife to dutifully fill a flask for their husband and put sandwiches and an apple in a Tupperware box? Am I wrong in expecting most women would have bought a Mars from the Co-op?'

'Most women I know would,' she retorted. 'Nothing to do with the macho and the dutiful domestic. Andy would do the same for me. But even if she's not the sort, what's wrong with him? Why can't he stop at the garage and buy a sandwich? Very odd if you ask me.'

'Get Raza and Tigger out to Bassingham,' said Darke. 'See what they can come up with. Ask in the shop, in the pub, butchers, and bakers, anywhere. Did anyone see him; in fact has anyone ever seen him out there? According to him that was the second day he spent there. I've put where he said he was exactly on the system.' He hesitated. 'And while they're at it. What exactly can you get out there? Coffee to go, a chippy, crisps? He was there for hours remember.'

It was Brian Daniels turn.

'Stew', he said to one of his Detective Constables. 'We need to talk to employees, and more importantly former employees to get the lie of the land. Don't want them spooked and come out with the company song. Can we ask about, see if we can find somebody with an axe to grind.'

'The more we uncover,' said Darke. 'The more likely it would appear to be just those three. Haven't had a sniff about any outside agencies wanting a piece of the action.' He looked across the room. 'Jake!' he shouted and beckoned the Detective Sergeant over to him.

'Yes boss,' said Jake as he rested his arm on a pile of box files. 'I want you to find out everything you can about TwinPrint. How did those two odd ball women come to run something like that?'

'Will do,' said Jake and sauntered away.

'And what's this I hear about you and some nurse?' Jake was shocked but tried not to show it. Dropped onto his chair and pretended to get on with his work.

'A nurse sorted out my leg that's all,' he muttered.

'Middle leg was it?' left Jake blushing as four or five had a good laugh. Craig Darke turned to Daniels. 'Put on your beret, dust down your easel and delve a bit deeper. Get somebody to find out what they can about Sebastian Quinn.' He slid a print out across the desk. 'That's what Intel came up with. Need a lot more. Pompous pillock who looks as though he gets dressed in the coal shed and has a piss easy life with a rich wife.' He looked up at Brian. 'And while you're at it. What's that awful car all about?'

'Being arty with a capital F.'

'It's shit!'

Jake had his head down looking at his screen surrounded by postits of every shape and colour. Some his gran had given him for Christmas. He was hoping the nurse comments had subsided when he realised his DCI was stood by him.

'PM says she died around eight,' said Darke as he plonked his hands down on the desk and leant in. 'Quinn was in Bassingham by then, so he says and Eimear was at work. Two things. When Raza and Tigger get back, work out a timeline for Quinn leaving home and arriving in Bassingham, and then cyanide. We need to know who supplied cyanide to whom.'

'And how he or she delivered it.'

'I've tried to get what I can from our pathologist friend, but she's away lecturing, so I'll pop and see her when she returns next week. See if she's any idea how you stuff cyanide down someone's throat?' He slapped Jake on the shoulder. 'It's similar in appearance to sugar. Apparently convulsions occur, and although the body initially suggests there has been a cardiac arrest the bruising and lacerations often caused by the convulsions illustrate likely poisoning. Death is as a result of hypoxia of the neural tissue. It was the bruising that confirmed it for the Doc. Have a look for suppliers. Check them against Quinn's phone calls, emails, texts. Need help, get hold of Toni. Might stop him picking his nose.'

Eilish's phone calls and use of her credit card had been of no use at all. Toni had discovered one credit card account, with both sisters having a card. Very little activity, nothing since her death, and the only thing of note had been a holiday deposit payment to Thomas Cook for a trip to Laos. They both had debit cards both linked to one bank account. Salaries in and normal run-of-the-mill payments out, plus cash on a weekly basis. Phone calls he had traced had all been business linked.

12

It was Saturday night, it was close to ten and what high life was Jake enjoying? Making a cup of tea in his kitchen was the best so far. True there was an all hands to the pump murder enquiry going on, and he'd been given part of Wednesday off in exchange for working the weekend.

Was his lifestyle conducive to having a pucker relationship? How many females would settle for him being at home on Wednesday for a few hours while they were at work, and then on a Saturday night have to wait for him to turn up, sometime, anytime to suit the force?

He had no preconceived ideas about his future. A pretty young thing to live with, to then marry and provide children was not the be-all-and-end-all as far as Jake was concerned. After all his boss survived without a woman at home to see to his every need.

As long as ten years down the line he didn't finish up overweight, slumped in a corner at the beer festival sipping yet another pint of Old Corn Knobbler. Dressed in a 3XL 'Mega Suicide Monkeys' emblazoned black t-shirt and baggy scruffy dirty grey jogging bottoms and gawdy trainers with laces undone he didn't mind.

He'd been going through a phase where he couldn't get to sleep, and had decided to make a cup of tea and listen to Rick Wakeman's *'Past, Present and Future'* very loud. So loud he only just heard his phone chirp. The screen surprised him: *'Sal'*.

'Hi,' he said and began to turn down the music.

'What's that noise?'

'Noise?' he threw back. 'That's Rick Wakeman.'

'Really?'

'I'll lend you it.'

'No thanks,' she threw out. 'You needn't bother.'

'Why can't they produce talent like him these days?'

'You really want to know?' she asked quietly. 'Anyway need to talk to you. Thought with you doing what you do, better confess.'

'What to? Armed robbery…?'

'Well if you're going to…'

'Hey, hey. Joke. Sorry, just a joke.' He heard her clear her throat.

'Used to go round in a sort of gang, and they were a bit manic sometimes. Girly nights out and Hen Parties. But it was either them or nothing.' He heard her clear her throat. 'At Christmas we went to Manchester for the day and one thing led to another and...'

'Last Christmas?'

'Few years back. Three I think. Anyway we'd go into big posh department stores,' Sally garbled. 'They used to play a game where one of us would pretend we were really interested in buying something very expensive, then at the last minute when the assistant thought she'd made a sale, we'd change our mind, have a good laugh and walk out.'

'Naughty nurses.'

'When we went to Manchester, I drew the short straw and had to chat up the assistant. Being Christmas it was very busy, and so I'm making a meal out of buying this jacket that was priced at about eight hundred if I remember rightly. Anyway we do the usual, and when we were outside and down the street laughing our socks off, they handed me a pure silk scarf.' She coughed. 'They'd nicked them, and stole one for me too. Hundred and fifty quid each. They were beautiful. I was mortified. I was scared stiff we'd been spotted and a cop car was going to race round the corner. We'd be on CCTV and I was shaking for days. I'm sorry. Sorry Jake I really am.'

'Hey, hey. Don't worry.'

'But I paid for them,' she said quickly. 'I sent back the one they gave me, and took money out of my savings and posted it all to the shop. Explained what they'd done. But I didn't give my name,' she said hurriedly.

'You need to calm down young lady. That's good. You did the right thing. But it would have been better if they'd sent theirs back too.'

'You're joking! They wear theirs.'

'They do this a lot?'

'No idea. We fell out over it. I couldn't tell them I'd sent mine back and paid for theirs, otherwise they'd have laughed at me. Daren't go out with them again,' she admitted. 'Sorry.'

'Why did you feel responsible?'

'They were my friends.'

81

'But why are you friends with such people?' she felt was not as sympathetic as she expected.

'It's not as easy as that. Two are nurses.'

'Listen very carefully,' he said slowly. 'You did right. The shop's got its goods back or the money and you've reported it to the Police. End of. Understand?' Was he on fast forward? He wondered if he'd missed a few instalments of Sally and Jake the new Saturday night drama. How had they gone from chatting idly over coffee to this?

'Thanks for that. Feel better now.' He sat there with his phone to his ear waiting. 'Right. Be off then.' Click and she was gone.

What had that been all about?. He was concerned at how had they jumped from that nonsense over coffee to a confession and then she was gone.'

Jake Goodwin never did watch late night television. He should have had that Ovaltine and when he climbed into bed something he'd read that day brought bad bedtime torments from his youth.

As a young teenager Jake had gone through a period when his mind in bed was controlled by a question. *What If There Was Nothing.*

This torment stayed with him for months before his brain moved him onto something else probably equally ridiculous.

Years before he was aware of boffins and geeks wasting billions building the Hadron Collider instead of feeding the starving, he was tormented by a world where there would be nothing to collide.

No the universe did not start with some sort of big bang, because in Jake's teenage world there was no universe. There was nothing. There never had been anything. No people here or anywhere in the solar system which itself would never have existed. No Earth, Moon, Sun or stars. With no Sun it wouldn't even be dark. No black holes, no planets billions of light years away, ever. No.... *think about this seriously and it will start to drive you insane!*

Those supporting the suggestion that some sort of 'God' had taken six days to create heaven and earth, miss out too. When there is nothing, that means precisely that. Nothing. No God. Just an empty space.....no! Not an empty space, even that would never have existed.

13

Their table was against the far wall in the restaurant, where they were not overlooked and could see everybody and everything. Craig and Jillie both ordered starters of Nachos, with cheese, chipotle salsa, sour cream and jacapenos.

Craig had never eaten Nachos before. In fact he didn't have a clue what to expect. There had only been three choices of Starter. Sweet corn soup. He didn't like sweet corn that much, boring toasted garlic bread, and these Nachos.

They both went for soft drinks as they were driving. Jillie would have preferred a red wine, but so be it, this was not Henry's Café Bar in the Wharf and he was the Police. Why are so many of these modern eating places so dark, she wondered. What's with the black walls, what are they hiding?

'Think we were set up,' he told her. 'Did your mother make a big thing about you going to the Spring Fayre?'

'Yes, come to think of it. I've only been back a couple of months, had nothing else to do, so I'd got no excuse.'

'We were set up then,' he smiled and sucked on the black straw in his drink that almost matched his mop of unruly hair. 'Want to know why you weren't the Wise Man?' She nodded. 'You were my favourite, even at that age with all that beautiful hair,' and she knew he was admiring it. His chocolate brown shirt matched his cords and the tan boots like his leather jacket were very shiny. 'You could never be a man, wise or otherwise and,' he lowered his voice a little. 'I needed one with the confidence to read the story. Thought I was giving you the special job.' He sucked again. 'Sorry.'

'Am I right in thinking you actually wrote the story?'

'Our version.' He admitted. 'Special Birthday Card.' Nervousness was running up and down her body. This man at seventeen (her mother had worked out) had an effect on her, now all these years later he was ravaging her. 'Extra jelly at the Christmas Party, piggy back rides at Hunstanton.'

She leaned towards him. 'How d'you mean special card?'

'They had a supply of cheap birthday cards we could use. When yours came round I went out and bought one specially.' Jillie sat there knife and fork in hand shaking her head slowly from side to side. He smiled away the hint of embarrassment. 'Now I'd need a CRB check and some other rubbish.'

'These days you'd have to sign the Sex Offenders Register for holding my hand in the coach,' she said and guessed by his look he was recalling the memory. 'And I'd have to phone Childline!'

'This is a bit hot,' he said about his food that they then concentrated on for a few minutes. Interspersed with memories of those days back in Sunday school.

Craig had already gone through a multitude of images from his past. Of Jillie and the other girls all frolicking in the sea on the Sunday school outing. Of them all splashing him and chasing him up the beach, and helping a couple of the younger boys with their sandcastle.

'Are you going to tell me or do I have to guess?' Craig peered up from his food as he came down to earth. 'Why you've suddenly appeared out of the blue.'

'I haven't. But I think you have.'

'You been checking up on me? That what you do for a living and can't stop yourself?'

'Hang on,' said Craig and motioned to their side as the waiter arrived with her Tagliatelle Carbonara and his Beef Stroganoff. 'Thanks,' he said as their plates were placed before them. 'No thanks,' was her response to a question about sauces.

This was the big dilemma. Should he go into detail about Katherine's death, right there and then, this early on? Was this too soon, would it put a real dampener on proceedings, or did she expect him to talk about her? In the past with women he had met he'd not said anything, then been accused of holding back secrets. Craig felt that evening just as he had many times before that he was in a no-win situation. Timing was everything.

Jillie knew from experience, sat there, that blokes like this do not grow on trees. Craig started to eat, so she let the matter rest. Why did he look so troubled? 'Where d'you live now?'

'Got my own place in Lincoln.'

'Lincoln?' she gasped. 'They all said you'd gone away. I've always thought it was away away, not just up in Lincoln.'

'Lived in Shropshire after uni. Been back this way a few years now.'

'Any specific reason why you moved back?'

His shoulders rose and fell before he spoke. 'Needed a change,' and they were back to stories about winning a three legged race and trying to remember who was the star of the pantomime they'd been to.

.Craig had finished his meal and put down his knife and fork. He lifted what remained of his cold drink and downed it all in one go. 'Want another?'

'Please, same again.' Craig motioned the waiter over and asked for a repeat on the cold drinks.

'I could be down here again next weekend,' he said in a hurry. The little voice in his head working overtime told him to slow down and take it easy. He still had a huge hurdle to get over.

'Wait a minute,' Jillie said. One minute he seemed only to want to talk about days of yore, now he's talking about another date. Was that all he needed, somebody to join him in his little world? 'What about me? What if I'm divorced with three snotty kids?'

He grinned. 'You're not. You said so in your email. Anyway is there a law against having a meal when you've been married, divorced and got three kids?'

'I haven't.'

He put up both hands in an act of surrender. 'You asked for honesty right at the start. So here goes.' He hesitated a moment. 'I know. Because Lavinia told me,' he said, and then added: 'She asked your mum, apparently. You've been in two big relationships, says they're both over. Used to work in the City, now got a job at that Golden Fitness place.'

Jillie wanted to tell him the second of those relationships wasn't anything real, nothing you could hang your coat on. The first was a real problem she knew at some point she would have to deal with. But not now. Honesty could just take a back seat.

'I was right, you have been checking up on me.'

'No,' he said firmly. 'Just didn't want to put my foot in it.'

85

'And how would you do that?'

'Make myself look a damn fool probably. Kiss you goodnight then find out later you're engaged and planning your wedding, and this was all just a bit of fun for old times sake. Spend a week feeling too embarrassed to show my face.'

'That the plan?'

'Plan?' he threw out with a breath, as Jillie took his fingers in hers across the table.

'You're blushing,' she chided and for Craig he felt this was all going terribly wrong. He dropped his head almost in an attempt to hide the pink of his cheeks. 'Will the cops be happy with you kissing your pupil?' Craig lifted his head and had to smile even though he was convinced she was having a laugh at his expense, as he searched for a change of subject in the midst of his embarrassment.

'Where d'you work?' he mumbled then corrected himself. 'Sorry. Where did you work?'

'USACorp,' meant nothing to him. 'Then with the German Munchen Bundesbank.' She smiled. 'I dealt in futures. Senior manager in screen based index futures.'

He smiled. 'Gobbledygook springs to mind,' he told her.

'Futures are contracts to buy and sell things at an agreed point in the future. Speculating on shares or oil and all sorts.' Jillie downed the last of her drink. 'Got any spare cash?' For a moment he thought she meant the change in his pocket. 'I'll invest it for you in oil futures if you like.'

'How long before I get my million pound bonus?'

'Very funny,' but he could see she really wasn't amused. She must have had so many dorks making crass remarks in recent times.

'Sorry.' Craig was fortunate in that a new subject popped up. 'Have you ever seen any of the others from Sunday school?'

'Once saw...' Jillie hesitated. 'Sue Greig with three kids. Few years back now.'

'Marie?' Jillie shook her head. 'Nearly forgot. Jill.'

'That's the obvious one. My mum might know.'

'Two Jills, turned into Jill and Jillie. You always use it now?'

'Most of the time.' Fresh drinks arrived and they both sat sipping for a while. 'Problems at work?' she queried suddenly. Craig looked left and right.

'Murders,' he said softly.

'You're kidding me. No wonder you're a bit pre-occupied.'

'It's not that. This is a night off,' got him a look that had explain written all over it. He blew out a long breath. In for a penny, in for a pound. 'I was married and my wife was killed. Got there ten minutes too late, saw her being dragged out of her car. Now you know, so that's buggered that.' Craig went back to his drink and as he supped his hand was squeezed.

'Why d'you say that?' was very intimate as she leant towards him.

'Women's reaction. Tell them you're divorced doesn't seem to be a problem, but a dead wife seems to freak them out. Couple of times I've been left to eat on my own.' Jillie was shaking her head slightly and had screwed her face up. He had learned the hard way how easy it was to be lonely in a crowd.

'I knew about both before I got here. I know about Katherine and you being a big cheese in the Police. I'm still sitting here. How long is it, you and I? I'll tell you how long it is, eighteen years, and I'll be honest I expected you to be totally out of reach. Happily married with at least a couple of kids, school run, swim lessons, football, fine house with a mortgage, holidays in the sun and all that. You were never going to be interested in that soppy girl with freckles from Sunday school.' She stopped to collect her thoughts. 'I lived with this stockbroker who turned out to be a real bastard. More interested in keeping his hoity-toity friends happy than me. Got fed up with banking, Been really pissed off for a while with being a woman in this ultra macho world. So I'm taking a sabbatical.' If only that were the whole truth.

'Got another confession. I don't go to church,' made Jillie chuckle heartily. 'Well, not very often.'

From there it was a case of her explaining in layman's terms about her role in banking. How Golden Fitness was just a stop gap, rather than sit at home all day with her mother. Craig talked about his work without going into case specifics, but his mind was completely on subject.

Jillie knew about Katherine. What did she know about Katherine? Craig wondered how much she had been told, and those who had told her, how much did they really know? Were they aware of the accident, aware that taking her to A&E was a complete waste of time with her head having been almost completely severed?

The inquisition had run its course and when the meal was over he walked her to her car at the rear of the pub. Then the awkward moment as she stood with her back to the open door of her new dark blue BMW, made worse by their conversation earlier.

'It's been really good,' he said down to her as his gentle hands cupped her face.The rush from her lips to her groin amazed her. Not one man or boy in twenty nine years had ever produced such a reaction from her body. A reference to the illicit nature of their former positions possibly. Teacher and pupil alone in the dark and a tender, soft and sweet kiss. Had she dreamt of this when she was twelve, secretly holding hands on the coach? Had those thoughts all come rushing back? Had she imagined what it might be like to be held in his arms to feel *him*, taste *him*?

Craig Darke's thoughts were elsewhere. On that motorway that dark wet evening that had changed his life forever. Katherine had no knowledge of Jillie Lombard with whom it could be said he had just been unfaithful or would she have given the kiss her full approval and support?

14

Craig Darke was sat in his small office, going through more paperwork when he sensed the presence of somebody at his open door before he heard the knock.

'Boss,' said Natalie Scoley quietly, as he looked up. 'Just had a thought.' Darke motioned her to a chair on the right of his desk. 'What if our killer is the real father of the kids?'

'Oh my bloody God!' he exclaimed as his hand went to his forehead. 'Brian!' he shouted.

'Gone to the canteen.' Darke was on his feet, and at the door.

He called out: 'Somebody get down to the canteen. Tell Brian Daniels to get his arse back up here, and to bring two decent coffees with him.' He walked back to his chair and slumped down. 'Where'd that come from?'

Natalie shrugged. 'Just came to me.'

'That would mean Gorich would let him in, and...' He stopped and looked at Natalie. 'We've got DNA from the women. If we get DNA from the kids and the two men we'll know if Gorich's husband and Hank Harding are the fathers. Or...or one of them is the father of both kids.' He hesitated as if daring to say it. 'Or somebody else is.'

'Would that give us our man's DNA?' Natalie queried.

'A child inherits half of his or her DNA from each biological parent. Not sure,' he pondered. 'Call it genetic inheritance.' He sat back in his chair. 'Bloody sure these days they can then come up with a DNA we can put through the system. The bloody hours I've spent trying to fathom who Gorich might let in.'

'And he'd know Petchey went out the back door all tarted up.'

'If you're right, he certainly puts it about.' Darke noticed how a hint of flush entered Natalie's face. 'Wonder what's so special about him?'

'Often wonder what some women see in men they go with.'

'You seeing someone?'

Natalie shook her head. 'Doesn't go down too well, boss.'

'What doesn't?'

89

'Being in the police.' Darke was not about to admit anything.

'Gives you your own in built vetting system. Useful I would think,' he said as Brian Daniels appeared at the door. 'Coffee?'

'Pete's bringing them. You wanted me?'

'Sit down,' said Darke and waited until Daniels was settled. 'Want to know why Gorich would let our Mr Who into her kitchen?' He didn't wait for a verbal response. 'Our mystery man is the real father of their kids.'

'Fucksake!'

'It's so bloody obvious when you think about it,' Darke retorted. 'Little job for you. Get hold of the Lovan Gorich and Hank Harding DNA test results. Then talk to Gillis about getting the two kids...er...' Natalie came to his rescue.

'Amelie Petchey or maybe Harding and Toby Gorich.'

'Getting them tested.' He smiled at Daniels. 'Put 'em together and what do we have with a bit of luck ?'

'No match and a new daddy.'

'Exactly. He growing this coffee?' he asked Brian.

Jake Goodwin took a seat in the main CID incident room between Ross Walker and chunky DC Toni d'Andrea. Weather wasn't as good as it had been the previous week. Across the grey table from him was second from the top of the squad Detective Inspector Brian Daniels alongside Rachel Pickard. To her right was young Harry Botting. As they waited for the DCI, Natalie Scoley appeared with a tray and mugs of coffee. Monday morning, Leeds lost to Watford at home on Saturday and Brian Daniels was like a bear with a sore head.

'I'm all ears,' said Craig Darke the moment he appeared in the doorway, took a mug of coffee from Natalie's tray and plonked himself down. 'Thought we'd just spread the word as most of us are here. I've got news on fingerprints, but we'll come to that.'

'Tigger and Raza?' DI Daniels snapped.

'Came back empty handed. Told them to get hold of that Quinn and get him to take them to the actual spot. According to Tigger if he was in the village, nobody saw him and nobody's ever heard of him.

90

All yours,' he said to the gathered throng as Scoley finished pushing round the mugs.

Walker responded first. 'Don't care where you go in that toy town car, some bugger must see you.'

'Sebastian Quinn,' said Jake from his notes. 'Forty two years old from Cornwall originally. No idea how he met the twins, but one assumes through his painting because at one time he had a small gallery in Mevagissey. Always possible they went there on holiday. Couple of touristy shops up here sell his paintings, but they are a bit pricey for what they are. They are all countryside views done in water colour. They're alright if you like that sort of thing. My guess is, he can ask eight hundred and seventy five a throw,' he waited for people to suck in their breath. 'Because he doesn't need the money. Because these pompous arty shops are awash with twerps' money anyway.'

Daniels took a sip of coffee from the white mug in front of him. To his credit he never attempted to hide his receding hairline, or his mood.

'My guess is', Jake continued. 'He somehow charmed himself into their lives, and somehow managed to prize one of them away long enough to form a relationship. Got no form.'

'Actually, pompous is how I'd describe Quinn,' said Darke. 'Pompous.' He looked across. 'Rachel, think what you've got will fit that nicely.'

'Fergus Kavanagh suddenly arrives around here nearly twenty year ago. From what I've been able to gather he and a work mate in Ireland took over a small printing firm in Wexford they both worked for, more than ten years before that.' Rachel Pickard looked at her screen. 'That would be back in the days of metal typeface and printing blocks, way before they then moved onto litho and the computerised systems we have today. Somehow that all went for a ball of chalk and this Fergus winds up around here. Found a local printer who was ahead of his time but in need of a cash injection, and set about building a business.'

'That's where the twins got their knowledge no doubt.'

'Exactly,' said Rachel. 'The chap who owned it originally retired. Fergus Kavanagh bought up his shares, formed a limited company

91

TwinPrint Limited. Ten years ago this Fergus also retired back to Ireland and left his girls in charge. Eilish has forty nine per cent and Eimear has fifty one.'

'Alarm bells…'

'I know,' said Rachel swiftly. 'Let me finish. This is serious printing. This is not running off a few business cards, wedding invitations or a leaflet for a new pizza place. This is big time. Apparently they are digital printers with integrated colour image processes and they print in millions. They print on demand and distribute their work worldwide. According to the last set of accounts they've submitted they made in excess of two million in the last financial year.'

She looked at Craig Darke.

'A couple of clever cookies,' he said. 'But at the same time that Eimear is one nasty woman. That how you have to be to get on in business? Be the biggest bitch of all time. Well done Rachel. What else?'

'Away from work nobody knows them. Literally,' said DC d'Andrea. 'They really don't socialise, don't use local pubs or even shops come to that. Window cleaner I spoke to told me he'd heard they don't even do their own weekly or monthly shop. Woman in the office at TwinPrint is given a list and does it for them. Same list every week. Never varies. Even get one of the lads to take their cars to fill them with petrol. Don't even do that themselves.'

'This all because a few nutters think they're freaks?'

'Could be their freak reputation has nothing to do with being dress alike twins, more to do with not socialising, never going to Morrisons or wherever. Never calling in for a paper, not buying their Lottery tickets.'

'That Eimear takes some beating. Wouldn't want her on my pub quiz team.'

'At two million a year, who needs Lottery tickets?'

'Is this the key? This why Eilish's been poisoned? Because she was a complete shit like her sister' the DCI needed to know. 'She upset somebody big time?'

'If that Eilish was like her sister, it wouldn't surprise me if people wanting to top her formed a queue. As we both know she is really nasty,' Daniels said to his DCI.

'You're absolutely right,' said Darke. 'Almost as if she's angry about something.'

'Weird,' was a one word description from Daniels to define the world of these strange sisters. 'Forensics as you know found a few anomalies at the house, but the strange bit is next door.' Brian Daniels took a drink from his mug. 'Remember these two houses are identical. Had them built to their own specification. Five bedroomed houses, and you have to ask what for? Especially Eimear who lived alone. Inside, both houses are exactly the same. Let me tell you, that's a bit creepy. Furniture, curtains, carpets. The whole lot are identical.' He put his mug down, folded his arms and smiled.

'Holiday,' said Daniels as a prompt to his boss.

'Oh yes.' Darke sat up in his chair. 'Two women who it would appear don't even go to the paper shop or the supermarket planned a holiday in Jakarta.' A few enquiring faces made him explain. 'Indonesia. Far East. Out past Singapore. Not on my holiday wish list.'

'Seychelles if you want to show off,' said Daniels. 'Jakarta? And soppy sod Quinn having...'

'Go on,' said Craig Darke. 'Out with it.'

'I think Quinn was giving them both one.'

'Get away.'

'Those old biddies?' tall Ross Walker shot out.

'Don't talk wet!'

'Were his fingerprints on the bed?' Craig Darke looked at Daniels who shrugged.

Brian Daniels got to his feet. 'Double bed in both houses are once again identical. My guess is, they share Sebastian bloody Quinn. And he gets a free trip to Jakarta as a bonus.'

He walked over and opened a window.

'And it's all gone wrong?'

'They're not old biddies,' Daniels snapped a reminder.

'The twins are only in their thirties,' said Pickard.

'You suggesting Eimear poisoned her sister?'

'Somebody did,' said Daniels grumpily as he took his seat. Was a football match that important?

'Tell you what I'll do with you all,' said Craig Darke seriously. 'I'll treat any one of you to a night out if you can come up with a way you could poison somebody without a struggle and without you being there when it happens, and at a time when you want it to happen.' He downed more of his coffee. 'Give that some thought. Carry on digging. Just keep this ménage á trios at the back of your mind, just in case.'

'Could be the pace is too much for Quinn, so he dumped one,' got Ross Walker a stern look from his DCI.

'D'you say Tigger and Raza came up with bugger all?'

'Sweet Fanny Adams, he might as well have never been there.'

'Perhaps he wasn't.' Darke picked up a sheet of paper. 'We've got all the fingerprints except four. Remember, there's just one set of prints at the house. Like somebody wiped the place clean, but missed four. Ross,' and Walker looked up.

'Missing five members of staff are away, one bloke off sick apparently.' He waved the paper. 'Got his detail here. Kenny Jones the Sales Manager's in Canada, been there a week so we discount him, woman on holiday and two drivers.'

'Check the sick bloke Ross and these drivers. That'll be all for now,' and Darke waved them all away.

As the remainder all dispersed to their various tasks the DCI caught Jake's attention.

'Surveillance job coming up looks like next week for City of London. Put your name down for it. I'll let you have the details. P'raps take one of the girls with you.'

'Having trouble looking into Quinn,' Jake told his boss once everybody was back to work. 'Myers is not easy, but I can knock on his door.'

'Kavanagh's probably our best bet for Quinn. She must know about him. Don't fancy the ideas to be honest, might call on her at work if we get desperate. Leave it with me. You concentrate on Myers.'

'Sarge,' said young Botting as he caught up with Jake in the car park. 'That Sally Conway woman.' Jake was all ears, but managed to curb his enthusiasm.

'What you on about?' he asked the young chubby faced DC.

'Sally Conway. You were asking.' Jake Goodwin motioned his acknowledgement. 'Morgan was seeing her apparently. But was shacked up with some bint from Gainsborough.' DC Botting looked all about unnecessarily. 'One of these Cougars.' It was eminently obvious he had to explain. 'These women who go with blokes young enough to be their sons.'

Jake had not given a great deal of thought to what he might be told. Had he done so, he was never going to come up with this scenario.

'You're joking,' he exclaimed. 'How old is he?' Harry Botting grimaced. He'd somehow caught the fitness bug or at least what purported to be an aid to fitness. At one time went to the gym twice or three times a week. In truth he'd be better of going for a run and eating properly, which if nothing else would save him a small fortune. Like everybody else the gym phase was something he'd grow out of.

'Twenty eight, thirty at most.'

'So she could be how old, forty?'

'More like fifty.' Jake Goodwin grasped his forehead with his hand.

'Let me get this straight. This Morgan shit is seeing Sally and this old biddie at the same time?' He took in a breath. 'Why?'

'Best 'o both worlds.' Botting had to go on. 'The old woman mothers him as well. Gives him all home comforts. Does his washing, cooks his meals and gives him a shag. Probably pulls every trick in the book to keep him. He thinks he's died and gone to heaven.'

'And this Sally found out?'

'Guess so.'

'That's gotta be hard to take. Being cheated on is bad enough, but bloody hell!'

'Thought you'd like to know.'

'Thanks, but there's no need to tell everybody!' Botting looked very sheepish as he strolled away.

That night Jake Goodwin checked his emails, then Googled 'Cougars'. He was amazed to find so many sites. Dating sites for young men to find these older women. There was chit chat about female liberation and nonsense about how this phenomenon from America had empowered modern feminism.

Officers all around the CID incident room were typing up reports of interviews. People in Saxilby they'd spoken to. Neighbours, the postman, the milkman who didn't deliver to them but might have seen something early doors. Paperboy and the pub landlord who'd never met them in their lives. Phones rang at intervals; mobiles chirped or made ridiculous sounds.

Jake had managed to slip the subject into conversation with young Botting struggling to tap his keyboard with two fingers, and discovered the big bust up between Sally and this Morgan shit had all happened eight or ten months back.

'So what's this man hater business?'

'My mate's woman's a nurse. Knows her like. Seems since then a couple of sods have shit on her too. Be gay before you can turn round.'

'What on earth are you on about?' Jake grinned.

'Thas what 'appens,' Botting said as if everybody knew. 'Birds get shit on by blokes, they turn gay. Without nobhead blokes there'd be no gay girls,' was an extraordinary thing to say.

'Yeh, right.'

'Thas what 'appens,' and he reckoned DC Botting was being serious. Misguided, but serious.

'You saying she's gay now?' He needed to know. Oh how he needed to know.

'Nah. Could be soon though. Won't touch blokes with a barge pole. Wouldn't mind touching it with mine!'

Jake had lost Beth after that one night stand with that Polish girl he met at that party he hadn't planned to go to. Truth he and young Beth were only seeing each other and his lack of effort to retrieve the

96

situation told him it was only a jog along relationship anyway. But it was cheating. You don't do that.

All part of his strict upbringing. In his world, discipline is a by word for everything you do. You do not speed in your car; you don't park in a disabled space. You do not drop litter. You put the right things in the correct rubbish bin. Self control to him means you put the right bin out on the correct week; you do not leave it in the street. You return a supermarket trolley back to the bay. You open doors for other people. You don't jump a queue. He would never tailgate or use his mobile phone in a car or in a public place. Jake could never eat or drink in the street, and had probably never even considered it. Always taxed and insured his car. Bought a TV Licence by direct debit. Things he learnt from his parents. He knew of no other way to behave.

He cheated on Beth. He has no idea why. Does not know to this day what got into him, apart from allowing his prick to be in command, and will remain eternally sorry for his sordid action. There is no excuse; there cannot be an excuse for such behaviour. In a decent society, in his idea of a properly ordered society Jake Goodwin would like to live in, which he was brought up in; you simply do not behave like that. Discipline an absolute watch word. Probably why he joined the Police.

He had let down Beth and himself.

Derek Morgan had no doubt done that deliberately loads of times. But then he probably did things every day that Jake would never do, would never ever consider to be acceptable.

That evening Craig was at home. Couple of phone calls so far that week had reassured him. Plans were made for them to meet for another meal. Another evening on soft drinks with them both arriving by car. He had considered booking a hotel room. Getting a taxi from the restaurant. Then that wouldn't be fair on Jillie, unless he arranged to pick her up and drop her back at her parents after by cab.

Sat there with a glass of red pondering the situation his mind wandered through his troops. What would they do? Would they mess about with a taxi here there and everywhere. Some would, but some he knew would have an altogether different plan in mind.

He couldn't could he? He couldn't suggest to Jillie that they both go back to the hotel like some of the lads would do. He knew some of the younger ones would take her home and their parents would turn a blind eye to goings on under their roof at night. He had to laugh. The thought of his dear mother welcoming Jillie into her home late at night before they trooped off upstairs to bed together, had produced more than an easy chuckle. Lovely mother, but no way.

15

Just one solitary name on the TwinPrint staff list matched anything on the Police National Computer. Perhaps they were all too good to be true, or the Kavanagh sisters were very careful who they employed.

Ross Walker had been to see the employee off sick and discovered him at home suffering from shingles. A check of the CCTV system at Twin Print showed the two drivers taking their vehicles out, and staff confirmed that they had both phoned in having reached their destinations. Phil Henderson had headed for Harwich to deliver a container and Brian Barry had said he was waiting with his Vivaro for a Eurostar train to Calais, and was then due to head for northern Italy.

Harry Botting and Toni d'Andrea had the task of getting background information on the company. Their one name turned out to be a company man and was very careful indeed in what he said. As the two of them gradually turned the conversation at Steve Kemp's front door away from the events of recent days to the history of TwinPrint he provided snippets. Their casual laid back attitude worked. When his dog came to the door, they both made a fuss of the scraggy mongrel. As they became matier Kemp provided them with information on the company's technical ability, linked with snippets on employees who had worked for the firm in the past.

According to this bald but hairy armed Steve Kemp, TwinPrint were involved in serious printing methods. One example they tried to understand was where apparently they electrically charge droplets of ink, about the diameter of a human hair at some incredible thousands per second rate. They were told how they do laser coding and are major global printing specialists.

'To give you some idea,' he told the two cops. 'Their printing techniques for the clothing industry are such that the ink is never a liquid. Solid yes, gas yes, but liquid no. So when people say they're a couple of top printing cookies maybe you'll understand. Those two ladies, let me tell you must be close now to perfecting a system for printing paperbacks for pennies. That will give this e-book nonsense a run for their money, when brand new best sellers cost just a quid, and probably less in Tesco.' He looked left and right down his street. 'Keep this to yourself but they won't be paper. Paperback size and look yes, but made of some new amazing synthetic stuff called Phlexodol they're importing exclusively from China. And ten times cheaper than paper.'

Somehow they managed to work their way indoors when Kemp's wife showed her face. Harry thought they might get a cup of tea, but it never materialised. Toni guessed Annie Kemp didn't like the idea of coppers stood at her front door. Out of sight and out of her neighbours mind was her choice.

'You thinking of throwing a sickie, then you might as well head for the Job Centre. There is no skiving at TwinPrint. It's what somebody once said. You play ball wi' them they'll play ball wi' you. And right to.' He had emphasised that turning up late for work or nipping home early would never be tolerated. 'Fag breaks' for the smokers were banned, but once you had been there a year, once they saw your value you were never on the minimum wage. No matter what role you performed. Most staff with more than five years service had at least six weeks leave that did not include Bank Holidays.

He never did reveal how and why he no longer worked for the twins.

The conversation at the first door they knocked on at Kemp's suggestion, started with "Don't mess with the Kavanagh's" and the second: "Bastard bitch! How can I help?"

Ronnie Mackinder provided little or no background, and anything he couldn't remember he said they would get from a Dan Scrimshaw he put them onto.

Dan Scrimshaw was a whole different ball game. He was angry. If what he said was to be believed Dan was three years off retirement when his wife discovered she was suffering from cancer.

Hour later the two DCs sat down with Craig Darke.

'Sorry we've been a while boss. This old fella invited us in. Wanted somebody to talk to. Poor bastard's in pieces.'

100

'Very disciplined company,' said Harry. 'No skiving, no fag breaks, no sickies. Wear full uniform at all times. Sign in, sign out.'

'But,' said Toni d'Andrea and stopped. 'This old chap worked for them until about two or three years ago. Wife had cancer, and when he wanted time off to nurse her, wanted to go with her for chemo. Twins said he had to take it as leave.' DCI Darke sucked in a breath noisily.

'Pay above the odds. Some of their top people apparently are on a very good wack, but they lack compassion. This old fella Dan was given an ultimatum when he ran out of leave. You work, you're sick or you quit. He left. Poor bastard.'

'Wife died.'

'Absolutely hard as nails.'

'Brian!' Craig Darke shouted and waited for his DI to appear. 'Lads say the twins are bastards.'

'I could have told you that!'

'Hang on sir,' said d'Andrea. 'Not both of them.' Botting was shaking his head. 'According to him it was Eimear who was the nasty bitch. He reckons Eilish was as hard as nails but always fair. Willing to listen.'

'Wrong bloody one was topped seems to me.'

Harry Botting repeated what they had found out, good and bad. Brian Daniels looked at his boss. 'We've met that Eimear. Are you surprised her pulling a stroke like that?' He received a shake of the head.

'Here's the good news,' Toni d'Andrea offered. 'TwinPrint used to be Hassett Printers. Bloke running it overstretched himself and advertised a business opportunity in the trade press. Suddenly according to this Ronnie Mackinder we spoke to, up pops this Fergus Kavanagh. Put money into the business so they understand, gave it a good shaking and before you can turn round he'd paid off this Hassett fella who owned it and changed it to TwinPrint. Then a few years later up pop the twins and there you have it.'

'Think the fella whose wife died knows more about all that, but he only really wanted to talk about one thing. Poor sod.'

'You took your time chatting to one old man?'

101

'Nah boss,' said Harry Botting quickly. 'Spoke to a Ronnie Mackinder and before him this Steve Kemp.'

'Where've I seen that before?'

'Mackinder?'

'Kemp,' and Darke was out of his chair. 'Steve Kemp,' he shouted from his door. 'Somebody remind me,' and he returned to his seat. 'Mackinder. Tell me about him.'

'This Steve Kemp put us on to him,' said d'Andrea. 'No love lost there.'

'With Mackinder?'

'No Mackinder and the twins, called her a nasty bitch or similar, and...'

'Boss,' said Jimmy Hatchard at the door to interrupt. 'Steve Kemp owns the grey Honda picked up on CCTV that morning.' Darke pointed his pen at him.

'Do a complete check on him. What's he do now? Why'd he leave TwinPrint?'

'Bit evasive at first boss,' Botting added.

'Go to it Jimmy. Thanks.'

The two women knocked on Dan Scrimshaw's door. It was as if the tall willowy man had been waiting for them to return. Not Natalie Scoley and DI Rachel Pickard in particular, just the police. He wanted to talk. To be honest to anybody who would listen and these two would do just fine.

Sending women was a Craig Darke clever stroke. A pregnant woman and an attractive young blonde, who put the kettle on, and pulled a packet of Hobnobs from her bag.

Dan Scimshaw's wife Lizzie had been diagnosed with cancer and had visited her doctor and the hospital, initially on her own. Then it was chemotherapy and visits to Oncology, the cost of parking and him taking leave to be with his wife of forty two years to cover his absence from work. He took his time, talked about his dear wife. How they first met, all about their wedding, their daughter and the treatment. Poor old soul even insisted on showing them photographs in an album.

102

Then he said, he'd run into problems. Took Lizzie away for a few days to the Lake District, never thinking that use of his leave allocation would come back to haunt him.

He asked his Team Leader for time off to visit Lizzie in Hospital, and was shocked to be told he had three choices. Put it down as unpaid sick with medical proof, which he wasn't. Take leave which he had run out of. Or resign. There was no other alternative, and since that day Kavanagh's words had rung in his ears, when he appealed to her better nature.

'I think you need to understand Dan, TwinPrint is not a charity. It is a choice you have to make. Not us.'

He resigned, to be with his wife Lizzie. To be able to visit her during the day as well as in the evening, and then for as many hours as he could when she was moved to a hospice for her final days.

Dan Scrimshaw was sixty three when Lizzie died. With meagre savings gone he had been on benefit for months. Now he was in a better state financially with his pensions, but he now had no Lizzie. Just his memories. Fit as a fiddle, but who would take him on now?

Dan seemed to know a bit more about Kavanagh's takeover than Ronnie Mackinder. According to the old man Fergus Kavanagh had been one of three people who responded to the advertisement Bill Hassett placed in the trade press. The fact that he had cash in hand probably swayed the decision so Dan understood. Compared to the other two who apparently planned to borrow the necessary. Very quickly Kavanagh established himself as a good printer and businessman and was there working day and night putting his ideas into practice.

Then one day old man Hassett announced he was retiring and Kavanagh took control, changed the name to TwinPrint, sacked four staff and brought in two new and very experienced printers.

Next major move, years later was the introduction of a twin.

Dan recalled how surprised he was that a family member had to start at the bottom and work her way up. Particularly as that family member was the only person in the place with a degree.

The two women tried to hide their soft laugh when sat together sipping their second cuppa, old Dan said that this Eimear was an utter bitch even when she was next to nothing in the hierarchy.

103

According to old Dan, Eilish then appeared out of the blue. She started off sweeping the floors, went to college at the same time. Neither of the young Kavanaghs would discuss their past or their present personal lives. Conversation with them was business only and the mystery surrounding them had been borne. Now the staff had one really nasty individual to deal with, and one who at times could be cold and aloof but very pleasant in comparison.

On the upside, business expanded and they moved into a new world of quality print they exported in massive quantities.

Fergus retired back to Ireland, and the two women took over. Business boomed, good loyal hard working dedicated staff, with good pay, but the rules were very strict. Work the Kavanagh way or you don't work at all was the maxim old Dan repeated.

'Mill Lodge @ 8 tomoz. Sal' was as much text as he got and it only added to Jake's concern. He spent all day hoping against hope that the boss or DI Daniels wouldn't come up with some evening surveillance idea. Point a finger at him to make Sally yesterday's news. It was a Thursday evening, inside the chain eatery they were doing a brisk trade but it was not full.

Change of menu since he had last been there and a bit of a shift around of furniture as these places tend to from time to time.

He had a glass of red wine. Sally's choice was white wine and soda. Something he'd never tried. To Jake, wine was wine, something you didn't mess with. They were sitting opposite each other in a corner both relating events from work since they had met previously over those coffees.

'Why here? You been before?'

'Loads.'

Her green top was stunning and Jake felt his Ben Sherman and jeans were too thrown-on. She looked good with just a touch of make-up and thin wooden bangles on one wrist. He ordered the chicken and BBQ ribs combo and Sally went for vegetable lasagna.

Then suddenly out of the blue, a complete change of tack. 'Confession time.' he said and sipped his wine as she played with the stem of her glass. 'This way nobody I know can overhear me making a complete ass of myself. If you get up and walk away, who's to

104

know? I'll just pretend I'm Billy No Mates, and I was on my own here hiding in the corner all the time.'

She hoped upon hope this was not going to be something bad again from another man. This time one she hardly knew. Please not a confession about being married, or going through a tricky divorce. The need to have two out of control kids every other weekend or some other story to beat her with.

'Didn't know this was the confessional.'

As stupid as it had sounded at the time, the idea that if he just let her go, one day, someday he'd bump into her wearing a Gay Pride badge and all would be lost, had stayed with him. He was not woman wise enough to realise the carefully crafted make-up, her collarless print shirt with striking coloured paisley pattern and black belted trousers gave out the opposite message.

'Think it's often best. Clear the decks, come clean.'

'You're very confusing,' she suggested and watched his expression. 'Why would I get up and walk away?'

Jake took a breath and crossed his fingers. 'I've been told you don't like men, and I thought if I confessed all, admitted my guilt and offered you a clean slate...' She waited. He waited. Was he trying to get off with a trainee lesbian? Her eyes as ever, big, bright and natural. Not black rimmed and tarty like most he saw these days.

'Maybe what?'

'Perhaps when we meet for coffee,' he had to look away towards the bar. 'It wouldn't end so abruptly. Then later have a meal, after which it seems to me if I leave it to you, it just might be another six weeks before we meet to feed the ducks in the park or something silly and...' He saw she was smiling, and pointed to his left. 'That's the way out....I know it's none of my business, but I've been told about you and Derek Morgan,' he suddenly rushed out and had to drink his wine. Silence and Sally had her head down. Her eyes had filled at the thought of him. 'If that's the competition, I'm sorry but I've never been on a sun bed, what use is a soft top in this country. I don't drive wearing flip-flops and if I catch him doing that he'll be done for driving without due care and attention.'

'That your idea of a confession?'

'No.'

105

'Well?' Sally drank from her glass, and was thankful that the tears were going away of their own accord. 'You confess, and then maybe I will too.'

This was different. It was usually a struggle to get men to confess to anything. To even talk at times.

'In for a penny, in for a pound. I won't be seen dead in flip-flops!' He chortled, and hoped she had more sense than to wear them. 'Seriously I was seeing this girl Beth. Went to a party with a mate. This Polish girl came onto me and one thing led to another, gave her a lift home, she invited me in. Two days later Beth told me to sling my hook. I didn't even know her name, never seen her since, so that tells you how good she thought I was. Hate myself for doing that to Beth.' He blew out his breath and looked at Sally. 'Sorry.'

She cleared her throat. 'I can do better than that!' she said and then made him wait. 'When you find out the other woman is getting on for twice your age, that's hard to take, let me tell you.' Sally put down her knife and fork. 'I don't have a high opinion of myself. I know I'm no glamour puss. So when Derek made a pass, I was flattered. Bloke like that had never come close to even saying hello before. So I was taken in by it all. Something inside sort of over rode all my sensibility. Yes he is too flash, yes he's not too bright, yes his tan comes from a machine and a bottle and he always wears sleeveless tops to flash his muscles. Don't know what came over me. Normally I'd have wanted to stick my fingers down my throat at the sight of him.' She lifted her hands. 'Don't ask me why.' She lifted her cutlery and went back to her meal. 'Men like him scatter their feelings far and wide, but always keep a load of it for themselves. That's who they really love.'

'First to take his shirt off sort of prat?'

'Got him in one.'

Jake paused, and then asked, 'Was he already seeing somebody else?'

'Of course,' she said firmly.

'You in love with him?'

'Just loved the flattery if I'm honest.' Sally wanted to take a look at the menu. There was a hint of something in her lasagna she didn't recognize.

'If he'd already got this other woman, why did he go for you as well?'

'What he does. He went for me instead of the usual painted tart because I was away from the mainstream. He didn't see me as part of the binge drinking circuit that marauds around town, causing havoc and leaving a trail of filth. His friends weren't going to tell the old dragon about me being out on the town with him. Truth is some probably don't know about her. Pretty sure they knew he was just using me. Probably did it all the time. I wasn't the first and I know I'm not the last.'

'How did you find out?'

'Friend told me. Male nurse knew two of his close buddies.'

'You live with him?'

'Don't be silly,' she said with a wide grin. 'Told me he lived at home with his folk. Truth was he lived in Gainsborough with the woman who did his washing, probably did it topless in Jimmy Choos and a mini...Haven't lived with anyone.' Sally looked at Jake until his head came up from his food and he looked at her.' You not happy with that?'

'What?'

'Living with someone.' He shrugged. 'You don't approve then.'

'What makes you think that?'

'Your face gives you away.'

'Too many folk are using people.'

'You think I should be at home with a mug of hot chocolate, a tatty old teddy bear, a *'Friends'* DVD and...'

'Better than being used as a substitute mother, or easy sex that most of the blokes are doing. Girls think there's wedding bells in the air, pretty bridesmaids, and honeymoon on some Pacific island. Ten years later they're still waiting. Truth is, he wants his shreddies washed and you in his bed at his beck and call.'

'And marriage is...'

He cut across her. 'He try to get you back?' Sally laughed and put down her knife and fork.

'And go back to living with mum and dad? Be serious!' she laughed again. 'Here we go then.' She took a swig of her drink. 'After Derek, this other guy sort of asks me for a date. Can't spend

107

my whole life wondering what if. I agree to meet him in a pub. Can't sit indoors moping for ever. Aaargh!' she exclaimed loudly. 'Hour I was sitting there, like a bloody tart on the pull. Bastard didn't show. Do I learn? No. Next tosser was classic. I'm working nights, it all goes quiet, and so I take a break. Somebody'd left a copy of the *Echo* lying around, so I borrowed it and went off for ten minutes. Scanning through the paper and whose picture jumps out at me but this slimebag I've been seeing. In court for beating up his partner.' Sally stopped, looked up and blew a breath up across her face. 'There but for the grace of God.' She stopped for a second. 'It's like a wake up call. It's get a grip girl. Banged up for six months and never ever said a word to me. Didn't know he'd had a partner, didn't know he was in trouble, certainly didn't know he was going to court for domestic violence,' she continued having noticed he was listening attentively. 'That's me back in the freezer...' She shuddered and took a drink.

Main course over they decided to leave a decision on pudding for later. Jake was a bit miffed. He really fancied a banoffee sundae but decided scoffing one down when she was loath to participate was not good form. Sally sipped her drink and looked around the restaurant at five couples of varying ages close by.

'Confession time,' she said softly and suddenly. 'That business after the coffee. That was me being immature. Derek and I used to meet in that café or went there together. Always had the same drinks, always had chocolate muffins. Hadn't been in there for a few months. All a bit too much for me. Too much emotion, too many nice memories mixed in with the bad. All so stupid.' Her big brown eyes looked at him. 'Forgive me?' she asked and her eyes had the same message. He nodded.

'You're not walking away then.'

'Can we start from now?' she asked and saw the sincerity in his eyes. 'Clean slates, all the nastiness gone away. New broom and all that.'

'Yes Sister,' he chided with a sprinkle of charm to delight her.

'Senior Sister,' she whispered and rested a hand on his arm. Just her resting her hand on his forearm for a moment or two, but it was a start. 'I've been all, go careful don't get your fingers burnt again. You don't know anything about him.' She moved her hand away and looked at him. 'When will I see you again?' was unexpected and Jake frowned.

'We finished for today?' she shook her head. 'Weekend?' he dared and she squeezed his arm.

'Haven't you got to work, or meet your mates, or play pool?' His look told her to explain. 'Always seemed to me that other things were more important to the men I've known. Decided when I left home tonight, just another date was my target.'

'Having heard what happened to you I didn't want some bright spark telling you I once cheated on this girl I knew. So I decided to come clean.'

At the end of the evening, Sally just talked incessantly all the way to her Micra. A quick 'I'll call you', car zapped and without as much as a puckered kiss she was in, backed out and was gone. Jake just wandered off to find his car. Would that bastard Derek Morgan have let her get away with that? He just leant against his car in the cool evening air to ponder the situation once again. Who could he talk to about her? Who would know what these strange antics meant?

Sally was fully aware there were certain aspects of her behaviour she could not control. It was as if she had never learnt the right responses to certain situations. We all have our faults. Some we admit to, some we never do. That night this Senior Sister was quite oblivious to how she had reacted.

16

'Tell me about Scrimshaw.'

DI Rachel Pickard shrugged and looked across at young Natalie, bottom propped against a filing cabinet. It was full to overflowing in the boss's office with the two women, Harry Botting, Toni d'Andrea and Jimmy Hatchard.

'Bloody sad, boss.' Darke's look told her he needed more. 'Sixty three?' she queried with another look at her young companion. 'He was when his wife died, couple of years back. That Eimear gave him no option. Go on the sick, which he wasn't. Clock on as normal and leave his wife to die on her own or jack it in.'

'First time we've heard the word motive.'

'Be serious!'

'I am being bloody serious.'

'He's an old man.'

'Don't be silly. He's what, sixty five. That's not old these days. Well built and…'

'Thin,' said Natalie. 'Looks like he could do with a good meal.'

'We're talking poison not six rounds with Mike Tyson!'

'But still, boss.'

'Want a check done on him and if you've already made your mind up, I'll find someone who won't be put off by his sob story.'

'It's not a sob story!' was DI Pickard. 'That bitch stitched him up. We're talking about an old man who's obsesseed about oncology. About chemotherapy, about metatistic coloreatal cancer and adenocarcinoma.'

'Suddenly you're an expert.'

'My aunt went through it!' she chucked at Darke. 'If you must know.'

'The more I hear, the bigger motive he has. Doesn't work, got all the time in the world. If he knocked on her door he's not a stranger. Might invite him in. All the makings seems to me. Now will you deal with it professionally or do I find someone else?'

'Leave it with us, boss.'

110

'Now Kemp,' he said to Hatchard

'Forty eight year old Steven Lionel Kemp worked for TwinPrint for six years until he got fired. Without speaking to him direct for confirmation from what I can gather he's still out of work. Married, two kids. It was his Honda coming out of Saxilby that morning. Behind him is probably a dead twin who fired him for slacking or being up to no good.' He looked at Botting and d'Andrea.

'Have a word. Bring him in. I want an alibi tighter than a duck's arse as to why he was out that time of day when he's no job to go to. Why wasn't he watching *Breakfast* like the rest of the unemployable or still in his pit?' He pointed at d'Andrea. 'You get the slightest inkling his alibi is not kosher I want to know.' Darke closed his eyes momentarily, then opened them again. 'Let's play this low key. Visit him at home rather than making a big deal out of an interview. Give him the usual bollocks about tying up loose ends.' He tapped the desk with his biro. 'Scrimshaw and Kemp, that's two. This is looking much better. That'll be all,' he said to dismiss them all, but Rachel remained seated.

Rachel Pickard rested her chin on her clasped hands. 'Remember DS Eoini Culligan?' Darke had not brought him to mind before Pickard went on. 'Bureau of Fraud Investigations for Garda in Dublin.' Darke clicked his fingers.

'Your very own Danny Boy.'

'One and the same.' Darke waited unaware just the thought of him made Rachel cringe. 'Fergus Kavanagh takes over the small printing business in Wexford he works for, with his mate. Then suddenly there's a fallout, and bingo he turns up here of all places with enough cash to buy into what is now TwinPrint. Why?' she asked as she got to her feet.

'Yes to coffee? I'll get them,' said Darke and left the room.

Rachel Pickard had been involved for two months or more a year ago in trying to track down a Lincolnshire businessman who had done a runner a couple of decades earlier. Been charged with massive fraud and then failed to turn up in court and had not been seen since. This local 'rogue' apparently suddenly surfaced in Ireland and rumour had it that all his business pals had helped him move around over the years. Morocco to start with, then Spain and

111

goodness knows where else then suddenly Ireland. During the course of her enquiries, Rachel had dealt over the phone with this Sergeant Eoini Culligan of the Garda in Dublin.

'What you thinking?' he asked as he walked back in with two mugs.

'Use my feminine charms, see what I can discover. Does he know anybody in the Garda in Wexford might point me in the right direction? Its twenty years ago, but somebody must know why Kavanagh suddenly upped sticks and set off for the bright lights, got lost and finished up in sunny Lincoln. Don't want to start looking for family, just in case they can get word to tip off our Eimear.'

As ever her work station was neat and tidy. No papers spilling unnecessarily from in-trays and lying across the desk. No amusing mouse pad. Standard plain black with matching service issue mouse. Only hint of frivolity was a pad of multi colour memo pads in green, cerise, orange and blue. Two star shaped postits stuck to her monitor as urgent reminders.

Pickard then recounted some of the stories Culligan had come out with in the past, all of which on reflection were seriously sad, yet they both found them amusing all the same.

'Possible he's matured. Could always have married and settled down.'

'Maybe he was married before.'

'Probably one of those who never change. Bloody sad when you think about it.'

'I'll assume he's still the same,' Pickard suggested.

'Good idea.'

'This whole thing's turning into a complete maze. Looked straight forward to start with.'

'I think we need a complete review of where we are. We go through all the evidence meticulously, and then we go through it all again. Except this time I want a different set of eyes looking at each bit. If Brian did an interview, then he doesn't do the second check. I'll start them on that in the morning; you see what you can find out.' He smiled at Rachel. 'Good luck with him.' She raised her eyebrows.

When she'd dealt with Detective Sergeant Eoini Culligan previously she was pleased there was the Irish Sea between them. He really fancied himself and spoke to Rachel as if she was a wee slip of a thing who would be easy prey to his Irish charms.

'Thank God it's not a video phone.' Craig Darke downed two mouthfuls of coffee, stood up and headed for his door. 'Off to play about with a bit more paperwork.'

'Dan Scrimshaw,' said Rachel Pickard. 'He's a non starter.'

'According to you.'

'Fair enough,' said Pickard and turned to leave Darke's office. 'Have it your way.'

'Sit down,' was firm without the need for him to shout at a pregnant woman, but all she did was turn to face her boss.

'How would he get hold of cyanide?'

'You tell me.'

'He didn't. I can find no evidence whatsoever that he bought any. Credit card, debit card, bank account.'

'Cash. What about good old fashioned pennies?'

'And where would he buy cyanide with the change in his pocket?'

'Someone in the pub.' Rachel laughed, and Darke knew she was laughing at him.

'Don't be ridiculous. A knocked off DVD player, cheap fags and dodgy vodka possibly, but cyanide? "Excuse me, anyone here know where I can get my hands on a jar of cyanide?" Don't be silly boss.'

'Motive and opportunity. Who else has them?' Darke put his hands up. 'Don't say Quinn. He lacks motive and the bloody gumption.'

'Scrimshaw had the opportunity to have a go at her at work. Could have gone bowling in her office and threatened her. He didn't. Well, according to people we've spoken to he just accepted it. He was so upset and down about his wife dying, he was in no mood to give her a mouth full or threaten to give her a pasting.'

'But now. In the fullness of time. His life is going nowhere without his wife. Time on his hands, all building up inside him.' Darke clicked his fingers. 'Wife's died, got to blame somebody. Time to get his own back.' He pointed at Pickwell. 'And if it's not him. Who the hell is it?'

113

'You've said yourself the sister's a nasty piece of work. There might be a dozen people wanting to top her. We just haven't worked out who yet.'

'But not Scrimshaw?' She shook her head.

'No chance.'

'Yes?' Darke spat at Harry Botting at his door.

'Kemp was fishing all night.'

'And?' was shot back.

'That was him coming home. Been with a mate fishing out at Dunham Bridge.'

'And what does the mate say?' Botting looked at d'Andrea who had joined him. Darke sighed. 'So the duck drowned.' Both men at the door looked confused. 'I said tighter than a duck's arse.' He hesitated. 'What are you waiting for?' the moment they moved away Darke looked at Rachel Pickard. 'Where do we get these from?'

17

'Governor,' greeted Craig first thing the next morning. 'Message here from someone called Mrs Lavinia de Costa-Jones,' said Jake peering up for confirmation that he'd heard it right. Craig almost snatched the postit note from his hand and hated the 'governor' term. He was not in charge of a prison or an American state.

'You got it right,' he said abruptly and stuffed it into his pocket. 'Down to business,' he said curtly. 'I've got here the Forensics report on the cyanide,' said Craig Darke as he walked to his office door.

Darke waved the folder in his hand.

'Good news or bad?' Daniels asked.

'Wont try to pretend I know what it all means, save to say that having looked at the metabolism and toxicokinetics,' he looked up from the report to shake his head. 'Apparently the thiocyanate was key, and they consider we have a match.' He looked at Jake. 'You're not going to like this. Where can you buy cyanide as a member of the public? Who has bought some? Quinn possibly or our Eimear? Get to it.'

'We bringing them both in boss?' Brian Daniels asked with little enthusiasm.

'I think we'll stick with our friend Sebastian. Think there was more going on than meets the eye,' said Darke firmly. 'I don't think anybody really knows what those two in particular were up to. That Eimear is such a nasty bitch. And it's not just us,' he said to Brian. 'We've also got the low down on how she treated that old boy waiting for his wife to die.'

'Can we have a couple keeping watch on TwinPrint when we pull Quinn, just in case he gets word to her and she decides to leg it.' Darke only had to look at Jake Goodwin.

'We'll go,' he responded and nudged Raza. 'We'll take the Honda, it's got better legs.'

'At least you won't have to take them to a nurse,' made Brian, Al and Raza turn their heads. Jake ignored the remark. 'Get yourselves organised,' said Darke and motioned Daniels into his office.

'What was that all about?' Raza asked Jake.

'Search me. Probably having a dig because I had to go back to the hospital about my leg.'

Rachel Pickard had never bothered to create a mental image of Detective Sergeant Eoini Culligan, and had she now been in possession of a video phone when she called the Garda in Dublin and asked for him by name she would have been shocked.

Eoini Culligan had taken early retirement was the official line to start with, and the idea that this smarmy man would be anywhere near that sort of age was a complete shock to her.

When Rachel explained exactly who she was and gave background information about her enquiry to an Inspector she had been put onto, he was more specific. He moved away from the party line. Sergeant Eoini Culligan of the Bureau of Fraud Investigations in Dublin had for some years suffered with arthritis. Financial troubles the whole world was aware of having beset Ireland, a slashing of budgets all round and once he had a hip replacement operation and four months off work the Garda took the opportunity to save a few euros.

Plain Eoini Culligan as he was now had been found a nice little research role and an equally unimportant office away from the real world of police work, where his particular expertise could be used as, when and if needed.

Dark, attractive married and pregnant Rachel Pickard had no idea when she finally located him, that the man she was talking to was sitting alone in little more than a broom cupboard. Nor had she any idea that he was bald with small wisps of hair covering each ear. There were signs of whiskey about his face and his weight was not helping his half hearted attempt to get back to full fitness. His demeanour on the telephone was still the same. He didn't sound fifty-two and spoke as if his new life was a step in the right direction. Truth was the powers that be hoped that a life of boredom just might persuade Eoini Culligan, him of twenty-eight years' service to just

116

retire. Get fed up, say thanks but no thanks and walk away into the sunset. No redundancy, no big lump sum. Just a pension to keep him in his nightly tipples.

Rachel had forgotten how difficult it had been to keep Culligan on subject. He really wanted to talk about himself, to up his self esteem and discover all he could about her. He talked as if they were just a few streets away. Could easily meet up after work, go to the movies, and dine together with his idea of fun to follow. It was as if the Irish Sea had dried up and he could just motor round to her place.

'Right then missy, what can yer mucker friend Eoini do for you dis time?' he asked when she finally got him down to business. Rachel went through what she knew about Fergus Kavanagh, reading prepared briefing notes from her monitor 'When are we saying he left Wexford?'

'Somewhere around ninety.'

'The name of the printers yer man owned in Wexford?'

'Sorry. Don't have a name. Can't be that many surely. One of their ex-employees has told us the story related to him by one of the daughters. About how her father bought into the business in Wexford that he worked for, then suddenly around ninety, give or take a year, upped sticks and ran this way.'

'Family still live in Wexford do we know?' Culligan asked.

'That's an issue. Quite frankly we don't know. The daughters are very secretive and we're a bit concerned that should people, possibly relatives in Wexford get wind of us asking questions they just might tip off somebody over here.'

'This murder yer say?'

'Yes.'

At that precise moment Rachel decided not to say who had been murdered, just hint that the sisters may be involved. She also kept twins out of the conversation.

'Not 'ad many murders to deal wi,' he admitted, when Rachel would have expected him to brag a bit. 'Specialised in fraud, so that took me away from the boring humdrum world of people topping one another.'

'Just up your streets then,' she told him. 'We think there may be fraud involved.'

117

Rachel Pickard spent a good ten minutes sipping coffee from a polystyrene cup, phone just to her ear as she scanned down the screen. Young Natalie was amused at the look on her boss's face. A picture really did paint many many words. Eoini Culligan had gone off on one. He was relating the whole dramatic scenario of a fraud case from some years back where he of course had played a major case solving role.

Naturally the villains had no idea he was onto them. They admitted years later that if it hadn't been for Eoini they'd have got away with it. He had sussed them very early on, but then that was often the way. He'd forgotten how many cases he'd been on top of from the early stages. Day One Paddy they used to call him, he suggested. It was a knack, and in fact some officers had often said he had a gift for the work.

Rachel was not listening to what he was saying, just aware that he was still speaking. What little she did take in told her, that according to him in his prime he had been a great copper and then she actually enjoyed the way he manoeuvred the story so that such successes had been a major factor in being chosen specifically for his present research role.

'Why Kavanagh left,' she managed when he hesitated for a second. 'That's what we need to know. And why he came here. It's hardly on the tourist trail. Wexford to Lincoln.'

While Eoini would never admit to anyone how depressed he was about his personal life, this one phone call had given him a fillip. For the first time in a long time he actually felt wanted. Somebody other than the dear old Garda was in need of his help and his experience, and he felt so good it was a young woman. A young pretty little thing he recalled he had imagined with long hair the colour of straw had need of him. Better than doing the crossword any day.

'When do we clap yer round these parts?' sounded more South Dakota than downtown Dublin.

'Depends how far you get,' Rachel offered as a taster. 'Could be you will make Dublin too good to turn down.' For the life of her she couldn't think of any Dublin tourism highlights, except for downing Guinness.

'Well if oi'm to git this sorted for yer, I'd best be off.' Rachel went to speak, to just say farewell and realised he was gone.

Craig had waited until he got home. All part of the in-built discipline that guided him through life. Never mix business and pleasure.

Lavinia deCosta-Jones was a sort of pleasure.

He was quite sure one day the church might not survive her demise. His parents had told him how she pumped money in over the years and since her husband had passed away it had become her whole life. When Craig was a Sunday school teacher she was a whole lotta woman to deal with. Big, bold and bumptious to say the least.

Shortly after moving back to the county his father had phoned Craig with a concern over church security. Mrs deCosta-Jones in an attempt to reduce the annual insurance had investigated the possibility of CCTV and other security measures. The wily old bird soon realized that the companies she had spoken with were trying to take her and her beloved church for a ride. Very few pulled the wool over her eyes and got away with it.

Craig in response spoke to a good contact and arranged a meeting which he attended. Lavinia and her church got all it required at a decent price, and it had proved to be the start of an adult relationship with the bombastic woman.

He phoned her and once the normal preliminaries were over and done with he got taken by surprise.

'If you and young Jillie are ever looking for somewhere for a night or two away from prying eyes, I'm quite often away, you know.'

He was gobsmacked. What can you say?He was wondering if Jillie's mother was privy to this suggestion and he had not responded when she went on.

'In fact I'm away this weekend. Saturday lunchtime to Monday morning as it happens. Shall I drop a key off to young Jillie?' He knew he had to do something, say something. What on earth would

Jillie say, think or do if old Lavinia turned up out of the blue at Golden Fitness to slap a door key in her hand?

'Can I call you back?' he threw at her quickly, then added: 'Just got a call from work coming through,' he lied and he was off the phone and sat back with his wine. He drank that back and poured another. Now what?

It was a full thirty minutes before he picked up the phone again. This time to Jillie's mobile.

'Don't know why, but Lavinia's been onto me. Probably realized it's a bit awkward you being down there and me up here. Don't fancy another glass of Fanta Saturday night, and she's said I can always crash down at her place. Makes life a bit easier. I can pick you up and drop you off by taxi so we can have a drink.'

'You're making me jealous.'

'Why?'

'Staying with Lavinia. Lucky old biddy.'

'She won't be there,' he'd said it before his mind was in gear. 'She's going away for a couple of days and…'

'Wow! That'll do nicely.' Had he heard that right? Silence for five seconds. 'Whoops,' was much softer. 'Have I jumped the gun, have I put my foot in it?' More silence as Craig felt himself colour up, as he searched desperately for the right words.

'Don't know what I'm supposed to say,' was a very obviously embarrassed tone.

'You can do what you like, but I'm staying at Lavinia's,' almost made Craig drop the phone, his wine or both.

18

Jake received a *Free Tonite?* text. Then after he'd said *yes,* he got a *Meet Me?* And his second *yes* got him a quiet pub out in one of the villages and a time.

Without actually asking her outright, Jake was left wondering at the end of the evening as she drove away from yet another car park what it was all about.

They had a relationship that was going nowhere. They had never met as part of a group. There was always just the two of them.

He knew many couples who had met when both were part of a group or groups and then over time had met up surreptitiously as a pair. This was somehow different in that it was always just the two of them. Maybe her feelings towards him were not strong enough to show him off to her pals.

They got on better each time he had to admit and their conversations were less stilted and they both talked more and more about work. What else was there? As far as he could gather Sally had no interests away from nursing. Knew she had a few friends she'd meet up with now and again for a meal, but apart from that it appeared to be cozy nights in with her mother.

Could be that was the problem. Was the mother domineering, was she a lonely control freak who wanted her daughter by her side all the time? Was Sally seen by her mother as her carer? Was there a problem, was her mother sick or an invalid? More questions than answers.

Whatever the issues, an evening with her was certainly a great deal better than another on his own at home.

Craig waited until he and Lavinia were in The Olde Manor House with the kettle on before he made any real comment. The Grade II Listed house had been in the DeCosta-Jones family since the middle of the 19th century.

'Somebody could have warned me.'

'And missed that look on your face, dear.'

'The transformation.' He sat down at the pine table in the large white kitchen, with two oak beans and red quarry tiles. 'You just never think do you? All that time ago, I never thought, one day young lady you're going to be a real beauty.'

'Been through the mill, I understand.'

His eyebrows rose. 'How d'you mean?' he wanted to know.

'Lived with somebody in the City, one of these high flying banker types. Probably a damn crook knowing the way they behave.' Lavinia poured the boiling water into her teapot by the AGA. 'Something happened apparently, turned quite nasty so I understand. All over now. Then she got mixed up with somebody else on the rebound, so her mother says, and then suddenly she's back home in Stamford.'

'Somebody told me years ago how she'd got all sorts of degrees, got a big job in the City.'

'Think that was probably me. You came down for our Dickens Dinner if I recall. Masters Degree in Economics at Oxford. Even in these enlightened times there are not many girls from a council estate get to go to Oxford. Ruth's really upset about it all.' Lavinia poured tea into two delicate cups. When she went to hand one to Craig she could see he was deep in thought. 'Penny for them.'

'Are you saying she gave up a good job in banking to work at that fitness place?'

Lavinia nodded. 'Apparently. Just turned up. So Ruth was saying.'

'And your interest?'

'Always knew you'd make something of yourself, and even at the Sunday school there was this special something between the two of you. Life of course works in mysterious ways. You went off to university joined the police and never really came back. Then later Jillian did the same and ended up in banking.'

'Now I mean.'

'Wicked old woman, that's me,' she chuckled. 'Just thought how nice it would be if the two of you, now both single for a variety of reasons could meet up.'

'You think she's a victim of the credit crunch and all the banking issues?'

122

'No idea. Her mother doesn't know, or if she does she's certainly not saying. Think our Jillian needs handling with kid gloves. You've both been through the mill.' Lavinia sipped her tea. 'Always possible it was down to a class clash.' Craig looked at her. 'My Robert always said the only money worth having is that which you actually earn, and the only position of any value is the one you achieve through your own efforts. Doubt if the people she was mixing with have ever gained anything that wasn't handed to them on a plate.'

'Wrong side of the tracks?'

'What a damn awful country this is at times,' said Lavinia as she nodded. 'I'd like to think this is the fresh start you both could do with. Drink up, and I'll give you the tour.'

Jillie Lombard drove from her parent's former council house into Stamford and out on the road to Market Deeping. Then down the lane that led to The Olde Manor House.

Through the big open black wrought iron gates, between the cedar trees and along the drive. Jillie parked her BMW at the side of the big house.

What was she doing? Right from the outset she had told herself this was a time to revaluate her life. Consider all her options without the influence of the opposite sex. Her next move could very well prove to be the most important of her life. Quitting the city would in some quarters have done her reputation no good. A wrong decision at this juncture would very well leave her floundering.

She had no need for men, and certainly no need for a relationship she had convinced herself. That was before Lavinia had tapped that tall handsome man on the shoulder in the church hall and her past came rushing back to greet her. To devour her and remove all her sensibilities and return her to a giggly schoolgirl state.

From a home with three windows and a front door onto the road, this delightfully imposing front of nine windows was a staggering contrast. An imposing building of great character and stature.

When she stepped out onto the gravel it occurred to Jillie how perfect her car looked, sat there outside this great home. Absolutely right for the marketing men, selling quality cars or grand houses.

It was with some trepidation that Jillie, pulling her case behind her, stepped into the deCosta-Jones big house, with beautiful wooden entrance hall and stone tiles. Craig took her along the entrance hall, through the lobby to the combined kitchen and breakfast room.

'Guided tour, madam?'

'How old's this place?'

'1850s I think she said, or thereabouts. Been in the deCosta-Jones family since it was built,' he repeated from what he could remember.

'Was the first one Lord of the Manor then?'

'Probably. Follow me. Cuppa?' he said as he switched on the kettle.

'Love one.'

'This is the kitchen, obviously.' He walked off down to the left at the far end. 'Utility Room,' he said as he opened the door, 'with a loo at the back.' Back out of there, he then opened another door on the right at the end. 'Pantry, she doesn't seem to use. Probably from the old days, before freezers and fridges. There are two fridges by the way, takes a bit of getting used to.' Craig then walked back down the kitchen and off to the right.

'Is the oven on?' Jillie sniffed.

'Chicken,' he said at her. 'Your meal. This is the conservatory through here,' he said while she was still trying to take in what he had said. It was then Dining Room, back to the entrance Hall and into the big Sitting Room. She trailed along beside him, like a prospective buyer being shown around by an estate agent.

She was given a tour by her guide into every room, nook and cranny except Lavinia's bedroom, before settling down in the big country kitchen for a coffee.

'Hope you like chicken?' she was asked, 'and cheese? We're having my own special cheesy chicken, roast potatoes, broccoli and peas.' Jillie was stunned. Never ever had any man in her life cooked anything. Jack simply refused, but then Jack wouldn't even put bread in a toaster or make a coffee, if there was anybody else there to do it. Denny would make hot drinks. On a good day, put bread in the toaster and spread his own toast, but that was his absolute limit. She doubted if either of them had ever shopped for food. Alcohol yes, food no.

124

Half an hour later she was sat across the big oak kitchen table from Craig. As she tucked into a great meal, she told herself that perhaps this is what life could be like. He had cooked the chicken well. It was moist, and she discovered covered with cornflakes and bathed in a delightful cheese sauce.

They talked about their day, neither of which had been anything close to interesting. She'd been particular about the clothes she wore. Her coat had been discarded and hung in the hall, and now her cardigan could follow suit. Now dressed in her white short sleeveless pure silk dress. The one with a myriad of tiny flowers around neck and along the hem. No tights – what a bother they can be – white bra and briefs. All designed for quick release.

'Tell me about your house.'

'What d'you want to know?' Craig queried. 'Detached, near to a park. Three bedrooms now, one en-suite, hall, front lounge, dining room, big kitchen,' he looked around. 'Not as big as this though, and a big office, utility room, downstairs loo and all lawn at the back, not really overlooked.' He smiled at Jillie. 'You could always visit.'

'I'll do that,' she told him and went back to the food. 'You said three bedrooms now.' The chicken really had been delightful, with roast potatoes, crisp on the outside and fluffy inside. Exactly as she liked them.

'Was four. Converted one over the garage into an office, where I can work from. Got my PC up there and a copier, big chair and a desk.' She'd said she'd visit thirty-seven, things were looking up. 'Don't know why I've got three bedrooms, nobody ever visits.' There was another putdown, why did he do that, she wondered.

'Why Lincoln?' she had pondered at home in her room.

'No particular reason. Got a transfer from Staffordshire.'

Meal over, washing up done by Craig, the kitchen looked spick and span and they'd had a cup of tea. Jillie had not lifted a finger. Sat talking to him watching him, taking in everything he did and said and slowly but surely becoming more eager for him. Craig in a light blue shirt and cream chinos walked behind her. He wrapped his arms around her, leant in and kissed her neck through her hair and snuggled his head against hers.

Keep this up fella he told himself, so far so good. If she wants to sleep alone, let it be. If she wants to go home so be it.

The big clock on the kitchen wall said close to 8.45pm. A long time to wait til bedtime, but Jillie knew it didn't have to be bedtime.

They moved together to find the sofa in the sitting room, with white the dominant wall colour as ever. They settled down with a glass of wine each.

Jillie was sat up with her legs curled beside her, glass in hand. 'Can I ask? How come you know Lavinia?'

'Did her a favour.' Craig knew he had to expand. 'Obviously visit my parents from time to time. Been to their Dickens Dinner a couple of times, been to church to please my mother and of course Lavinia is always there. Few years back they were looking at security. Had a few minor thefts and my dad asked if I could help. Got to know her through that. I was last down here around October time for my mother's birthday, then again near Christmas. Then we were talking on the phone and she mentioned this Spring Sale.' He looked at Jillie at the other end of the sofa. 'Seems to me Lavinia had spoken to your mum, she'd said you were back home and she obviously put her plan into action.'

'Have you ever met anybody else from Sunday school?'

'Few times I've been to the church I've looked around to see if there was anyone I recognized, but it's not easy. A twelve year old and a twenty five year old are completely different. Except if they have all this,' he leant across and played with her ginger locks. Jillie put down her wine and moved towards him. When his soft lips met hers it was perfect. Their hunger quickly became so obvious.

'That bed looked comfy,' was all she whispered and she soon found herself in penetrated ecstasy. Kisses that had begun as tender were now more eager, and her bliss was shaken by an approaching orgasm to make her shudder as she strangled her first cry. She sobbed; she dug her nails into his back, arched her own, and squirmed her body, shouted and cried out again. His deep release she felt, and her tears rolled out and dampened the pillow.

'You're crying, I'm sorry,' he gasped into her ear as she clung to him with such force, his exit was impossible.

126

Jillie couldn't speak for crying, and Craig was there with the duvet to dry her eyes, she blinked and smiled at him. Still there, still inside her still worried.

'Craig,' she managed, sobbed and gasped for air. She had never ever had an experience to match that, no way shape or form. Jillie Lombard had found herself a great lover. They squeezed each other and rocked from side to side and fell apart, but held hands. Jillie so wanted to talk to him about their shared experience, but the words were difficult. There was no need to mention other men at a time like that, yet she craved to. Those before him had done the deed and left her to pick up the crumbs. Craig had made love to her, had made her feel part of the whole gambit of emotions that now cradled her.

'What just happened to us?' he asked in his breath. How had that happened? One minute he was telling himself to go easy, everything is fine and let her sleep alone and wham! He had never ever experienced anything like that. He had been with five or six women in his life. No, one girl, five women, but none of them had been made like that, had been like that towards him, or as it appeared enjoyed him like that.

'We were so good,' she managed from a dry mouth. He wanted to tell her she was the first he'd brought to tears. 'It felt sort of naughty.' Jillie giggled. 'With my Sunday school teacher,' and bit her lip like a innocent naughty schoolgirl.

'Why did you cry?' was what worried him. He guessed everything he did was being monitored for his end of term marks.

'Simply the most beautiful love,' Jillie moved the few inches to kiss him until it hurt.

'Thought it was me...'

'It was you, you were an absolute joy. Fabulous and you're sexy and have a great bum.' She didn't need to tell him she'd had a body tumbling climax, but guessed he must have known. 'God you can fuck.' A moment of total silence. 'Oh shit I'm sorry. Oh dear, oh no...idiot!' Jillie turned her head away.

'Shhh. You're fine' he whispered. 'I'm okay. Be yourself.'

'I know, but...

'Hey, hey it's only us. We're not in Sunday school now. Great compliment.' He kissed her cheek. They both chuckled.

127

'Say what you like. Be honest, feel free.'

'Still great,' brought laughter from both of them as they wrapped their arms tightly.

'Thank you madam,' he pulled himself free and rested on one arm. The duvet had fallen away and their upper halves were very obvious. 'Imagination destroyed,' he said. 'I've been imagining what you might be like, but never ever this beautiful,' he squeezed her breast gently. 'So good, so loving and you look so happy. Would a glass of wine suit?'

'Perfect,' and to her delight he kissed her softly, rolled over and was out of bed and walking to the door, naked.

Craig skipped around the house, closing curtains, checking the doors were locked before picking up a bottle from the cool pantry and two glasses. He needed a minute or two to himself, so he put them down on the kitchen table. They'd gone from chatting, to bed, to absolute bliss in no time. How had that happened? Stood there in the kitchen naked he suddenly felt vulnerable, but had no remedy. All his clothes were up in the bedroom. Were thoughts of a twelve year old with freckles allowed at a time like this? 'Jillie Lombard' he said to himself. 'Jillie bloody Lombard'. He was smiling when he left the kitchen and climbed the stairs.

Jillie had laid there looking at the beamed ceiling, at a white vase of flowers on the chest of drawers. She parted her legs to find cooler parts of the pale blue sheet and savored that moment of ecstasy all over again, when Craig returned with a bottle and two glasses.

'I've closed all the curtains, everywhere, so it's our entire world.' Jillie watched this naked man open the bottle and pour wine. That was damn cool.

'Can I just say, I'm not looking for commitment.' Jillie hesitated as he walked towards her glass in hand. 'Well, not now anyway.'

'I'll not make demands,' he said as he handed her the glass. 'Just let it be,' he said as if trying hard to justify their actions.

19

'Breakfast in fifteen minutes,' she heard. 'Breakfast,' she heard again and turned over. Jillie opened her eyes and there was Craig dressed in a British Lions polo shirt and jeans. He bent down and kissed her, but she wouldn't let him stand up again.

'Craig,' she whispered, and tears rolled down her cheeks.

'Hey, hey. What's the matter?'

'You're – making me so happy…' he had to wait for her to dry her eyes. 'It's like you've switched me on.'

'I love you,' he whispered. 'And I love making love with somebody so beautiful.' He pulled himself free. 'Breakfast in fifteen,' he said. 'Or you'll be late for Sunday school.' Jillie giggled as he pulled back the duvet and walked away. At the door he glanced back at her lying there naked, winked and was gone.

Down in the kitchen his mind immediately went to the body and the beauty he had left lying naked in the bed. He hoped to God he would not suddenly wake up to find it had all been a dream. If it was, then it had been the wettest dream he'd ever known.

Jillie finally slipped from the bed, showered in the en-suite and threw on her clothes before she remembered her phone. She sat on the end of the bed and checked her texts. Just two. How they had diminished in a matter of weeks. One from Rita who had little to say and the other from him downstairs in the kitchen: N*obody has ever made love with me that fabulously and never been so beautiful. C*

She'd heard the radio start when she was in the bedroom, and halfway down the stairs she stopped. Tristar's haunting *'Daydreams'* but not just the trio. Craig was singing along. *"You must know my sweetheart that my love's for you. Just wait a while my love, for the day to come…"* Jillie crept further down and peered into the kitchen. That man cooking and singing. She waited for the song to fade away.

'You sound happy,' he turned and felt embarrassed as he so often did. He went to turn the radio off. 'Leave it on,' she told him. *'I'll be there beside you, making daydreams true'* he smiled at her.

The words from that text were still sinking in. Her legs a bit wobbly, as she looked at two places set, across the big wooden table from each other. Two rounds of golden toast, each with a beautiful sunny side up egg. A pot of coffee, a cup each of coffee already poured. More toast, milk, cut bread, jam, marmalade, butter and spread. Brian Matthew and 'Sounds of the Sixties' on Radio 2 gently in the background.

Jillie was ushered to her seat, a napkin placed on her lap and her eyes followed him. Washed, shaved, those great eyes and that mop of black hair.

'I didn't hear you get up.'

'I did cheat,' he admitted. 'Used the bathroom, not the en-suite.'

'Was I supposed to use the bathroom?'

'No. I just did so as not to wake you.'

'This is lovely,' she said as she picked up her knife and fork. 'You always live like this?'

The white casual fit top was enhanced by eye-catching embroidery of peacocks and flowers down her left hand side. Black leggings and small black-heeled shoes were perfect. Her enigmatic smile completed the picture.

'Here?' he asked when he had swallowed his first mouthful of toast and egg. He couldn't help but look at that great red hair tumbling down in cascades onto her shoulders.

'No. At home.'

'Hardly. Make a coffee, bit of toast, grab the paper and go up to the office.' Craig continued as she did, with his breakfast and when he had eaten his first round of egg and toast, he put down his knife and fork, picked up his cup, held it in two hands with elbows on the table and looked all around then at her. 'We need to talk,' he muttered.

'That sounds serious.'

'It's difficult to talk about my work. I don't want you to feel I'm shutting you out from part of my world.' he said and then took a sip of coffee. 'To be honest it's my whole world. Work is what I do. I really don't do anything else. Yeh I've had a few dates that all turned into disasters.' He shrugged. 'Everybody said it would get easier with time. Probably gave it too much time and I filled that time with

130

work. Waiting too long was probably wrong. Got too engrossed in it all, and it probably showed and women I went with thought I was the Gestapo or thought police or that I'd do them for not wearing their seat belt.' He took a drink of the coffee and put the mug down. He nodded. 'In the end I didn't bother. For four years I just haven't bothered.

'I don't understand.' Jillie rested eight finger tips on her forehead and looked down at the table. 'Can we get this straight? You're a policeman who went to Bristol University.'

'I studied law.'

'My car's taxed and insured and I've got my licence in my bag. Anything else you want to see officer?' made him smile. 'Why would there be a problem, unless I was a drug dealer or organized kids birthday parties and invited paedophiles?' Craig shot to his feet and walked over to lean back against the sink.

'This is not real,' he said to her. 'I've been worried bloody sick that you'd have second thoughts about me.' He stopped and looked all about. 'For years it was as if I'd picked all the wrong women. I've had one or two first dates and nothing else. I'm sorry, but I've had so much nonsense thrown back at me the moment I say the word police.'

'I see knowing you as a real positive.'

'There was the one who lectured me loudly in a wine bar about aggravated trespass being an infringement of human rights. Said she wanted nothing to do with me because unless I supported it I should resign on moral grounds. Another had a go about us being brutal to innocent students, before she flounced out of a restaurant.'

'Innocent students!' Jillie chortled. 'That'll be the day. We know. We've been there! Used to work with someone who was really worried when the bloke she started dating told her he was a gynaecologist. Guess she's got over it. She's got three kids now.'

. 'Last date I had must be four years ago now.' Craig crossed his legs at the ankle and folded his arms. 'I'm investigating a series of break ins. Went to see the boss of this firm and the receptionist apologized that he was out, said he wouldn't be long and offered me a cup of tea. Sort of against the rules, I invited her for a drink. Next it was a movie, then a meal. That was a real achievement, three

131

dates. Dropped her off at her place, drove back home, got out my car. This van pulled into my drive; three blokes got out and gave me a good kicking.'

'You're joking!'

'Eighteen months they got and I spent three days in hospital.'

'Because you're in the police?'

'No. Because the receptionist was married!'

'Married?' Jillie threw at him.

'Separated. I didn't have a clue.' Craig smirked. 'Separated because he used to knock her about. Probably saw it as his chance to give a copper a smacking as well. Now I have a golden rule, check they're single first. Sorry, but three dates is not worth a kick in the head.' He pushed off from the sink, took a few steps, stopped and rested his hands on his hips. Craig went to compliment her looks, but changed his mind. He doubted whether most of the women he had ever been with looked as good at night all dolled up as Jillie did right there at breakfast. 'I've got nothing planned for today. Thought we might go out for a meal tonight. There's a new Indian opened apparently. Up near the station. Book while we're out?' he suggested. 'Unless you know the number.' She shook her head. 'I could get used to this,' he said, and she smiled at him. It really was delightful, and maybe, just maybe that was a good idea.

20

Sunday morning and Jake Goodwin faced a whole day of nothing. Nothing that is apart from a bit of a hoover round, stuff his dirty clothes in the machine, iron it all later and cobble together some sort of meal.

When his phone rang he was still sat at the table in the kitchen drinking coffee and reading the Sunday paper he'd nipped to the shop for.

'You doing anything?'

'Not exactly.'

'Want to pop round?'

'Where?'

'Here. Home,' was out of the blue.

'Yeh, fine.'

An hour and ten minutes later Jake knew exactly where all Sally's attributes came from. Tess Conway was her daughter's mother of that there could be no doubt. An extra pound or two here and there, slightly fatter in the face, but she had given her girl her deep brown hair, chocolate eyes and great legs.

They were back to the slightly nervous Sally for ten minutes, and Jake struggled to offer assistance in a slightly tense atmosphere. When Tess suggested she make a cup of tea, Jake offered to give her a hand in the kitchen, but actually did nothing more than lean back, arms folded against the sink. Their initial chatter was about his role with the Police, and she initially made little attempt to produce tea.

'I suppose you still live at home do you?' Tess asked Jake directly as she eventually poured water into three plain white mugs in the kitchen. 'Part of the why generation, no doubt.'

'Why?' he sniggered.

'Why should I move out, why should I buy my own place, why should I tidy my room?'

'I am buying a place as it happens.' Tess looked towards the door and dropped her voice.

'In my day, there's no way my parents would have approved of the way they behave these days. Now parents are stupid enough to let their kids sleep together, get drunk, smoke goodness knows what. All in the family home. No wonder they don't want to move out.' She sighed. 'Where did it all go wrong?'

'Progress?' said Jake as he felt a hint of a blush.

'Regress more like. Anyway,' she said and hesitated. 'Why is she still living here?' amazed him and it must have been obvious. 'Take her with you,' she said quietly as she moved a pace or two to push the door closed. 'Or is commitment a foreign language these days?'

'Actually…well…erm…'

'You don't need my permission.'

'Think you've jumped the gun a bit.'

'In what way?'

'We're a long way from…' now he was flushed and embarrassed.

'In this day and age? Surely not.' What the hell was she suggesting?

Tess turned back to her task and put the three mugs onto a tray.

'Possible she thinks you wouldn't approve' he blurted as his mind searched for the right thing to say.

'Deep inside,' she tapped her chest. 'I know there's a proper way to behave, but for now the world doesn't see it like that.' She looked towards the door. 'I can't dictate at her age, nor do I have the time to wait for the world to come to its senses.'

'Well, I…erm..'

'Just promise me you'll treat her decently. You treat her right and my Sally could be the best thing that's ever happened to you. She's a very astute young woman, and even if I say it myself very grounded. She'll not be found wasted in the gutter on a Friday night, won't spend money on ridiculous high heels and certainly doesn't support the larding of celebrities. Sally is an original in her own right, not a photocopy like so many are today.' Tess Conway folded her arms, to create a serious stance. 'But men have been her weakness. Made all the wrong choices.'

'Thanks.'

134

'No,' said Tess and took hold of Jake's arm. 'I could spot the others a mile off.' Tess Conway stopped for a moment, removed her hand and Jake waited. 'Not having a father hasn't helped. Had nobody to set a standard.'

'I'll look after her,' was what he said, what he wanted to say and what he felt he needed to say. Tess moved away to open the door.

'There's two old suitcases in the loft if you want to borrow them,' she called out to her daughter sat cross-legged on the sofa. 'We'll have this tea, and then I'm sure this young man can get them down.'

When the pair of them appeared from the kitchen with mugs and Penguin biscuits on a plate, Sally's face was a picture. Dumbfounded, amazed and confused all rolled into one and looked up at Jake from the cream sofa for help.

'You lived here long?' Jake asked Tess to annoy Sally.

'Since this one was about seven,' her mother said from a comfortable chair. 'So how long's this been going on?'

'Not long,' said Jake. 'Had a certain nurse tend to my leg in A&E.'

'Senior Sister, if you don't mind.' Jake grimaced at Tess.

'I take it you didn't go to Alice's then?' she threw at Sally.

'What?'

'Last night. You told me you were off to see Alice.'

'I did.'

'I didn't float down the Witham on a biscuit young lady. Young man like this, place of his own and you're having a cozy girl's night in with drippy Alice,' she laughed heartily. 'I don't think so.' She laughed again, this time more softly. 'It's only sex,' almost made Jake choke on his tea.

'Mother!'

'Why are people so damn coy about it? Billions of people do it every day. It's nothing clever. At least now I can invite Russell round.'

'Russell? You're joking!' Sally gasped and didn't know where to look.

135

'Did you really think I belonged to a Scrabble club?' Jake took hold of Sally's hand but didn't look at her. He knew she would be blushing probably more than he was. How outlandish was all this?

'How long's this been going on?' Sally managed, as if roles had been reversed.

'Must be a year.'

'Why didn't you say?' Sally asked.

'Didn't think you'd approve,' said Tess, drunk her tea, picked up a Penguin and tossed it at Jake. 'Didn't need you moping around with a long face. Past year with you has been bad enough.'

'Hang on,' said Sally and put down her mug. 'I'm the daughter. You're the one who's not supposed to approve.'

Jake glanced at her and she flicked him a quick smile.

'If it was some of those others you've been with I'd not be too happy.'

'But a policeman must be all right?'

'Detective Sergeant,' he popped in.

'Yeh. Whatever.'

'I don't know if he's all right,' her mother shot at her. 'You're the one who's been sleeping with him.'

'Mother! I haven't been sleeping with him!'

'Well, doing it then.'

'This when I get a score?' Jake asked Sally to make her mother laugh. 'This what happened to the rest? They got to this point and you gave them three out of ten?'

'Three!' exclaimed Tess. 'I doubt whether some of them were that good, by the look of them. Bunch of self opinionated ragamuffins.'

'Stop it!' Sally shouted and got to her feet. 'This is terrible. Why d'you have to do this?'

'Do what?'

'Make out I've been...you know,' Jake stood up, walked the few paces to her, took Sally in his arms and kissed her. He could feel how hot and flushed her face was. Suddenly she pulled herself free, grabbed his hand and almost dragged him into the kitchen, and kicked the door closed. 'I'm so...' Another kiss stopped her.

'Want me to go?' he whispered.

136

'No,' she replied and clung to him, then moved away enough to look up at him. 'Been hurt a lot. They've been unfaithful, been married...and I miss my dad.'

'Can't replace your dad,' Jake said softly. 'But I could be everything else you'd like me to be.' The kiss was their first real passionate experience together.

'Better find these suitcases,' said a slightly embarrassed Sally and pulled him back into the lounge. Tess and Jake exchanged glances and grins.

On the landing Sally had used a pole to pull down the steps from inside the loft in an irritable fashion and went to climb up, when Jake took hold of her.

'You all right?'

'Yes,' she shot at him and tried to pull herself free.

'I know your mum was a bit over the top, but in some respects you're just like her. And because you're like you are is why I'm here. Think she now feels she can have a life without worrying what her little girl will think.' He kissed her. 'This because she's seeing someone? What's wrong with this Russell?'

'Nothing,' she shrugged. 'Why couldn't she tell me?'

'In case you didn't approve.'

'How did we get from making a cup of tea to suitcases?'

'Think she sees me as the way of getting rid of you, so Russell can come round. Stay the night probably. Asked me if I've got my own place.' Jake stepped onto the ladder. 'Suitcases, madam.'

Tess and Jake left Sally to pack the suitcases herself in her bedroom, while he answered all the woman's questions, about his family and particularly about his job. He carried both cases to his car, while mother and daughter chatted on her doorstep.

As the car pulled away, Tess Conway stood alone in the drive. Was this the last layer of motherhood being pulled from around her?

Was Sally really happy about Russell when she expected emotion about Peter being cast aside? As she waved the couple away Tess felt tears behind her eyes.

'I never ever thought I'd have a conversation like that with my mother,' said Sally as Jake pulled out of her road. 'She's been going round his place two or three times a week for a bit of nookie. Why is it so difficult to imagine your mother, you know.'

'She's an attractive woman.' got him a slap on his thigh.

'There was me really worried in case she disapproved. Worried it might cause a rift between us. Truth is she couldn't get rid of me fast enough.'

'I bet she's phoning Russell now.'

What had occurred to Tess while they were retrieving the suitcase was their holiday. Tess and Sally holidayed together, had always holidayed together after losing Peter. First two years they didn't, then the year after they'd gone to Whitby in a caravan. As the years passed by, their holiday adventures progressed. For ten years or more they had always holidayed in September. Away from the worst of the heat and more importantly away from the badly behaved children whose parents allow them to think they own the world.

An attractive typically French farmhouse on the outskirts of Nice had been booked since February. What now? Would Sally still want to spend ten days with her mother? Hopefully not, if Tess had anything to do with it. Nice just round the corner from Monaco with Russell would do just fine, but she'd not mention it to him yet. She had work to do on Sally first.

21

Two men were somewhat disappointed on Monday morning. Jake was first in and nobody asked him if he'd had a good weekend. Mid morning, not one soul even mentioned to Craig Darke that him arriving after ten was almost unique, and they didn't ask about his two days off.

He and Jillie had thoroughly enjoyed their meal on Sunday evening. King Prawn Kor-Rye for him and she went for the Prawn and Mushroom Biryani. Red wine, ice cream, coffee and a taxi back to the Olde Manor House made it a perfect weekend nobody asked about.

Must have been something in the water, for there was no 'top of the morning to you' just a plain simple 'Eoini', when Rachel Pickard picked up her phone. Immediately she sensed all was not well, in that her Irish friend skirted around the subject. He didn't go in for his usual sexist silliness. This time it was as if he was reluctant to talk at all, then he suddenly spouted something in Irish she didn't understand.

'You've lost me now Eoini.'

'God forgive me. Tis a dreadful business to be 'onest so 'tiz.'

'What is?'

'Wi' the girls.'

'The twins?' she guessed.

'Eimear Kavanagh.'

'How d'you mean?'

'Being sent away loike that.'

'Sent away where?'

'Don't rightly know yet,' was of little help.

'Why was she sent away?'

'Yer know,' was very sheepish.

'I don't know Eoini, you tell me.'

'Pregnant' he said as if the word would set his lips on fire the moment he dared to utter it.

'Eimear Kavanagh was pregnant.'

'Holy Mother of God.'

'And she was sent away?'

'Shame was too great for himself. Poor man he couldn't stan' it.'

'Who couldn't stand it?'

'Fergus.'

'The father?' Rachel heard Eoini mutter something. 'Let's get this straight,' said Rachel as she scribbled notes. 'Eimear Kavanagh got pregnant and her father was ashamed. Then what?'

'Sent 'er away. De wee lass.'

'How old was she?' she waited.

'Fourteen or thereabouts. Maybe fifteen.'

'Sent her away to where, do we know?'

'Not yet. One scayle says they went ter Liverpool.' Rachel Pickard wrote 'DCI' in big letters on her pad and waved it at young Natalie and gestured.

'You've done a great job Eoini. You must have worked hard on all this. This all come from Wexford?'

Truth was Eoini Culligan's life since his wife walked out was bereft of anything. That is until this delightful young lady from Lincoln popped up on his phone.

'Must be the luck of der Oirish,' he said, and for the first time in a long time felt good about himself. 'The printers was in a small village outside Wexford, made it easier.'

'And this is where he worked and eventually with a mate took over the business.'

'Georgie Doherty.'

'The mate?' she asked as she scribbled.

'Yes. Sauld his shares to a fraudster who ripped himself off.'

'Ripped Fergus off?' she asked as DCI Craig Darke walked up to her desk.

'No,' was sharp. 'Georgie Doherty got ripped off and finished up wi' nathin. Ran the business into the ground. Not there now.'

'Let's see if I've got this straight,' said Rachel Pickard for the benefit of Craig Darke and the other coppers listening in. 'Fergus Kavanagh worked at a printers near Wexford. He and...'

'Tollsford.'

140

'In Tollsford.' Culligan grunted. 'He and this Georgie Doherty eventually took over the place. Then Eimear gets herself pregnant, and Fergus sells his share to some passing rip off merchant, packs his bags and heads possibly for Liverpool.' She looked across at Craig Darke as she said it. 'And he sent Eimear away. Do we know where?'

'I'll keep searching.'

'That's brilliant Eoini. You really are one heck of a researcher. How did you get onto all this?' She winked at Craig.

'Luck of the Oirish missy.'

'More than luck I should imagine.'

'The moment I was onto Tollsford and then to Georgie Doherty it was easy pickings. wee community loike that, one of their own ripped off. Not something they forgot in a 'urry.'

'Where is this heading you next?'

'Back to Tollsford.'

'I have to say this is a cracking piece of work Eoini. What an asset you must be across there.'

'Wouldn't jist chucker it fer anybody.'

'Ah thank you Eoini.'

'Tanks. Til the next toim.'

'I'll be waiting.' Rachel replaced her receiver and clapped her hands. 'Bingo!'

'Flattery will get you into big trouble one day.'

Rachel patted her tummy and smiled. 'Think it already has.'

22

Craig Darke was back to meeting Jillie in pubs to drink J20 all night or restaurants with unimaginative menus. No deCosta-Jones mansion to wallow in. No sex, in fact he had noticed not very much at all and in the way his mind used previous experiences he sensed that all was not well and she'd had enough of him already and the end was nigh.

She always appeared relaxed enough, but beneath that exterior Craig perceived a seriousness that might make really knowing her and loving her difficult. As if she would never completely lower her drawbridge.

On his way down the A46 to meet her in Newark, Craig had decided that when this came to an end, he really would not bother any more. If he couldn't make it properly with Jillie, then he couldn't make it. As his depression had slowly taken hold during the week he had felt increasingly angry with himself. Angry that he had given in to the desires he had probably had for eighteen years. He was angry when he admitted to himself that quite possibly he really had wanted to have her when she was just twelve, and now he had and that made him angry too. It was entirely possible he had been involved in abuse by mind and then by body.

Craig told himself he should have left well alone. Gone for a coffee that Saturday of the Spring Fayre out of politeness and left it at that. Not listened to his hard cock talking, not made love as he had that weekend.

Should he strike first, tell her it was all over before she could dump him?

'We need to talk,' arrived early in their conversation. 'I'm back at home with my parents because I don't know what I want to do with my life. I'd got my personal life in such a mess. Went from one bad relationship to another. Then career wise I have particular skills and experience the banking industry is crying out for. But is that what I want? Do I need immature remarks every time I go to the toilet, do I need oafs in braces commenting on my periods, do I need disgusting screen savers of private parts thrust in my face? You think

28banking's bad from the outside. Let me tell you, being on the inside is worse. A whole lot worse. Grown men crying on a regular basis, suffering threats about their futures. Being bullied by people who probably invented the word, and all just for the sake of money. More money than they know what to do with.' She took a healthy swig of her cold drink. 'I planned to take six months out, take a complete break and make a decision.' She just looked at him.

'And?' Perhaps he should make it easy for her, take himself out of the equation right now.

'And now it's all been thrown up in the air.'

'How?'

'By you.'

'Me?' he threw back.

'There was no man in my life once I got myself free of all that rubbish. I had no plans to get tied up with another lousy bastard...'

'Thanks for that!' Jillie Lombard clenched her fists, shook them, screwed up her face, then suddenly released all the tension and fell back into her chair and looked up at the ceiling. This was not the woman he loved. This was the hard businesslike Jillian with all that gorgeous hair pulled back tight into a pony tail.

'That's the problem,' she said slowly. 'You're the problem you're the bloody opposite.' she said to the ceiling, through clenched teeth.. 'Up to two or three weeks ago it was, do I go back to banking? Perhaps for somebody who speaks fluent German a move to Germany might not be a bad idea. I could work in Frankfurt or on the other hand take one of the London offers I've had. Then what happens,' she imitated her mother "please come to the Fayre Jillian, dear"..."you will be coming on Saturday wont you"...'Sitting behind my mother's cake stall was a damn long way from lunch at the Dorchester or cocktails in the latest swish Sushi bar.' She lowered her head slowly to look at him.

'So this is goodnight Vienna.'

'Only if *you* want it to be.'

'London or Frankfurt can't include me. I'd try to transfer to the Met at a push, but not the Bundespolizei or whatever it is.'

'Let me ask you the million dollar question, and I want the absolute truth, the honesty I hope you and I have been running with.'

143

Craig waited while she cleared her throat. 'Are you really interested in me, is this anything like serious or has shagging the ginger kid from Sunday school been a good tale to tell all the lads and...?'

'Stop it!' he was sure all the pub heard, as he leant across the low wooden table. Craig looked deep into her beautiful green eyes.

'Sorry,' she sad sadly with her head lowered. 'It's just that...well since I walked out on my ex I've been told he got his kicks out of telling all his Little Lord Fontleroy posh boys he mixes with how he'd gone from Charterhouse fillies to a council house bit of rough.'

'The bastard.'

She peered up. 'Had to ask myself the same question. Is that what you're all about? Ginger kid from way back. How many brownie points do you get from your copper friends for me I've been wondering? Do you just see this as legal paedophilia?'

'For your information young lady, nobody knows I've been seeing you. It's none of their business. But I do have to say it seems to me as if you're the one who has had a taster for old times sake, and are now off to pastures new.'

'Sorry,' she said again.

'D'you want the truth, the no holds barred honest to God honesty I don't think you're ready for?' She nodded and he saw her bite her red bottom lip. 'Then marry me.' Jillie turned into a statue, her mouth slightly open, her eyes just staring at him, no flicker until she had to suck in a breath.

'You're joking!' He shook his head.

'You wanted to know.'

'Was that a proposal?' she asked quietly.

'No,' was no more than mouthed. 'That's just so you know the truth about me. This is not notches on the bedpost. This is not bragging in the canteen on Monday morning. Coppers I work with I'm pretty sure think I'm a boring old bastard who lives alone, and gets his kicks out of reading post mortems. I don't socialize because it's all wives and partners. Talk is about their spoilt brats, school run bollocks, school league tables, ballet classes and gym clubs.'

'I feel stupid. I thought...' she closed her eyes and Craig expected to see a tear. 'You'd had your fun and...'

144

'No, no, no.' She looked at him.

'I need to sort this out in my mind. Spending time with you would put unfair pressure on me. I need to go back to where I was before that damn Fayre. Back to looking at everything on my own without any outside influences. Now I know where you stand, now I don't have that as an added worry I can decide on my future, but I need time to weigh up the pros and cons.' She put her head on one side. 'Please.'

'This all about money?'

'No it's not!' was very sharp. 'I realized I lacked the motivation I once had. I need a new challenge,' was not the whole truth.

'What we talking time wise?'

'Give me a month. Max.'

'So this may be goodbye?'

'It means that I have more options.' Told him clearly she probably meant yes.

'How will I know? Will it be all trendy and I'll get dumped by text?' and the look on her face told him that was the wrong thing to say.

'Look at it this way. Twice in my life I've made hasty rash decisions about men and in both cases I've been hurt very badly. With my career I've always taken my time, considered all the options and each time I've come up trumps. Even if I didn't need time to sort out my career, I wouldn't rush into anything with you. Had my fingers burnt twice. I won't let it happen again.'

'That means it's me against the bankers, and it doesn't matter what they do, they always win. They always get the bonus at the end of the rainbow.' Craig lifted his glass to take another drink of mango and melon or whatever it was, as Jillie suddenly got to her feet picked up her bag from the next chair and looked down at him.

'Give me a month.' She turned and walked a few steps. 'I'll be in touch, I promise,' she said, walked away, pushed open the door and was gone.

There he was again the lonely man sat on his own in a pub, just like it had been so many times before. The sad git all those at the bar were now no doubt chuckling about.Would go home and tell their family about.

It was at times like these when Craig really hated himself. Would probably have cried had he been on his own. He missed his wife. He missed Katherine like mad, and missed what they had shared. He hated himself for not missing her more. When life was gently trudging along, when work was good he had to admit he didn't think of her. Now when it looked as though another woman had cast him aside like an old sock, it was Katherine he went to for comfort.

Oh how he just hated that lorry driver. Doug Sardeson, a name he would remember for all time, had killed Katherine. Taken her life away from her and now it seemed had also destroyed his. Why he asked himself again as he had done so many times before. Why was a dead wife so much of a hurdle for other women to deal with compared to an unfaithful one?

Jillie Lombard knew, in fact had always known that at some juncture she had to come clean. Maybe not with Craig if she decided the world of banking was still too hot to resist and he fell by the wayside, but one day with a man.

Life with her stockbroker had been good in a materialistic sense right from the start. Emotionally it had been almost barren for some time. Jack Crampton more then ten years her senior was a partner with LeFevre-Connaught. A position not earned of course, like almost everybody he mixed with in business and pleasure he had been parachuted in by his family and friends as part of his inheritance. Somewhere along the line all to do with Contracts for Difference he and one of Jillie's senior bosses had fallen out big time. A broker had accused Jack of underhand methods, of double dealing and worse of insider trading involving CFDs to take advantage of a falling market, or 'going short'. The row had escalated to such an extent that some said that had they come across each other at any time it was more than likely that Savile Row suits would have been involved in actual fisticuffs.

Then up pops Ralph Doré one of Jillie's senior bosses to side with the broker Crampton was at war with.

City investment banking is hard work, and to compensate they play hard. This is not just a myth one reads about in the tabloids, this

146

is real. Usually on a Friday in a bar, and at the end of this particular week it was different. The moment Jillie walked in she sensed an atmosphere brought about by the unusual and unexpected presence of said Rupert Èdouard Doré.

She made the mistake of downing two glasses of Mount Koinga Pinot Noir very quickly and then when her third was spilt all down her white blouse and grey suit jacket, chaos reigned. The bar was noisy and packed, and there was more than one pair of hands attempting to help her deal with the 'accident'. People were pushing and shoving and all of a sudden there was a wild stench of old whisky and Doré was slobbering all over her, and as she struggled to free herself an unwelcome hand intruded.

Despite her cramped situation Jillie manage to somehow raise a knee and do him real damage. Before he was down she slapped his face pushed herself free and was gone.

Worse was to come.

Back home in their apartment a distraught Jillie Lombard told all to her partner, expecting a combination of outrage and sympathy. None was forthcoming, in fact totally the opposite.

Jack Crompton harangued Jillie about her behaviour, demanded that she apologise profusely and more than simply disregarded the sexual assault. He suggested instead that she had in some way brought it upon herself. At one point so heated had the situation become she was convinced he was about to hit her. This was the public schoolboys all sticking together, despite their differences.

Angry and isolated Jillie Lombard packed her bags and walked out. Found a small hotel and stayed there, alone and humiliated. Jack Crompton the whole while simply sat there in his big brown leather chair sipping Lagavulin single malt and talking to his old school tie chums on his BlackBerry.

Monday morning instead of apologizing to Doré profusely as Jack had demanded, an angry Jillie stormed into his office to loudly demand a public one from him or else. Or else she would go to the nearest police station to accuse him of sexual assault.

An aggressive and bullying Doré at first tried arrogantly to bluster his way out of the situation by suggesting that what she saw as sexual assault was no more than a drunken attempt at a kiss. Jillie

147

was having none of it, and had reached the door when he and two colleagues stopped her, sat her down and called in their legal team.

She knew right was on her side, not to mention the bank's code of conduct that strictly forbade any intimate or sexual behaviour between senior and junior employees. Jillie was no junior, but she was certainly a rung or two down from rotund Doré.

Banking embittered and under the cosh from Parliament down, had to ensure that the matter never saw the light of day. Within forty eight hours, Munchen Bundesbank's head office in Germany had issued a statement to the effect that Jillie Lombard had left the company to pursue new and exciting interests which she did with their blessing and good wishes. A six figure bank draft payoff left a nasty taste in her mouth, and she was back in Stamford drinking weak tea from a china cup with her mum in her kitchen.

Since then colleagues who had not come forward at the time for fear of recrimination had been in touch to admit that it had all been set up to get at Jack Crompton. It had been Ralph Doré's mission to 'finger' Jillie as a warped form of point scoring in their trading wrangle.

Back home in the very bedroom she had slept in as a twelve year-old and a Sunday school regular, Jillie considered how luck for once had not been with her.

Now just a few months later she faced another of life's dilemmas. When do you admit your past? Right from the start and end any chance of a relationship? Wait a while or keep it all taboo? Are hidden secrets any way to blend a liaison? If only old Lavinia had got them together at her Autumn Fayre, by the time she had been assaulted by bloody Doré she would have had a kindly policeman she could have called on, to explain it all to. To seek advice and receive a cuddle in return perhaps.

23

Detective Sergeants Jake Goodwin and Raza Latif were in the Honda outside a environment equipment supplier on the industrial estate with a good view of the TwinPrint car park. In particular they could see the red Lexus of Eimear Kavanagh. They received the call to tell them the DCI and DI had phoned Sebastian Quinn, when there was nobody at the houses in Saxilby. Then a call on the radio from DC Ally Sutton advised that Quinn was being interviewed back at HQ.

Arrogant was a new word for Craig Darke to use to describe Sebastian Arthur Quinn, when he offered him legal representation, to go alongside his pompous nature.

Darke and Daniels one side of the tables, Quinn the other. PC Reynolds on a chair by the door, tape recorder and video on.

'Shall we start with the cyanide,' Darke suggested. 'What use do you have for cyanide?'

'I have no idea what you are talking about,' replied Quinn. He made a big issue of yawning and flapping his hand in front of his face. 'Just remember you have to prove all of this, and if you are unable to. I win. It really is as simple as that. I will remind you every day, have no fear of that mister policeman.' Arrogance had clearly landed, but Darke was able to ignore him.

'Cyanide – you can buy an ampoule on the internet. 25grammes for £110. You had it delivered to your Gallery in Mevagissey.'

'Is that so?'

'Cornwall Police are interviewing your sister under caution at this very moment,' Darke lied. Yes, they said they were going to, but it probably wasn't at that precise moment. 'Perhaps you would care to think of her for a moment or two.' Darke looked at Brian Daniels. 'Perhaps we should have a moment's silence for Mr Quinn to digest that snippet of information.' The pair sat in silence, arms resting on the grey tables looking at Quinn, and his nerves were suddenly evident in a small twitch. They waited. 'Your sister Melanie being charged with aiding and abetting murder, Mr Quinn.' The stoic Quinn moved his gaze to look through the gap between them. 'Do

149

you think she will find prison life to her satisfaction? Be some whore's bitch within a fortnight. Could be ten years of that Mr Quinn.'

'What sort of state do you think she will be in when she gets out,' Daniels pursued.

'And her partner James, their son Robert and daughter Mary-Anne. How do you think they will enjoy the process? The court case, the media intrusion and visiting hours. Imagine sitting across a table from her, watching her grow older with every visit. How do you think they will greet you when you get out?'

'How long d'you think James will hang about? Divorce is easy when your missus is in the slammer. He and the kids'll be long gone.'

Quinn sighed. 'And your point is?'

'My point is Mr Quinn,' said Darke rather louder, mentally giving the pompous bastard credit for his calmness. 'That right here and now you can stop that pain. You can deal with her suffering; you can be a man for once in your life and step into the firing line. Admit your guilt and pay the price.'

'Women's prisons,' said Daniels, who had remained fairly quiet. 'Are not at all like a seaside art gallery. You don't get the twin-set brigade and retired colonels in there.'

'Well, not many,' said Darke as an aside.

'I fail to see what my sister has to do with this.'

'Apart from signing for the cyanide, you mean?'

'The cyanide your sister ordered,' Darke opened the brown folder in front of him and lifted a photocopy of an invoice. 'The cyanide paid for with a credit card in the name of Melanie Quinn.'

'Sorry Sebastian,' said Daniels. 'But the name Quinn was like a beacon. If you'd had the stuff delivered to David Davis in Aberystwyth or Mac McAloon in Aberdeen, we'd never have put two and two together, probably.

'Either your sister Melanie Rose Quinn who signed for the package or you Sebastian Arthur Quinn had a use for that cyanide. Use a lot of cyanide in an art gallery does she?' Both men laughed. 'The cyanide that matches the same batch, particles of which we found in the stomach of Eilish Kavanagh.'

'Would you like a bit of time to digest it all Mr Quinn?' Brian Daniels asked calmly. 'Maybe get you a cup of tea, let you contemplate your situation. Consider your options. Do you take the rap for this; do you remain silent and be told what sentence your sister has got? After all a jury may decide that she killed your partner. What will you do about Eimear?' They watched Quinn's eyes.

Sebastian Arthur Quinn did not admit to anything, asked for a solicitor he named and by the end of the day he was not charged with the murder of his partner Eilish Mona Kavanagh.

'He's so shit scared about going to prison, that bastard will let his poor bloody sister take the rap.'

Eoini Culligan had his own personal demons to fight, and these would be more prevalent when he visited Tollsford again, which he had to.

In his research already passed onto Rachel he had come across talk of young pregnant Eimear being sent away. Sent away it had been suggested by an embarrassed and furious father to a Catholic home. Culligan guessed if might be one of a series of establishments he had heard about; a place of punishment and degradation any religion should be ashamed of. Places he hoped by now a decent society would have done away with.

He had gradually had to accept that his dear mother had over the years become an entrenched religious fanatic. She saw evil in only one sector of society. In her little world religious punishment homes did not and had not ever existed. Even if they did it hardly mattered as in her eyes those dreadful girls deserved all they got. Evil stories of sexual abuse by priests were to her just filth spread by the enemy.

Slowly but surely over the years, and particularly after he joined the Garda he realised that the Orange and the Catholics were probably equally responsible for the powerful hatred, irrational bigotry and unexplained intolerances that still exist. Intolerances that were increasingly evident in his dear mother every day of her life.

Now as a mature being he felt they had always been equal sides of the same now battered coin. The coin of course was kept spinning by bigots from both sides. Centuries of religious illiteracy and neither side could face the prospect of a final spin.

Having grown up observing religious bigotry so often for its own sake day in, day out, Eoini now had those demons to contend with.

Stay loyal to his mother, to his estranged wife and to the religion forced upon him or move on. The disputes he had with the women in his life, both servants of their faith had been to the detriment of their lives and relationships. A mother and son relationship was barely held together by the merest fragment of strained and tormented love. The husband and wife would never be together again. In fact did not even speak, controlled as Mary was by *Rome*. Edicts she latched onto, held firm and would never discuss.

It was all so ingrained in his Mother's psyche. She had spent a lifetime ignoring anything and everything that showed her beloved religion in even a hint of a bad light. A local parish priest could be interfering with an altar boy in her parlour in front of her eyes yet she would never acknowledge it. Nothing untoward ever happened in her little world.

Eoini like the world, now saw bigotry as being primarily based on ethnicity yet his mother and wife, simply and vehemently expressed hatred for just those of other religions. Colour of skin was never an issue. They simply displaced their own sense of low self-esteem by expressing this ghastly hatred.

Eoini was nobody's fool. He could read between the lines. He knew his days with Garda, even as a civilian were numbered. Now with the free time that provided he was working on a dream he had held for some years. He knew there was room for a good experienced private detective. Someone with fraud experience that was with the internet becoming more prevalent. A pension to fall back on when times were hard, but bags of experience when needed. He was absolutely sure he could succeed where others he knew had failed in the past. That Rachel Pickard from Lincoln he knew would never become a client, but she was good practice. Do a good job and he'd quote her as a reference.

When he thought of Rachel he smiled on two fronts. First he really would love the opportunity to meet her, and the second he had

152

not suggested, would not bother to ask. He had no idea whether this lovely copper from the flat lands of Lincolnshire was a Muslim, a Jewess, a Seventh Day Adventist or what his mother would only accept, a good Catholic girl. He didn't know and had no intention of asking or finding out. In the new world his mother's bigotry had forced him into it was just irrelevant.

Botting and d'Andrea started off with TwinPrint. The woman in HR – with volumes of arse and more spare tyres than Michelin, was adamant. Talk of human rights, staff confidence and data protection. That is until Harry Botting phoned Craig Darke, he phoned Kavanagh, and she buzzed down to tell the woman to stop being silly.

Steve Kemp had been implicated by a Ruby Palethorpe. Systematically she had been removing rejected copies of paperbacks destined for pulping. Placed them in her bag alongside the day's banking, hid them in her car when she headed for Barclays and sold them at car boot sales.

Somewhere along the line he had sussed what she was doing and in exchange for remaining schtum she rounded up his overtime or added an hour here and there to keep him sweet.

Ronnie Mackinder with his little wife at his shoulder throughout was of little or no help at all. He admitted when pressed that he had been fired for turning up late for work consistently. Knew that Kemp had been given his marching orders, but put it down to Kavanagh cutting costs or firing somebody on a whim.

Old Dan Scrimshaw was different again. He cheekily told d'Andrea he would have preferred chocolate Digestive biscuits, but was forthcoming. He had the basics right about the books being filched, about Palethorpe's husband selling them at car boot sales, but then his reading of the circumstance was different. Old Dan suggested that Ruby Palethorpe and Steve Kemp had been having an affair. The Kavanagh's had got wind of it, took the moral high ground and were looking for any excuse.

'And if the old man is right,' said Darke, when they returned to the crew room. 'Chances are Kemp is all forthcoming about printing techniques to put us off. Wants us to think he's very helpful and

153

don't get suspicious about anything else he might have done.'
Botting had created an elaborate grimace. 'Go on.'

'He's more worried about what his wife might find out than us
going from nicked books to murder in one leap?'

'Even if we did, how in God's name did he do it?' Darke threw
back. 'This is not cutting her windpipe with a Stanley knife, blowing
her head off with a Glock semi-automatic or a heavy object we're
talking about.'

24

A society so lacking at times in standards or good old fashioned morals still has strange sexual orientated quirks.

When a woman on her own walks into a hotel to meet a man staff know is already ensconced in a room, they have a look of amusement about them. A 'we know what you're doing' attitude. If truth be known for many of them it is nothing more than pure jealousy.

So it was when Eimear Kavanagh in her business suit, white blouse and heeled black shoes climbed the stairs and pushed open the door and the man waiting was laid on the bed watching TV.

'Any problems?' she asked as she slipped off her grey jacket and checked the kettle.

'Smooth as silk,' he advised, without taking his gaze from *Pointless.*

'Wish I could say the same,' she said.

Eimear made them both a coffee, as she managed to move him away from Alexander Armstrong to the business in hand. They enjoyed delightful oat crunch biscuits she produced from her bag, rather than the standard shortbread all hotels feel obliged to provide.

First it was catch-up time.

'Take it the books reached Bergamo. How is Luigi?'

'He's fine.'

'Hope he didn't ask too many questions?'

'Just appeared to accept the story.'

'Does he know she's dead?'

'Never mentioned it.'

'And the van?'

'One of his lads will bring it back next month, when I've gone.'

'With a full load I hope.'

'Lovely set-up they've got over there.' He sipped his coffee. 'Wonder if I set off any alarms when I flew in?'

'At East Midlands? Don't be silly. Anyway they're looking for a van coming through one of the ports, if at all.'

155

They laughed at the antics of some as she brought him up to date, chuckling about their own contributions. Eimear with a built in lack of respect for authority talked at length of police incompetence and what she saw as their muddled thinking.

'Major failings of modern police forces,' she emphasised. 'Is their indifference and disinterest dependent on social status? I've not come across it before. But they don't like me, that's very obvious and so their judgement is clouded by a desire for low social status and servitude.'

'Happy dealing with low life. They're happy cuffing some druggie and telling him he's banged to rights, son.'

'They can deal with the lower echelons of society. Somebody like me, intellectually superior leaves them struggling. So obsessed are they, they take their eye off the ball.'

'Didn't you say that first interview was all about them trying to score points.'

Eimear winced slightly and stroked her stomach.

'Problem?'

'Haven't felt too good for a couple of days,' she said as she sipped the last of her coffee. 'Probably something doesn't agree with me'.

'We still going for a meal.'

'Would you mind if we didn't? Just stay here and talk.'

He was hungry. In fact he was famished, but he wouldn't protest. After she'd gone he'd find somewhere on the main road for a tuck-in. Fancied an all day big breakfast with bread and butter to soak up the egg yolk.

'You ever done anything like this before?' he asked, laid beside her on the bed.

'You must be joking.' She just looked up at the ceiling. 'Good to just get away from it all.' She turned to look at him laid there and stroked the back of a finger along the stubble on his chin. 'You've no idea how good freedom feels.'

'Any news on the funeral?' he posed.

'Not yet. Police say they'll tell me when. P'raps they're still trying to work out how. It's a blinkered approach. They are looking for evidence to fit their pet theory.'

156

'What about dear old Sebastian. Any news on him?'

'I've no idea to be honest. I've banished him. Packed all his stuff into boxes and gave him a deadline to collect them. They've gone, but sod knows where he is. Always possible he's gone back to Cornwall. Can't see there's anything to keep him here.' Eimear ran her tongue across her lips and winced.

'You all right?'

'Just catches me now and again.'

'You need to see a doc.' He sat up and looked down at her, at her shiny black hair. 'I'm worried about you.'

'I'll be fine,' was what she said but not how she felt.

25

'Now the hard work begins,' said DCI Craig Darke to start his morning briefing. 'We need as much evidence as we can muster. Even if that means we go back to Bassingham time and again until we find someone, anyone who can confirm Sebastian Quinn was there.'

'Or wasn't,' Brian Daniels contributed.

'I'm not going to court with the assumption that because nobody saw him, he wasn't there. We say he was back at home bumping off his partner. Then suddenly his bloody barrister comes up with the local baker who swears our friend Sebastian called in every day for a hearty oat loaf and a hot cross bun.'

The trill of a phone stopped him. Jake glanced at his mobile.

'Take it outside if you must!' was his anger at no doubt being thrown aside for a banker. Craig Darke went on: 'Did anyone see him leave his house? So far enquiries in that direction have come up blank, bearing in mind from their place he can be out and down to the A57 and on the bypass mixing with the traffic in no time.'

'That way's not past the CCTV,' DC Hatchard reminded him.

'Exactly.'

'Sorry boss,' said Jake as he read *Phone urgent Police business Sal.*

'What now?'

'Sorry boss,' said Jake, as he got to his feet. 'Urgent Police business,' he offered as he strolled from the room and went into the corridor. He pressed *Reply.* 'You rang,' he said when Sally answered.

'Think you need to be here,' she said quickly. 'Miss Kavanagh. Something's come up. Meet you at the front door.'

'Can you tell me what?'

'Could be serious. She was brought in last night. Just get here,' was the Senior Sister in her.

'On my way,' he told her, walked back into the office phone in hand. 'Sorry boss,' he said to disrupt a disgruntled Darke yet again.

'Just had a message from the hospital. I'm needed urgently. Something to do with Kavanagh being admitted.'

'What?' Craig demanded with more than a hint of annoyance. 'Kavanagh?'

'She's in hospital. They're waiting for me.'

'Let's go,' was not what Jake expected, as Darke slipped his jacket on. 'Ross. Phone TwinPrint we still haven't taken prints off that driver.'

'He was on his way to Italy.'

'And how long ago was that?' Darke said as he followed Jake out. 'Just do it!'

He saw Sally stood in the sunshine at the County Hospital main entrance the moment Craig parked with his hazards on.

'Sir, this is Sally. Senior Sister Sally Conway,' he said and she nodded. His use of her title having not been lost on her. 'What's up?' Sally looked all around and ignored those patients in dressing gowns having a crafty fag.

'Kavanagh was admitted last night. Head of Nursing's waiting,' she said and lead the way. The two detectives followed her along corridors and up stairs. Finally they were shown into an office.

'Good morning gentlemen,' a short woman said. 'Molly Brewster, Head of Nursing,' and motioned for them to sit down. 'All yours Sally.' The Senior Sister picked up a brown folder from the desk.

'Miss Kavanagh was brought in around half three this morning with stomach pains. When I came on duty I was briefed and then when Mr Chandrasekar came to do his rounds he asked if we had any medical records. Our Ward administrator had been for them, but although we have a Miss Kavanagh, it's not the one you'd expect.' Sally lifted the folder to show the name: *Eilish Mona Kavanagh.*

'That's her dead sister,' Craig Darke told her, but that was met by a shake of the head.

'The lady downstairs in my ward has a scar.' Sally opened the folder. 'In August 2002 Eilish Mona Kavanagh was admitted for an appendectomy.' She handed the folder to Molly Brewster.

'Are you saying…?' Sally's nod stopped Jake.

'Oh my giddy aunt,' Darke sat there with his eyes closed, a look of total disbelief across his face. 'We nearly charged him with the wrong murder,' he said almost to himself as his eyes opened. The look he gave Jake told his sergeant that his boss was now onside with name swapping.

'Looks very much like it detective,' said the Head of Nursing, with a wry smile. 'I also have to tell you that we have had the body in the mortuary checked. That body does not have any scaring anywhere.'

'We're sure about this?' he wanted to know.

'I've asked a surgeon to find a reason to have a look at her,' Molly Brewster told him. 'He will confirm whether or not he considers the two are a match. But as one has no intrusions at all, its only confirmation really. While we wait may we offer you a coffee?' Both detectives declined.

'Do we know what's wrong with…the patient?' Jake enquired.

'Probably psycho sematic. Reaction to her sister's murder, arrest of…' Molly Brewster stopped to chuckle. 'I was going to say arrest of her partner.'

'Let us assume for now, she is Eimear and it was Eilish who was killed,' said Darke as he pushed himself to his feet. 'I've got a team all running off in the wrong direction. Between you and me, we came damn close to charging her sister's partner with murder.' He looked down at Jake. 'You stay here. You've never come into contact with her have you?' Jake shook his head. 'So she won't recognise you. Get word to me as soon as you know, and,' he turned to look at Molly Brewster. 'Can he wait on the ward, just in case she decides to go walkies?'

'Of course. I'll have to pass this all by the Chief Executive, but I'm sure under the circumstances.'

'Thank you,' said Darke and clasped Sally's upper arms. 'Good piece of work.' He looked at her and then at Jake as he rose and back to her. 'Have I got this right?' Sally smiled.

'Yes you have.'

'Excuse me,' said Molly. 'Is there something I should know?'

'Jake's my partner,' said Sally proudly.

160

'Off you go then,' said Molly. 'Well done Sally.'

'I need your assurance,' said Darke to Molly and Sally. 'That this goes no further. And please ensure your chief is aware of that.'

Craig Darke and then Jake Goodwin shook her hand and all three left the office.

Before he left to take the news back to base, Craig Darke spent a few minutes with Jake alone.

'She's swapped again,' he said as if he needed assurance.

'Looks like it.'

'Why?'

'This just her swapping back? Possible Eilish didn't want to swap back to who she was. Now she's gone Eimear can do what she likes.'

'Has to be more to it than that. Easy way to get a degree. Change your name's a way of avoiding tuition fees.'

'Any chance that Irish bloke might find out why Kavanagh changed their names in the first place?'

'He's never going to run around telling all and sundry why he's changed his girls names. People back there won't know, will they? And besides, they hate his guts.'

Left alone Sally made her way back down the long corridors and then downstairs to her ward with Jake in tow.

During their walk together they decided to keep his presence there low key. He was not the police and he most certainly was not Jake, the man in her life. Sally showed him to the waiting room, plied him with coffee and introduced him as Russell Clements, the name of her mother's fancy man, a journalist gaining background material for a hospital feature.

The room was small with a Coke machine, ten wooden chairs with blue seats, plenty of leaflets on fun matters such as Blood Clots Kill, Breast Cancer and MRSA.

On one wall was a copy of a painting of Lincoln Cathedral suggesting how it and the surrounding countryside may have looked centuries previous. There were also photograph of aircraft and buildings at RAF Cranwell for some reason.

Jake got the best of the deal at the hospital. Within ninety minutes it had been confirmed through the surgeon and her GP that the

161

woman in the ward was indeed Eilish Mona Kavanagh, and the scenario back at Police headquarters had been turned on its head. The reasoning behind the murder had taken a sudden twist.

Sebastian Quinn if he indeed was the murderer had killed his partner's sister not his partner.

'Understand this and let there be no mistake,' said Brian Daniels the moment he was told. 'This remains with us. The hospital know, we know. Nobody else is to know she is not who she says she is. If the press get a sniff, somebody will be hung out to dry!' He received a series of nods and grunts.

'I'm bloody confused already!' was Toni d'Andrea.

'You still putting money on him shagging them both?' Latif asked his DI.

'It brings that theory back to life, but it doesn't tell us why. Unless.' Daniels stopped talking and spun left and right in his chair. 'The relationship was on the rocks, and they cooked it all up between them.'

'Didn't need to kill her sister if she had control, boss,' said Latif. 'She could just get rid of her and move him in.'

'Enough theory,' said Daniels. 'We need the warrant for Quinn's place, and another one for Eimear's house, two teams to go through them like a dose of salts with the crime scene guys.' He stood up. 'Let's get it done.'

'We've been through them once.'

'That was before we knew they'd swapped identities and before we knew it was cyanide.'

'And if my bet's correct, could be it's simply a case of Eimear wanting a shag every night.'

'Hold your horses,' said DCI Craig Darke as he walked in the door. 'CPS are getting jittery about Quinn. I've admitted we very nearly charged him with the murder of a woman who is very much alive.' He sat down at the desk nearest to him. He looked at Brian Daniels. 'Get in touch with Jake. Make sure nobody but nobody knows it's a dead woman alive in that bed.' He looked around. 'And by the way, that nurse of his is very nice. Very nice indeed.'

'Boss,' said Ross Walker. 'That driver's still in Italy.'

162

'Still?'

'According to TwinPrint, Brian Barry's working from their Italian base, because their main van had an accident and he's helping out with his.' He looked down at his desk. 'Bergamo, just north of Milan.'

'Fair enough.'

.

26

Detective Superintendent Kenneth Gillis always had this supercilious look about him. Slumped in his chair behind his over large desk.

'In words of one syllable Darke, explain this cock up to me.'

'Let's go back to square one, shall we sir?' he suggested and knew by being called *Darke* his boss was not in a good mood. 'Eilish Kavanagh's body was found by a driver from TwinPrint who called us and an ambulance. She was pronounced dead at the scene. Dr O'Carroll did the PM and concluded she'd been poisoned...'

'How did this driver know who she was if they were so bloody identical?'

'She was in her house, and Eimear was at TwinPrint, she had...'

'Yes, yes man, get on.'

'Last night Eimear Kavanagh was taken ill, called an ambulance and was admitted to the County. Today a very bright nurse in looking for any medical history happened to notice that her sister Eilish had been in there ten years ago having had an appendectomy. The Eimear Kavanagh currently languishing in a bed up there, has an appendix scar. I've since been told by head of nursing that a consultant has looked at the notes and at the scar and confirms. Eimear Kavanagh is alive but is she really Eilish? But Eilish Kavanagh is in the mortuary, but is she who the tag on her toe says? And I might add, the County has no record of ever having seen Eimear before, even as an outpatient.'

'And her husband?'

'He's her partner.'

'Bloody good job you didn't charge him with the murder of a woman who's still alive! His lawyer would have loved that. How the hell is this turning into a mess?'

'Be fair boss. Eilish is dead on her kitchen floor in her house. Her sister is at work and later identifies the body. What other conclusion would you have come to? But now it seems the woman walking round at TwinPrint that morning was wearing her sister's badge.'

'What d'you mean badge? Don't they know who she is?' Ken Gillis laughed.

'Sir. They are identical. Let me tell you when Eimear identified the body that was a creepy as it gets; almost put the fear of God into me. Like she was looking in a mirror. She doesn't just look like her sister. She's the dead spit.'

'DNA? Or didn't we bother Chief Inspector.'

'DNA is the same. I've been through that with Dr Bronagh. They are monozygotic twins. Absolutely identical. Identical twins are always the same sex and as a result have their entire DNA in common. Non identical twins are formed when two sperm cells fertilize two ova...'

'So what are you doing about it now?'

'I've got two teams one at each house, going through them with a fine tooth comb. And that's another thing, their homes are also identical. And that's bloody weird as well.'

'Let me get this straight,' said Gillis as he pulled himself up in his chair. 'Are we now saying that this Eilish was killed in her sister's house?'

'Not necessarily, sir,' said Craig Darke. 'Could be Eimear and Quinn killed her, then moved her body to Eilish and Quinn's house to make it look like she was the dead one. Or Quinn did it. Waited for Eimear to go to work before he moved the body. But in reality the two women are the other way round.'

'But I thought you went through the murder scene at the time. What's this all about?'

'That was when we thought Eilish was killed in her own home. Now we know it was Eimear in her home, and probably moved.'

'And she's still in the County?'

'Goodwin's up there keeping an eye on her.'

'And you?'

'Off to the houses, see what we've found.'

'It had better be better than the Pikka Parcels fiasco.'

'There was over a hundred grand's worth in that van. That's a good day's business.'

'But nothing at the depot. Not a sniff and Mackenzie's going to plead bloody innocence and blame it on the driver.' He pointed at

Darke. 'That was a major drugs route and we've told the world we're onto them. Brilliant.'

'But they sure as hell won't come on our patch again, and two illegals going home.'

Gillis just waved Darke away.

Back downstairs, Craig Darke poked his head into the incident room just on the off chance. For once it lacked the noise of a busy section, empty save for Rachel Pickard, head down intently focused on a pile of interview forms, eating a small square of white chocolate.

'Coffee?' She looked up.

'I bet you need something stronger than that,' she said and stood up. She really was getting bigger on a daily basis. Yes he could do with something stronger, but it had nothing to do with his chat with Gillis. A sleepless night with just one subject on his mind. Jillie.

'What's a bollocking between friends?'

'Bad?' she checked.

'His usual bluster to be honest,' admitted Craig as Rachel walked past him with a tray. 'You know what he's like.'

Craig plonked himself down when he really should have insisted he get the coffees.

'I reckon my Eoini is working on this in his own time,' she admitted when she returned with two coffees and two packets of biscuits. 'Just bits and pieces he's said, and said he'd be in touch again after the weekend.'

'He really think old man Kavanagh had Eimear put in a home and then hot footed it over here?'

'So he reckons.'

'Need as much as we can get from him now.'

'Do I offer an incentive?' There was no need to wait for a response. 'If he really is doing this in his spare time, even if it's only to impress me, a bit of petrol money might oil the wheels.'

'Whatever it takes without going mad. Enough to keep him on our side.'

'Something's troubling you,' said Rachel. 'And it's not just old Gilligilli.' Darke sucked in a breath.

166

'Brian and I have met this Eimear. She's as nasty as they come.' He leaned forward, fingers intertwined. 'According to that old man you spoke to, Eimear is the first class bitch, but Eilish was quite nice.' He clasped the sides of his face. 'It now turns out it's Eilish we've met. If that's being quite nice I'm a soddin' Dutchman. And what the hell was her bloody sister like then? This one's bad enough!'

'Wait a bloody minute!' said DCI Craig Darke stood in the conservatory of Eilish Kavanagh and Sebastian Quinn's home. Everybody stopped their searching. 'When I wanted to know what capsules Eimear Kavanagh might have been taking, Dr O'Connell checked with her GP and told me Eimear had been taking some digestive pills. If Eimear has been taking the pills, how on earth did Quinn persuade his partner to take one? Wait for her to say she had a digestive problem and 'hey why not take one of Eimear's pills' or has their GP been fooled as well?'

'This what they've always done boss, pretended to be each other?'

'Thinking caps on everyone,' said Darke. 'Have a good think. What advantages can you gain by being someone else?' He went back to the drawer he had started to search. 'Answers to me on a postcard.'

'If I pretended to be my sister, it opens up a whole new world,' lightened the atmosphere. 'Swimming pool changing rooms...'

'Can we just be serious for once? According to Branagh O'Connell their GP was adamant that he had prescribed the medication to the correct sister.'

'How the hell did he know?' Brian Daniels asked nobody in particular. 'These days you can book an appointment on line. Knew her sister's login and password, booked an appointment as Eilish. What's the doc have? A list? Or is that on his computer? Eilish on his computer, say. "Next please" and in walks a Kavanagh sister he assumes is Eilish Kavanagh. "Got a jippy tummy doc. Here have some pills," runs off the prescription. All done.'

'But how do they get Eilish to take pills she hasn't been prescribed?'

'Says they're for a digestive problem, and then makes sure Eilish has the very same problem. Low dose of something to give her a jippy tummy, Eimear says take one of these, they did me a power of good. Identical twins where's the harm and Bob's your uncle.'

'You're making this bloody complicated. Lots of ifs and maybes.'

'Want me to check the system with my quack?'

'Might be an idea.'

'What else we got? There's no DNA.'

'Am I right in thinking identical twins also have identical fingerprints?' Raza Latif asked.

'Urban myth.'

'You sure, boss?' Toni d'Andrea queried.

'Harry!' DCI Darke shouted. 'Do identical twins with matching DNA also have matching finger prints?'

'No,' came back from a white hooded suit near the back door. 'Not connected.' DCI Darke's phone rang.

'Yes,' was closer to a shout of annoyance. 'Hold one,' he said in the phone. 'You lot. Have we come across Eilish or Eimear's purse or wallet? Have we still not found her credit cards?' Blank looks, silent gestures. 'Well thank you very much. Jake, there's a DC coming up to take over. See you back at base.' He slid the phone back together. 'Our Jake's been through her effects in the hospital when they took her for an x-ray. Guess what?' Nobody did. 'That woman in hospital has credit cards and everything else in the name of Eimear. Her wallet says Eimear Kavanagh, her credit cards say it and what have we found here? Our Eilish has been killed and Eimear has turned into her, and there's bugger all we can do to prove otherwise. Bollocks!'

'But why for fuck's sake?'

'Language Timothy!' Was Darke's stance against bad language him standing up for public morality? His team knew it wasn't. The great man on occasions used bad language, but he simply could not abide the constant use of some four letter words, when their inclusion was totally unnecessary.

168

'And you can bet your life they had the same pin numbers.'

'If the clowns who were dead set against ID cards had to do this job for five minutes they'd soon change their chuffing minds!'

'Just a thought boss,' said Raza Latif. 'Have you seen things like her driving licence?'

'Anybody?' said Darke loudly. 'Driving Licence? Cheque Book? Any of that?' The response was silence. A couple of his team quickly double checked drawers. 'Job for you Raz. When we get back check them both with DVLA, then....bugger!' he said with frustration. 'I was going to say Home Office. They're bloody Irish. Whatever, see what you can dig up. A will is something we need to have a look at and life insurance.'

'But we do know nobody has used the Eilish credit card since her demise.'

'That bitch is probably using Eimear's.' Craig Darke screwed his eyes shut. 'God I'm sick of all this!' When he opened his eyes Raza's face asked the question without a word. 'We have Gorich which is trouble in itself. Then along comes Petchey to double the trouble, now this. Double trouble is doubled again with bloody twins, then one of them swaps to being the other. Talk about double or quits. Right now I'd like to quit.' He blew out a breath as he smiled. 'Tigger,' Darke called out. 'Do a check on Eimear Kavanagh's credit card. And while you're at it show young Ashley the process.'

'Tigger' Woods stuck his hand up as if he was trying to attract the teacher's attention.

'We got the mobile record for Eilish before we knew she'd swapped...'

Darke clicked his fingers. 'I'm ahead of you...'

'Now we need Eimear's. That's the one people will phone, and if she's got any sense the one she'll use.'

'Good man.'

Twenty hours later Craig Darke and Jake Goodwin were back in the office at the County Hospital to meet Molly Brewster and this time Sally had been replaced by consultant Mr Rupert Jenkins.

169

An articulate and impressive man, but short in stature with what would be described as a pencil moustache, but was in effect as thin as a matchstick and appeared totally pointless.

He explained as carefully as he could that he considered Eimear Kavanagh to be suffering from Ulcerative Colitis, a form of inflammatory bowel disease. What was of particular interest was that the disorder is presumed to have a genetic component in that it tends to occur in families and identical twins. If one has it, the other usually does. Jenkins was unsure of the severity at that stage and treatment could be anti-inflammatory drugs or if need be the excision of the colon may be required.

Molly Brewster advised that Eimear had been moved from the assessment ward while she waited for a colonoscopy that would give more precise details of the severity.

That information was passed to Dr Bronagh O'Connell who a day later confirmed that the person she assumed to be Eilish had suffered a less severe form of the condition. Not a diagnosis she had missed during the post mortem, but one that bore no relevance to the woman's death by poisoning, and was not included in the highlighted areas..

27

Eoini Culligan, hundreds of miles away in County Wexford had no idea how by the end of the weekend he would have information to muddle the waters even more.

He had already established through contacts he had made by phone that the Kavanaghs left Tollsford in very much of a hurry back in 1990.

Eimear Kavanagh, the eldest of the Kavanagh twins had got herself pregnant and in no time her distraught, embarrassed, angry and volatile father had packed her off to a home for wayward girls. Out of sight and out of mind. Handed over to nuns to deal with in their own particularly insidious and disciplined way.

In no time Fergus Kavanagh had sold his interest in the printing business in Tollsford and with his wife and one daughter set off to Britain and a new life.

The people of Tollsford were shocked and dismayed at their reaction, but did not personally encounter problems for a few months. Then the first man was laid off. It happens. It was hard on Padraig Brennan to be shown the door, and his colleagues, friends and neighbours sympathised with him. Then young Siobhan in the office received her abrupt marching orders mid-afternoon one day, out of the blue. That was the thin end of the wedge.

Tollsford Printers had been housed in a large run-down country house in its own grounds, with stunning views across the open countryside. Very quickly Fergus Kavanagh's partner Georgie Doherty had found himself sidelined in a company increasingly devoid of work as staff were tumbled one by one onto the scrapheap. A new pricing policy made them uncompetitive, and in time the only work they did was done on the cheap solely for associate companies of this Michael Sheehan who had bought up Kavanagh's shares. Inside fifteen months there was no Tollsford Printers. Every one of the employees lost their jobs, and very soon many were having difficulty paying their mortgages and rent and the lives of so many small town folk had been turned inside out.

The house was still there having undergone a refit and inside two years it had been sold, with planning permission in place to develop the whole grounds.

That was why the name Kavanagh was like a red rag to a bull, when Eoini mentioned the name in the pub in Tollsford. The whole town had decided that Fergus Kavanagh had known all about Sheehan's intentions. Taken the money for his share of the business and ran before it became a huge property development.

That weekend, asking questions about the whereabouts of Eimear Kavanagh brought him into direct conflict with his mother's beliefs. Eoini knew she would pray the Rosary every day. Had created a nightly prayer routine and was most likely currently going through a fad about eating food she really didn't like as part of her commitment of faith.

She would be beside herself and do nothing but kneel for days had she known the questions he was asking about the nuns and their corrective establishment. It was not a subject the locals in Tollsford were willing to talk about openly, and when he established that whilst the big house remained, it was no longer any sort of asylum he moved on.

A couple of women in the town had in their teens become pen pals with Eilish after she left with her parents, and whilst that had gradually faded as such relationships do, they were able to help build up a little more of the story.

Before he made his way back to Dublin on the Sunday afternoon, Eoini took a drive out to the west of the town to where Tollsford Printers had once stood. In its place a magnificent house in cultivated grounds fronting a huge development.

He cheekily stopped at an elegant four bedroom house for sale. A glossy brochure in the estate agent's window told the whole development was highly regarded, and with a west aspect to many of the five bedroom properties, the stunning sunsets were to die for. This long established development offered so he was told, potential buyers luxurious living, with seclusion and security of paramount importance.

Monday morning before Rachel Pickard could attempt to establish whether Eoini was funding his enquiries himself, a request for her to phone him at home that evening told her she probably was on the right lines.

Eoini Culligan admitted to Rachel that evening, how he was working independently of the Garda. He lied when he said they had refused to co-operate, but had told him he could help if he wished, but in his own time.

They arranged for Rachel to send him 'expenses' to at least help with his petrol costs. When she asked for an invoice, he knew any chance of choosing a fancy name for his fledgling detective agency had just been blown away. It would have to be "Eoini Culligan PI" on an invoice he could create on his PC. Money Eoini had not expected, but he wished she would deliver personally.

Eoini went through everything he now knew about what had happened to the Kavanaghs from Tollsford. Rachel received more detail than was really necessary about the demise of Tollsford Printers, the loss of jobs the effect that had on a small community and the development of the huge estate.

'Trouble is da trail runs cold when Eilish went ter university…'

'You mean Eimear.'

'Naw missy. Eilish.'

'I think you're wrong Eoini.'

'Eimear was da one who got up de spoyt. Eilish moved with 'er auld pair and went ter university.'

'Whatever.'

'Dat's when the trail runs col' when she went ter university.'

'Do you know where?'

'Nottingham,' said Eoini. 'Two friends ov hers from dohs days were sort of pen pals, but when she went ter university she just never replied ter letters anymore.'

'Different world, Eoini. Not something you'd admit to as a lager swilling protesting student that you've got little pen pals back home.'

'Waaat nigh?'

'That's about it for now Eoini. I'll pass this onto my boss, and we'll see what he wants to do next.' She took a last swig of cool tea. 'That's a good job done Eoini.'

'An' when chucker we clap yer roun dees parts?'

'Need to get all this out of the way first,' she said. 'Better go. Give my boss a call.'

It had to be the first thing she said to Craig Darke next morning. Forget Tollsford Printers; forget Fergus Kavanagh, Georgie Doherty and Michael Sheehan. Sackings, redundancies and the destruction of people's lives were way down the list.

'Which one went to uni?' Darke looked at her. 'Which twin?'

'Eimear.'

'You sure?'

'Why?'

'Danny boy says it was Eilish.'

'They both been?'

'You tell me.'

'Brian!' he shouted out into the incident room. 'Which twin went to uni,' he held a hand up before Brian could say Eimear. 'Not what you think, not what we think we've established. Get someone onto it now.' He looked at Rachel. 'When?'

'Eighteen in ninety three,' she called down the room.

'D'we know where?'

'Nottingham.'

'Onto it now,' said Brian as he turned to look for Toni d'Andrea, and was gone.

'According to Eoini,' said Rachel as she moved to a chair to ease her back. 'Eimear got herself pregnant. Got sent to some nasty Catholic asylum place for naughty girls...'

'Be serious!'

'According to the locals, she went there. At the same time Fergus Kavanagh sold up, came over here and Eilish went to uni in Nottingham.' Craig Darke was on his feet, round his desk to a filing cabinet. He opened a drawer fingered his way back through folders and pulled one out.

'PM doesn't mention Eimear having had a child,' he said, looked at Rachel and sucked in loudly before he put the brown file back.

'Was that the service the nuns provided? Abortions?'

174

'Catholics?'

'Stupid me.'

'D'we need Eoini anymore?' Darke shrugged. 'I'll keep him dangling, just in case.'

An hour later Eoini Culligan was needed again. Craig Darke had everybody's attention. Had even called in one or two who were out making enquiries.

'I'll take this slowly, just so you all understand. According to a source in Ireland the elder of the two sisters Eimear Kavanagh got hers....' He stopped. 'Cut the cackle, I've not got this wrong, just listen up and take it in. The elder of the two sisters Eimear Kavanagh became pregnant back in Ireland. She was shifted off to some asylum outfit run by nuns to have the kid. From 1990 to 1993 Eimear Kavanagh was also at Robert Pattinson School. Clever trick if you can do it. In 1993 Eimear Kavanagh went to Nottingham University and has a First Class Honours in business management. Her father sold out his interest in the local printers, took a boat over here and finished up running TwinPrint. According to laughing boy painter Quinn his partner Eilish was murdered, a fact confirmed by her sister. In fact it was Eimear who told us who was dead. Quinn had to go along with it. In the County Hospital we have a woman we are told is Eimear with a scar on her torso that clashes with hospital records that show Eilish should have an appendectomy scar because she was treated there at one time. If the body in the morgue is indeed Eilish then according to the PM she has not had any children. I have asked our forensic pathologist if she could have had an abortion and she says no.'

Brian Daniels was scratching his head furiously. 'Who the soddin' hell is who?' he demanded and raised his hands. 'This could become more confusing than that muppet on the tele last night saying black holes are invisible, but we have proof they are there. For our purposes it is Eilish Kavanagh who is dead and Eimear Kavanagh is the nasty bitch running TwinPrint. Understood?'

'I'm not buying all this,' said Craig Darke and all eyes were on him. 'Are we seriously saying old man Kavanagh told his teenage daughter she'd got a new name? Her sister's name? No way.'

'We're talking about a nasty autocratic bully,' said Rachel firmly.

'And your point is?'

'We've seen dozens of cases of cruelty and child neglect and you wonder to yourself how parents get away with it. Why don't the kids rebel, why don't they tell someone? Then you meet the parents and you know why. They're shits of the first order.'

'Boss,' was Brian. 'Cases where the father rapes his daughters for years. It happens. It's probably happening now.'

'What's that to do with anything?'

'In those cases the kids are so terrified they don't tell anyone. Eilish Kavanagh is told her name's now Eimear. What's she going to do? Who does she complain to? She's living in bloody Lincoln then. What good would telling a teacher do? Can't nip round and cry to her auntie down the road. If she could, she'd get a bloody thrashing.'

'We're not talking rape here,' said Rachel firmly. 'As far as we know,' she added. 'We're talking a change of name. Someone like that tells me I'm called Rachel, that's who I am. He then tells me I'm Sharmishta Chakrabarti.' She stabbed her own chest. 'I'm bloody Sharmishtra, don't you worry about that!'

'He had to do it to both,' was Craig trying hard still to dismiss the idea.

'She gets put in a home, and Kavanagh tells the nuns she's Tallulah. She's bloody Tallulah! What's she going to do? Argue with the Mother Superior?' Rachel needed white chocolate, but had run out. This craving annoyed her. It was dark chocolate she loved.

'If I accept what you're saying, answer me this. Why?'

A lot of sighing, one or two gurns, a grimace, a shrug but no answer.

'Spoke to my doctor,' said Daniels. 'Popped in yesterday. Apparently there's a list of the patients for the day with appointment times on his computer. Start of shift he just does a quick check, has a look at any he knows have a history. So he's briefed before they walk in.'

'She turns up, says she's got guts ache. He has a chat, pulls her up on the screen, has a quick check and prints off a prescription.'

'He's none the wiser.'

'Probably asks how her sister is.'

'More than bloody likely.'

Rachel Pickard was supposed to be taking things easy, but now it seemed that she could only deal with Eoini at home in the evenings and weekends. She reminded him to invoice her for services rendered and then set him another task.

She and Craig were agreed, she would establish beyond all reasonable doubt exactly who it was who fell pregnant. Establish with her two old school chums who it was they were writing to in Lincoln before she went off to university. Attempt to establish how long it might be that Eimear had to spend with the nuns.

Eoini Culligan took a 'sickie' but it was doubtful if anybody noticed, and was back in Tollsford before dawn. He met up with Niamh at the baker's shop where she worked three days a week. She confirmed and so did Caitlin when he caught up with her later, that their friend was indeed Eilish Kavanagh, and it was Eilish they wrote to in Lincoln and then at Nottingham. It was from there letters were returned as "Not Known at this Address," weeks later.

From there he tried the best he could for most of the day, but people wouldn't talk about 'The House' as they called it. The evil place the nuns had run set back off Slaney Road had been closed for a decade or more. One person reckoned young girls stayed there as long as their parents decreed. Some apparently just until the birth was over and the baby had been farmed off out somewhere, anywhere. He was told they could be there working in the laundry for upwards of five years as punishment for the dreadful deed. One woman reckoned it was a seven day a week hard labour the girls had to endure. Nobody had a clue how long Eimear Kavanagh had spent at the house.

He was back too late that evening to phone his friend Rachel, but on the Wednesday he did.

'Tis certain it was Eimear Kavanagh who got up der spoyt,' Eoini told her. 'Tis also certain it was Eilish who went ter live in Lincoln an' went off ter Nottingham University when de letters ran dry.'

177

'I'll tell you something now Eoini, strictly between you and me. Eilish Kavanagh has been murdered.' She thought she heard her ex-Garda man gasp. 'The body in the mortuary has never been pregnant and never given birth. So it has to be Eimear you say was up the duff all those years ago and brought shame on the family. But. And Eoini this is the big but, it was also Eimear who went to Nottingham University and got a degree.' Rachel waited for a reaction that never came. 'I'll leave it with you. You get any bright ideas, you know where I am.'

'Be Jeezus, this is…'

'I know.'

'Did is not idle blather.' said Eoini firmly. 'When I first went in I mentioned Fergus Kavanagh. Dat wus the key. Luck av de Oirish finding their weak point. Years av training mind, years av training.' Rachel had to be careful he didn't go off on one as he sometimes did. She was paying for the call. 'Suggested yisser Peelers were after 'imself. Didn't say it wus fraud, but gave dat impression. They 'ate 'imself with a vengeance. They believe yer man knew what sort of crook Sheehan was. Yer paddy who almost single handedly destroyed dat community. And,' he said quickly to assure her there was more to come. 'They weemen new who their mucker was. They know who got up der spoyt, an' if you want probably know who was responsible.' Rachel waited.

'Was that a question Eoini?'

'Do yu need ter know who the lad was?'

'Right now, no. What I need from you now Eoini, is what sort of education would a girl like Eimear get in this home for pregnant girls. If she was fourteen when she got pregnant, chances are she was fifteen by the time she had the baby. Was she studying?'

'It was a laundry,' he said quickly. 'Seven day a week been towl.'

'And still had time to study well enough to qualify for university in Nottingham. How did she do that Eoini if she was in Ireland?' Rachel waited for a comment. 'If you come across a name for the father, make a note of it, but for now it's irrelevant.'

'Gaff is a different matter. Sum admit ter it, probably knew all about it at the time. Others don't admit ter it, never can.'

178

28

The text Jake Goodwin received half way through the morning turned his plans for the evening on their head.

<Mums sprained her ankle. Not 2 bad. Meet her place>

Jake had never been with Tess Conway when she was unwell and he was gearing himself up for a sob story, not really thinking of anything in particular when he pulled of the main Lincoln road, took a left and left again when he saw it. Thought he saw it was more accurate.

Sebastian Quinn's car. There in the drive of a large white bungalow as he drove past. How many powder pink and sky blue Smart Cars are there in Lincoln? What was it Toni d'Andrea called it? Jake continued on, and was pleased when he found his way back to where he had spotted the small vehicle. Made a note of the number in his mind and drove on to Tess's place. He phoned before he went in and young Natalie promised to check it out on the national computer and call him back.

Tess Conway had indeed sprained her ankle. It was strapped, and she was laid back on the sofa with her bad leg on a pouffe. As Sally's mother went through the graphic details his phone rang. He got up, left the room and took the call.

He was right. Sebastian Quinn's car. What was he doing in Washingborough?

With Tess's annoyance self evident, Jake briefed the two women on his reason for making a call. She appeared satisfied with his explanation and he expected that to be the end of the matter.

'Good morning Jake,' in his ear next day had him ready himself for Tess Conway's needs. *Could you pop a bit of shopping in if you're passing? Could do with a paper, there's a pet...* was the sort of thing he was prepared for. Instead: 'That's Ruth Rushton's fancy man's car.'

'What is?' he queried without thinking.

'Pink and blue you said, on the corner near the Monkey Puzzle tree.'

179

'Yes.'

'Ruth Rushton's fancy man.'

'And who might Ruth Rushton be?' Jake asked as he wrote down the name.

'After his money if I know her. Husband has that big farm out towards Heighington. He had an affair with this slip of a girl. Ruth received massive maintenance and a lump sum. Bought the bungalow about four years ago.'

'Now she's hooked up with Sebastian Quinn?'

'If that's his name.'

'May I ask how you know all this?'

'Marie Slater lives next door but one,' he was told. 'Old friend. Known her years.'

'And he's a regular.'

'To be fair,' said Tess in the form of a rebuke. 'It is only one at a time.' She hesitated. 'Need to know more?'

'Can we just cool it for now?' Jake didn't want this Ruth Rushton getting wind of anybody asking questions. 'If I need to know any more I'll come back to you.'

'Thought you'd like to know.'

'Yes. That's very useful. How are you today?'

To be fair to Tess, she wasn't a moaning Minnie woman. 'Be up and about before long. Can't be doing with crosswords and daytime television.' Jake said he'd see her with Sally for their evening meal.

'Boss,' he said as he entered Craig Darke's office the moment Brian Daniels and Raza walked out. 'How about if our Sebastian Quinn only went to Bassingham to take the photos? Didn't actually do any painting. What if he doesn't do any painting out in the woods? What if he does his painting indoors, in his ladyfriend's bungalow?'

'Ladyfriend?' he said as if it was an odd description. 'What's given you that idea?' Darke chuckled out.

'Seeing his Brabus tailor-made Smart Car outside the bungalow of the ex-wife of a rich farmer in Washingborough.'

'Technically, could be he's telling the truth,' said Darke as he rested his chin on clenched fists. 'Always possible he did go to Bassingham that morning. Took the photos. Raza took photos of the place and the painting. What he didn't say was, he was only there five minutes and then buggered off round to...'

'Ruth Rushton.'

'And if this Ruth Rushton testifies he was with her, we're probably going to find it difficult to place him at the house at eight o'clock or thereabouts. He wanted the early morning mist and if he put his foot down he could've be eating cornflakes with his piece of stuff when we think Eilish died.' His eyes were fixed on Jake. 'Both he and our Eimear just might be innocent. In which case that means were looking for a third party.'

'And we have no suspects.'

'Except all the people Eilish upset over the years. And take it from me, if those two women are both parts of the same egg. From what I've seen of Eimear, that Eilish could upset anybody without even trying.'

'Former employee?'

'And where do we start? With the old boy whose wife just died of cancer? You fancy dragging him in to answer questions?' Jake grimaced.

Craig Darke drove and explained his sudden decision to Jake Goodwin on the way.

'Carry on as we are, we'll just be going round in circles. We've pretty much confirmed that Eilish came over here with her father and for some reason he changed her name to Eimear. In the meantime Eimear got herself in the family way, finished up with the nuns, then came here as Eilish. Together they work for their father. He then retires back to Ireland and leaves them to it.'

'And you think Quinn will fill in the missing bits?'

'Who else is there? Fergus Kavanagh didn't go back to Wexford, because he couldn't. They'd have strung him from the lamppost. The only people we have left are Eimear who used to be Eilish in Hospital and Quinn.'

When they reached Saxilby, the gates were closed, both houses were locked up. Nobody in sight.

'You know where in Washingborough?' Darke checked as he spun the car round.

'Yes,' said Jake at the very moment his phone rumbled in his pocket. 'Hi' he said into it.

'Discharge are sending Eimear home.'

'D'we know when?' Jake asked Sally.

'This afternoon.'

'Thanks. Talk to you later,' he said into his phone and then closed it. 'Hospital are releasing Eimear this afternoon.'

'Bugger!'

'Problem?'

'Quinn will probably be running round after her. We just might be chasing rainbows.'

The Smart Car in the drive was not quite all the colours of the spectrum, but pink and blue was a start. The sky that day was a blue wash Quinn would have been proud of, with not enough breeze to even lift a limp flag.

'Mrs Rushton?' Jake asked at the door when it was opened and held up his warrant card. 'Detective Chief Inspector Craig Darke, Police Major Incident Team.' She confirmed who she was, he introduced DS Jacques Goodwin and without hesitation she allowed them in. There was an uneasy silence with unspoken messages and glances between the couple for a few moments when Sebastian Quinn realised who had walked into the conservatory.

It was ghastly. Craig Darke could not stand conservatories at the best of times. Like a garish whitewashed carbuncle stuck on the back of a house, he regarded them as cheap tat.

'Thought we'd have a chat Mr Quinn. Off the record, so to speak,' said Darke, once he had sat down.

'Can I perhaps get you gentlemen a tea?' Ruth Rushton in her pink framed glasses asked at the door. Elegant woman, wearing what was obviously a very expensive jogging suit in cream and lilac that was never likely to encounter sweat. Her red manicured nails and lipstick matched.

'That would be very kind,' said Darke. 'No sugars, all round,' he added. The cane furniture had hideous white foam filled seats and cushions with large black flowers.

182

'Tell me about the Kavanaghs,' he directed at Quinn, who peered up at Ruth Rushton, and she nodded. He avoided the question.

He rambled on about TwinPrint and how successful they were, how hard they worked. How it had been built up from nothing. Darke let him waffle on and waited for a break.

'How about what we don't know Mr Quinn?'

Elegant Ruth Rushton walked into the room with a tray, four cups and saucers, and plate with biscuits. She placed it on a square glass topped coffee table.

'How would I know what you do not know,' he waffled again, as Ruth Rushton handed round the drinks.

'What about their life back in Ireland? What do you know about that? About why they just upped sticks and came over. Why here?'

'Advertisement in the trade press and a business opportunity is my understanding,' said Quinn. 'Kavanagh was looking to invest; he had been involved in printing all his life apparently.'

'But when they came over, there were only three.' Quinn and Rushton exchanged looks without trying to hide the fact.

'Out with it,' said Rushton suddenly and then sipped her tea.

'Well....'

'Tell them man,' was direct, and Quinn looked very sheepish.

'Eilish was pregnant,' he blurted as if the subject was taboo.

'And?' Darke asked when Quinn didn't go on.

'Had to stay behind with relatives. Came across later.'

'Three years later,' Jake added. Quinn frowned and looked at Rushton.

'That can't be right,' she said. 'She told you she followed on after. Had the child adopted.'

'What school did she go to over here?' Darke asked quickly as he digested the fact that Quinn may not know about the nun's asylum.

'School?' Quinn repeated. 'Robert Pattinson probably or NK.'

'No,' said Darke with a shake of his head. 'Eimear went to Robert Patt, and then Nottingham University. Eilish never went to school over here. By the time she arrived over here she was too old.'

'She worked for TwinPrint,' Quinn offered as an alternative.

'We know that,' Jake Goodwin told him, as Darke picked up his cup and saucer, sat back and began on his weak tea. 'Learnt printing from the bottom up.' They both saw a slight nod of the head from Rushton, and Quinn frowned.

'Either you tell them or I will,' said Rushton firmly.

'I got the cyanide for Eilish,' was rushed.

'Did you know what for?'

'Said she needed it for a new revolutionary experimental process, but didn't want it to go through the firm.'

'What was it for, do we know?' Rushton asked Darke quite quietly.

'The cyanide?' Rushton nodded. 'Printing apparently. Not at all sure in what context.' He turned to Quinn. 'Why did you involve your sister?'

'She uses it.'

'Cyanide?'

A self satisfied look on his face came first. 'My sister is a metallurgist. She creates jewellery from scrap metal that she sells in the gallery. There is a blacksmith shares the workshop next door. She uses cyanide for gilding and buffing. Has done for years.'

'Did she not query why you wanted some?' Why the hell hadn't the clown said all this before?

He shrugged slightly. 'Said it was for a new process.' Quinn hesitated and took in a breath. 'I did not,' said Quinn suddenly, hands gripped tightly together knuckles white.

'You did not what Mr Quinn?' Darke asked slowly.

'Go to Bassingham.'

'Tell them!' Ruth Rushton almost shouted. 'Can't you see where this is going, you stupid man?' Quinn looked bemused. 'With all due respect,' she said. 'These men will pin this on you if you're not careful,' she told Quinn and turned her head to look at Craig Darke. 'Sebastian had nothing to do with killing that dreadful woman. If you must know, he came here to be intimate with me,' she said quite casually, but Quinn looked horrified that such a thing should be revealed. Spoken of in polite company. 'Well, didn't you?' she asked him.

'Yes,' was almost a whisper, as he coloured up.

'Look Inspector,' she said as she slid her cup and saucer onto the small coffee table. 'We were planning for Sebastian to leave her and move in here. It was just a matter of choosing the right moment. Then all this happened.'

'Why the hell didn't you say?' Darke demanded. 'We've spent a great deal of time and effort trying to confirm you were where you said you were.'

'What's the problem?' she posed.

Quinn looked up, then sheepishly at Ruth Rushton. 'Protecting you,' he muttered.

'You never said,' was an annoyed Ruth. 'You silly man,' she said and looked at Craig Darke. 'He didn't tell me what he'd told you or he'd have been back pretty sharpish, I can tell you.'

Jake asked, 'Can you tell us what was wrong with life with Eilish?'

Quinn's spokeswoman was in before him again. 'The twin business. I'm sorry but nobody can live like that. Mothers dressing little twin girls the same, I can understand to a certain extent. But grown women? I'm sorry it's not an acceptable way to behave. Have you been inside their houses?' Darke nodded and grinned. 'That really is beyond belief. They go to extraordinary lengths to ensure everything is identical. It's unnatural.' She looked at Quinn. 'Tell them what you think.' When Quinn just looked embarrassed and failed to respond she went on. 'Seb thinks that on more than one occasion he was conned into having sex with the wrong sister.'

A blushing and obviously embarrassed Quinn sat forward, rested his arms on his knees and looked down at his feet.

'I have known Eilish about four years, and we have been together getting on for three. Started going wrong,' he stopped to clear his throat. 'Whereas before she would never socialise, Eilish had been going out more and more. Said it was work of course. Meetings to attend, people to meet. Breakfast meetings,' he chortled. 'Do you not think that sort of nonsense is seriously sad?' Darke agreed with him. Sort of thing some twerps like to brag about.

'Anything else in your life seem strange?' Goodwin asked while Darke wondered why none of this had been revealed before.

'How can it not be strange?' Rushton suggested. 'Living with a woman and a mirror image. Identical clothes, identical homes, cars, offices.'

185

'Do you know where the parents live now?' Goodwin asked in hope.

'No idea,' came back Quinn quickly. 'Like they are taboo.'

Darke had decided not to broach the subject of the hideous home for fallen women that had housed Eilish at one time. It was likely that the girls wanted nothing to do with their father for treating her in that way. It was also very likely they had discovered why he had swapped their names over. Knew what scam he was involved in. What fraud that maybe had initially brought him into contact with the swindling Michael Sheehan.

'Does Eilish have an appendix scar?' Goodwin threw in a Darke-like gesture. Quinn just looked at him.

'Yes,' he replied in a way that suggested he was strangely embarrassed at having to admit he had seen it.

'Medication. Was she on any medication?'

'Stomach ache. She got pills from the doctor.'

'She did?' Quinn's head went back on his neck.

'Yes,' was accompanied by a slight nod.

'Eilish went to the doctor and she got the pills.'

'Yes, well I think she did,' was tentative as if he was saying the wrong thing. 'Eimear might have picked them up. Or one of the drivers.'

'On the day Eilish was murdered. When Eimear phoned you...I was going to say out at Bassingham. When Eimear phoned you. Here I assume?' Rushton nodded. 'What did she say?'

Quinn looked at Darke out of the top of his eyes.

'Said something like Eimear here. I am afraid there has been an accident. I understand Eilish has died.'

'And?'

Quinn shrugged. 'Said I had better get over there.'

'That it?'

'Think so,' he looked at Rushton and she nodded her response.

'Can I ask you this?' said Darke. 'When she phoned, how did you know it was her?'

'Said who she was.'

'And if she hadn't said who she was, who would you think it was?'

'Eimear.'

'How?'

'Because it was…'

'It was either her or Eilish and she told you Eilish was dead.'

'Pretty much.'

Craig Darke put his cup and saucer down and was on his feet, as part of another one of his interview techniques. End it suddenly. Leave them guessing. 'Thank you Mrs Rushton, thanks for the tea,' he was almost at the door before Jake was off his seat. 'We'll see ourselves out.' Then he turned back to them. 'Want to show me where you paint when you're here?'

'What about the funeral?' Quinn asked.

Darke looked down. 'Be a while yet I'm afraid. Won't Eimear organise that?' Quinn looked at Ruth Rushton.

'She will,' he was told. 'You know she will. You know what she's like' Quinn got to his feet very slowly.

'Where is it you paint?' Darke asked.

Sebastian Quinn looked down at Ruth Rushton as if he was in need of her permission and took Darke into the bungalow, out through the kitchen and round the garden to a large six sided pine summer house set amongst trees at the back. Quinn opened the door with the key already in the lock, but Darke moved him down the side of the summer house to the back and out of sight. Darke slammed him up against the wall.

'Austin Myers,' said Darke inches from his face. 'Tell me about Austin Myers and why you gave us a false address.' Quinn spluttered so much, Darke had to wipe spittle from his face with the back of his hand.

'I…I…panicked.'

'Why did you panic?'

'Thought I was in trouble.'

This was a weak little man, not the one who had been in control and chosen his words carefully.

'What had you done?'

'Nothing. Just worried.'

'About what?'

'Ruth.' Darke just looked at him. 'What she would say, what she would do.'

'Such as?'

'Be all over. Then what would I do?' Darke released his hold and stepped back a pace. 'I would be homeless and on my own. That is why I could not admit where I was the morning Eilish died.' he said looking down. 'Thought if Eimear found out...'

'She's still kicked you out.'

'Never a proper relationship, you know. There was always three, never just the two of us. Not sure Eilish and I ever had any secrets from Eimear.'

'Talking of relationships. Has Eimear got a chip on her shoulder? What's her problem?'

'Dominated their relationship.'

'And Eilish. What was she like?'

'Like chalk and cheese. Delightful woman. Amazing really, so much alike, so much effort to be the same, yet in private they were so different. Loud, domineering on the one hand and calm, almost serene Eilish.' Quinn put his hand up. 'Don't think the real Eilish ever came across at work. Think they both felt they had to be nasty. Their way of coping, because they felt people would never take them seriously otherwise. But I never saw that with Eilish.' Darke could see talking about her had an effect on Quinn.

'Listen fella,' said Darke gently. 'Don't piss us about anymore. If you do, I'll have you for wasting Police time. Then you might well be in the shit with her indoors. How would she explain that at the local Ladies Circle?' He pushed Quinn back towards the front of the building. 'Right. Show me where you paint.'

After a mile Craig Darke stopped the car.

'That worked,' he said. 'Thought if I saw him in his own environment we might get more out of him.'

'And her.'

'He doesn't know does he? He really thinks Eilish is dead.'

'All he has to go on is what the voice on the phone told him.'

'And that means unless I'm completely up a gum tree, our Quinn is not involved. Acted a bit stupid, told a few porkies, but he never topped his woman. Or rather his partner's sister. And we can't put him right.'

'How many does that leave us with?' Jake asked.

'Just Eimear or Eilish or whoever she is.' Craig turned to look at Jake. 'Quinn goes off for an early morning shag out here. Eilish has to be still alive. Then Eimear goes to work. In between or after that somebody does for her.'

'It's not as if one sister is bigger than the other. One overpowers the other. Not a catchweight contest'

'Nor Quinn, come to that. He's not much bigger.'

'If she did it. How did she get that cyanide down her throat?' Craig looked out of the windscreen.

'Or somebody else was involved.' Darke forced out his breath. 'Here's something else to throw in the stewpot. Eilish who is now Eimear, according to Quinn back there, was a very calm serene woman.' He sucked in loudly. 'Is this even more complicated? Have they always given false names? Did Eimear go into Hospital for her appendix as Eilish? If so, like changing names when they came over here. Why? We're missing a bloody trick here somewhere!'

'We know it was Eilish who had the operation. Quinn confirmed she had a scar, and the one in Hospital was checked for a scar. The cadaver doesn't have a scar.'

'You explain then, how the nasty bitch at TwinPrint is described by Quinn as a lovely lady.' He turned the key. 'I rest my case. It's like blackjack. Twist, twist, twist. Somewhere somebody has to shout stick.'

189

29

'What on earth do you think you are doing?' Eimear Kavanagh demanded of Craig Darke when he walked into her big office. He didn't respond immediately, just strode across to the window that overlooked the factory floor.

'Good to see you up and about,' he said with his back to her.

'I asked you a question Darke.'

'Just having a look round,' he said as he watched a team of fifteen at work below. 'What would you use cyanide for?'

She blew a breath out noisily through her nose. 'I have no idea,' Eimear told him from her chair.

'So why order it? Why order it on the sly?'

'I have no idea what you are talking about.'

'But you do,' said Darke as he turned to look at her. According to Quinn, Eilish had asked him to get cyanide and he had got it from his sister. Problem now was that the Eilish he had given it to was now Eimear. Technically he had no evidence that *Eimear* was involved, and *Eilish* was in the mortuary. How would he prove she killed her sister? 'Did you really think we would be less than vigorous in our investigations?'

'Be what you like, it's of no concern of mine. And for your information potassium cyanide is used in silver plating and in analytical chemistry.'

'And what were you going to do with it?' Darke didn't know that, and wondered if that was general knowledge. If you stopped a hundred people in the street and asked them what cyanide was for, would they know? He guessed analytical chemistry was a pointless answer.

'I,' she allowed to hang in the air, 'was not planning to do anything with it.'

'New printing process we've been told.'

Kavanagh chuckled. Was that the first time he had seen anything resembling a smile cross her face.

'And if cyanide had been next on your priority listing you're so keen on, what's the system then?' Darke waited just a second. 'Would you have to admit you didn't have a clue? That what happens when you get the task you know nothing about in this wonderful management style of yours?

'We have a very tight schedule Mr Darke,' she said without as much as a glance. 'Play your silly games if you must, but please do not disturb our production.' She really was a cool one. Cold as ice and nasty with it. So how come Quinn described her as a lovely serene woman? 'Close the door on your way out,' and she continued to flick through paperwork on her desk in a way that illustrated that she wasn't actually doing anything.

She hadn't asked him if he had a warrant. Did that tell him she had expected him to call? Darke guessed what that did tell him was, if cyanide had ever been in TwinPrint it was long gone. Surely this crafty bitch would never leave something like that lying about. He decided to annoy her. Leave his team searching for a while. Knew, somehow their presence there would have an effect on production systems.

He left the office without another word, went back downstairs and chatted to a few of the lads. Told them not to be in too much of a hurry, noticed Eimear watching him from her office and headed for the canteen with three of his men.

They paid for and casually drank coffee, nibbled and dunked biscuits. Those who returned to their search which by now was not a lot more than going through the motions were replaced by three others. This Darke repeated until he had wasted an hour, all were refreshed and then as suddenly as they had arrived they left, except him and Raza.

Craig Darke didn't stand on ceremony when he just barged into Eimear Kavanagh's office upstairs, to find it empty.

'I told you,' said tall Maureen the women's secretary come goffer. 'Now if you'd wait outside,' she said and gestured back the way they had come. 'I'll see if Miss Kavanagh is available.'

'It's not if, dear,' said Darke as they walked slowly back to a small area at the top of the stairs outside Maureen's office. He then went on through the door he knew must have been Eilish's office, with this soppy Maureen woman trotting along behind him. Identical. He just wandered around and left again and waited at the top of the stairs. Creepy again. Creepy enough to bring on a shiver. The office was an absolute mirror image of Eimear's. All this identical business was not easy to take. When he'd waited ten minutes Craig Darke knew the bitch was playing silly buggers.

'Now then Mr Darke what can I do for you?' said Kavanagh as she reached the top of the stairs. 'Find what you were looking for?'

'You can provide me with certain documents or I can get a warrant and be back later with a team to turn this place inside out again.' He hesitated. 'No, Miss Kavanagh. I'll tell you what I'll do. Next time I'll shut you down for a couple of days.'

'You wouldn't dare!'

'Try me.'

She blew out her anger with her breath; spun right and walked quickly back into her office. At her desk she spun back to look at him.

'Let this be a warning. My lawyer has a team of PI's who've all been in the Met, all served at a rank you can only dream of. If you don't get your disclosure absolutely spot on, woe betide you.'

'Driving Licence, Certificate of Insurance and Passport,' Darke said as calmly as he could manage. Then added. 'For you and for your sister.'

'I don't have my sister's, you'll have to…' She stopped. Stood hands flat on her desk and waited a moment. Emotion. A very rare commodity for this woman. When she stood up, she was back in control. 'We've been over this before Mr Darke. I was not her keeper. She was covered by the company's insurance to drive our cars, and I'll get Maureen to look that out.' She bent down and lifted a black handbag onto her desk, and produced her driving licence. Clean British driving licence, no penalty points.'

'Passport?'

She produced that from a drawer in her desk. Darke spun through the pages, stopping, checking then on he flicked.

'Satisfied?'

'I will be when I see your sister's.' Eimear just shrugged. 'When you look for that, perhaps we could have her credit cards, cheque book and anything else you think might be appropriate. Like her will.'

'Will?'

'Your sister's will,' said Darke.

'You'll need to see our solicitor. But I can tell you what it says,' she said. 'It is very simple. I leave my whole estate to her; she leaves her whole estate to me.'

'And now?'

'Now?'

'You get run over by a bus. Who gets it all now?'

'That Mr Darke is none of your business.'

'It's a murder enquiry. Everything is my business.' He held his hand up and pointed to fingers in turn. 'Will, passport, driving licence, credit cards, cheque book. They'll do for starters.' He turned, took three steps and then looked back. 'We'll be back for them and we'll see ourselves out.'

'What about the victim?'

Darke spun round to look at her.

'Your sister?'

'No you fool. Me.'

'How did you become the victim?'

'Because I'm the person who has suffered a loss. It's my sister who some bastard killed.'

'The sister you couldn't be bothered to check up on? The sister who was lying dead on her kitchen floor while you fiddled about with paperwork.'

'How dare you!'

'I deal in facts Miss Kavanagh.'

'Not got your dog today I see?' she threw at him. 'That puppy dog who normally trails after you.'

Darke treated her remark with the contempt it deserved, but wanted to laugh all the same. He'd not tell Brian what she's said.

On his way out he stopped at Maureen Pearce's office, and after checking with her boss she allowed Darke sight of the company's insurance policy that covered all vehicles, including the two red Lexus. Both of which he noticed were side by side in the car park.

Craig hadn't realized it, but he had very quickly returned to working morning, noon and night. Back to having absolutely nothing else in his life. Gone were the phone chats, the texts, the drinks in quiet country pubs and the meals out. What he did know however was that this was day twenty three of his thirty one before he got Jillie's decision. He also knew that was only as guide. He doubted whether 'a month' would mean precisely that, thirty one days. It could be quicker than that if she'd received a fabulous offer from a bunch of Germans, or had fallen head over heels in love with some smarmy pretentious git from Barclays. Might even be six weeks. There again he might never hear from her again.

30

Eimear Kavanagh left work early and followed her favoured route. Travel from the complex off Doddington Road to any of the city's large supermarket by the back roads. Park up and wait. That day it was the turn of Waitrose to the north of the city. No vehicles followed her in, and from where she parked she could spy on any arriving.

After ten minutes she ventured into the shop. First into the toilets to change her clothes. Off came her business suit, blouse and heels and quickly she was dressed in her walking gear complete with Green Bay Packers baseball cap pulled down. From there she purchased wraps, bottles of water and fresh fruit. Paid cash to hide her identity, and soon she was out and back en route for her destination. This time heading east on the Skegness road and then cross country in order to keep sight of any vehicles following her.

Eventually she was able to park up near the church at Temple Bruer and wait.

When he arrived, neither of them acknowledged the other until they were away from the road. Eimear with her new backpack strode out in front. Initially their planned route took them along a farm track that in time brought them to Brauncewell, then to Ermine Street part of the Viking Way. They were able to relax, embrace and sit down for a quiet snack.

They shared their experiences since their last meeting, and made plans for their future.

This was a whole world away from life with TwinPrint and in particular how life had been for years with her sister. The treadmill of further development of long meetings discussing strategy as part of a never ending need to succeed. Creating new open channels with partners.

Sitting together on a grassy bank with the new man in her life, just enjoying her hoisin duck wrap and his company. Listening to him talk about his past, his upbringing and his plans for their future together.

This was so far removed from the trivia of management speak that Eilish had taken to her heart. There were no longer best-in-class operations or standardised agile services to get her head round. No integrated in every meeting, no leverage.

Just sit and chat like normal educated human beings.

It had not been a particularly good day and the high temperatures and sunshine of the recent past had gone into hiding, but Eimear didn't seem to notice or care.

She spoke at length about the police, about their tactics being so obvious. She chuckled at the naïve way they hoped to upset her, when the opposite was true. That Darke seemed like a nice bloke.

'Asked him where his puppy dog was,' she said. 'Should have seen the look on his face,' she smiled at her man. 'Spoke volumes. I could see he wanted to agree with me but had to toe the party line.'

'No woman.'

'Really? How d'you know that?'

'Looked him up on the net. Had a number of commendations.'

'He gay d'you think?'

'Shouldn't think so. His wife died.'

'Really.'

'Car accident.'

'Recent?'

He shrugged his reponse. 'He a waste of space too?'

'No, far from it,' Eimear told him. 'Probably the best they've got though.' She stopped talking to savour her second wrap. 'If I was his big fat controller or whoever bosses him I'd tell him he uses his switching tactic too often.' She ate more of her wrap. 'And if I was his boss I watch out for him pinching my job.'

'How do you mean switching tactics?'

'He suddenly changes subject. Can be quite off putting at first and I can understand how numbskulls get taken in. Hardest thing was pretending to be Eilish. Remembering to be this belligerent somewhat offensive woman.

'Has she always been like that?'

'Developed over the years. Father drilled it into us in the early days. Regard everybody as no more important than yourself. To some extent he was right. So many people regard their view of social

196

status as being all important, when in truth the majority don't give a toss. But on the other hand my mother prays day and night to somebody who doesn't exist. Strange isn't it? Eilish quite rightly derided self-importance including of course people like kings, queens and bishops and all their bowing and scraping nonsense. On the other hand we had mother treating them like...I don't know what. Being in awe. Getting down on her knees to them if the truth be known.' She chuckled.

As Eimear sat there with a slight breeze in her face she couldn't help but think about how her life used to be. How this simple act was a million miles away from how her life was until very recently. How Eilish insisted on the stereotypical lifestyle that so many pseudo successful people are for some reason desperate for. The planes and trains the sheep have to jump on and off when a phone call would suffice, and the technology that goes with it. No sit back and enjoy the ride. No coffee from the trolley dolly. Top of the range laptops out, the best and latest smart phones to fiddle with. Work, work and more work. The stares, the remarks in the Quiet Coach she had to ignore, even though she agreed with them wholeheartedly. Those suits Eilish insisted upon, the bags they always had to lug about and those boring seminars.

'Do you think they checked up on me?'

Eimear came back down to earth. 'One of them phoned me, asked when you were due back. Told him they had transport problems and you were helping out for a while.' She looked at him. 'Then it was as if you were off their radar. Didn't mention you again to me, and human resources say they've been asked but nothing lately about anybody.'

'Any news on Sebastian?'

'Not a word. Suppose he's shacked up with one of his old buddies. Could have gone back home to that dreadful sister of his. God knows.'

'She really as bad as you paint her?' she was asked.

'It's all long diaphanous skirts you could shoot peas through, scraggy long hair, flip flops and an arm full of bangles. Two hearts tattooed in her cleavage. Pink scrubbed chubby cheeks and no make-up. Thick washer woman's nails.' Eimear sat there picturing Melanie in her mind.

'He religious at all?'

'Not particularly. Seen the light like most people.' She played with a leaf in her fingers. 'Don't understand how people get taken in by it. We all know about the big bang and yet so called educated people still talk about heaven and earth being created in a few days and pray to what? In effect nothing. As if the bible's events really happened.' She looked skywards. 'Billions of years. Six billion not six days and nothing to do with a man with a beard.' She chuckled. 'Wonder why they get taken in? These religious freaks are all as daft as a brush, with centuries of in fighting and bigotry. Being a priest has to be a cop out, what sort of a job is that? Vatican is as bad if not worse than any corrupt nation or major company. Power mad insanely jealous religious bigots full of half baked centuries old ideas. But then all these churches have all got more money than they know what to do with,so I guess that's a clue to what it's all about. Could be it's like chocolate, smoking or cocaine, once hooked...' She shrugged, chuckled and looked at the leaf laid out on her hand. 'Think we'd better be on our way before it gets dark.'

He grabbed her backpack. 'I'll take this.' Eimear didn't argue as she scrambled to her feet, brushed down her jeans and they set off eating apples to complete the walk.

31

Knocking on the door of Ruth Rushton's bungalow for Jake Goodwin had an element of déjà vu about it. The same elegant well groomed woman went through an identical procedure of showing him through to the conservatory and offering a cup of tea, just as she had done when the boss was with him. Teas without sugar and biscuits on a tray. Except for one thing. No Sebastian Quinn. Jake wondered what it was his boss didn't like about conservatories. The black and white furnishings were a bit garish, but apart from that.

'Delivering a painting,' she said and sipped her tea, when he asked his whereabouts.

'Pity that,' said Goodwin. 'Wanted a bit of background on life with the Kavanaghs.'

'Try me, sergeant.' She balanced cup and saucer in the palm of her well manicured hand. She stirred slowly with a silver spoon for no reason.

'It's the domestic arrangements really. We understand staff at TwinPrint do their supermarket shopping. We're told one of their drivers fills their cars with petrol. Wondered about things like gardening, cleaning.'

'There's a gardener and a cleaner.'

No jogging suit this time. Not that she had probably ever jogged anywhere. This time a beautifully patterned fawn, purple and cerise jumper, fawn tailored trousers and a swish of a cream scarf in her neck. Hair looked as though Vidal Sasoon had been there moments earlier.

'Don't suppose you know what the cleaner actually does. Bit of hovering, dusting here and there and...?'

Ruth Rushton's shaking head stopped him.

'Everything,' said the woman before she put down her cup and saucer and allowed himself to fall back into those dreadful black and white cushions. 'She makes the beds, does the hoovering, washing up, and does their washing, ironing, cleaning, and dusting. Puts out

199

the rubbish, puts the bins out once a week probably.' She picked up her cup and saucer again. 'Lazy doesn't come into it.'

'Dusting and cleaning,' said Goodwin. 'How often are we talking about?' He had to wait for Ruth to stop sipping the weak tea.

'Monday to Friday. Every day. Seb says the place is like a new pin all the time.'

'Have you ever been there?' Goodwin threw in. Ruth made a face. Craig Darke could do it so well. Throw in a question to put people off guard.

'Yes.'

'And?'

'One time earlier this year they were off in Birmingham for a conference. Seb suggested I poke my nose in. He'd told me all about it, said I should see it for myself.' she shook her head, sipped tea and just looked at Jake. 'I was staggered. One is fine. A bit old fashioned and tired. Quality stuff mind. When you go next door, dear me. That is quite unacceptable.'

'I know.'

'Nothing out of place. Not a magazine lying around. Not an empty cup and saucer in the kitchen. I swear to God the toilet rolls in both bathrooms were brand new. Folded like you get in some boutique hotels. All prim and silly.'

How wrong can you be? Jake if asked would have plumped for Ruth Rushton appreciating pointless little touches like that. Taking time to fold pink paper some hairy arsed smelly bloke will wipe his arse with.

'That'll be the cleaner.' Goodwin decided to drink half the tea, and then leave it to go cold. It was so weak and milky and hot milk was something he really didn't like.

'Guess so,' she laughed amusedly. 'Can't see Seb doing that!'

Jake Goodwin would never put Ruth Rushton on a list of possible targets, but she was certainly a good looking woman. No doubt the money helped. Has the best manicures and pedicures. Hairdresser every week no doubt. Make up done perfectly, quality clothes suited her figure.

'Do you think there might be a case of obsessive compulsive disorder or something like that?' Her cup and saucer were back on the coffee table again.

'Nobody's ever mentioned anything.'

'Has Mr Quinn ever mentioned an obsession with dirt, or a need for exactness in how they organise things?'

'You'd have to ask Seb. I've never met them, never been in their company.' She lifted her hands. 'Has anybody?'

'How did you come into all this?'

'How do you mean?'

'Meeting Mr Quinn?'

'Exhibition at a hall in the Bail. Seb was exhibiting there. Began chatting as you do, said he took on commissions...' she just shrugged the ending.

'And if you don't mind me asking. Your background?'

'Brigadier Lionel Rushton's second wife,' she said as if his name meant something. It didn't. 'Farms out the other side of Heighington.' Jake just looked at her and she got the message. 'Ran its course fairly quickly. We had no children, but I have a son at Sussex University from a previous relationship.' She smiled. 'Don't have a good track record, really.' Goodwin was smiling inwardly having heard about Craig and Brian's meeting with Eimear Kavanagh, so he had to ask.

'Brigadier still serving?'

'No,' told him Eimear would not approve of him being called Brigadier when he was no longer any such thing. Wondered if Ruth knew how she was over titles. There had been considerable discussion back in the office on the issue, and Goodwin himself did wonder why the military have a penchant for continuing to use their rank long after its usefulness has waned.

'Has Mr Quinn ever suggested there was conflict between the two sisters?'

'All the time,' said Ruth as if it was well known, as if Goodwin should know that already.

'Over what?'

'Being top dog. It was permanent.' She crossed her good legs. 'I think that's why they have been so successful. Striving to be top dog,

201

trying desperately to be better than each other has pushed TwinPrint on.'

'You think that's always been there? Back to when they were girls.'

'I wouldn't go as far as that. Remember, Seb hasn't known them that long.' She smiled. 'Think there's probably been a nasty streak.' She leant down to lift her cup and saucer again. 'You know he can't gain access to the house.'

'Mr Quinn?'

'Not been back since the murder.'

'Why?'

'She had the locks changed. All his things were stuffed into a couple of packing cases and left in the garage.'

'Do we know why?' Goodwin queried.

'You tell me. She was downright nasty. Told Seb on the phone he was no longer welcome and his things would be in the garage for twenty four hours, after that they'd go to charity. He had to hire a van at short notice. Most of it, apart from his clothes is still in the boxes at the back of my garage.'

'What made Sebastian a likely suspect,' said Goodwin. 'Was his lack of alibi. When we couldn't find anybody in Bassingham who had seen him, have to say we became very suspicious. Couldn't see how he'd spend six or seven hours without a drink. Thought he'd take a pack up or call in the local shop.'

'This may sound sexist, but I'm afraid Sebastian wouldn't know where to begin. Doubt whether he's ever made a sandwich in his life. Not what he's used to I'm afraid. Father was a vicar. Not the sort of thing the local reverend does is it. Take a box of sandwiches and a banana into church.' She gave a soft laugh of disdain. 'And Eilish? I'm sorry, that evil woman would never lift a finger to do such a thing. As much as she would do to make a cup of tea. You do know they never eat at home.'

'How do you mean?'

'They eat out every evening.'

'Every evening?'

'Hotel restaurants in the main. Doubtful if either of them could even boil soup or make toast. Three of them dined out.'

'And he never called in the local shop.'

'Had no need,' she said quickly. 'To be honest with his new digital camera he takes all the photos he needs, and then comes back here. Days of sitting for hours in a field have long gone. And as far as people seeing him is concerned. He'd be round here soon after six.' Goodwin waited. He sensed there was more. 'Sebastian is a rather naïve man. Brought up in a rather cloistered over protective environment. Having said that he has such a kind nature. He really is an absolute gentleman, last of a dying breed I'm afraid. Illustrated that once again by trying to protect me, when there really was no need.'

'Her being nasty about his belongings and access to the house. Was she always like that?' This was such difficult ground. Talking about someone who people regarded as being dead, but knowing she wasn't.

'In a word, yes.'

'Has he met her mother?'

Ruth shook her head. 'Not aware she's ever been back. Seb has certainly not been to Ireland.' She lifted her empty cup. 'More tea?'

Sebastian Quinn never did return while Jake Goodwin was there.

He learnt that apart from eating out daily and normal household expenditure, the Kavanagh's only luxury was foreign holidays. At least four, sometimes five times a year. According to Ruth the pair in the past year had been to Bhutan, visiting Thimpu and Amankora Punakha. In Vietnam they had cruised the Perfume River, visited Hanoi and Ho Chi Minh City. A safari in Botswana and a week in Jakarta were planned. The holiday Toni had found out about.

It was always just the two sisters. Poor Seb had to remain back in sunny Lincoln. Nowadays in the arms of Ruth. A very strange relationship.

The summer house at the bottom of the extensive garden was to be upgraded for him to use as a Studio all year round. As far as he knew, Ruth Rushton had never said it, certainly not to him, but Goodwin was convinced that she was sure Sebastian Quinn was quite innocent. There were no signs about her that she was concerned for him, or doubted him. After all, from her perspective when the sister

203

died, he was in bed with her. The Kavanagh death had nothing to do with him.

Ruth Rushton and Quinn of course were quite unaware that it had not been because of the demise of his partner that he had been thrown onto the streets. This was his partner doing this to him.

Back at base, the moment he mentioned the cleaner, Darke demanded to know why nobody had mentioned a cleaner in the early days of the inquiry. Before he could catch his breath Goodwin was given another avenue to go down. He phoned Ruth Rushton to ascertain the name of the cleaner. She agreed to phone Quinn, and in no time she was back to him and he headed for the Kavanagh houses.

Rachel Pickard was leant against the doorpost when Craig Darke finished reading yet another report.

'Why didn't she want Quinn back in the house?' he asked as he looked up, and ushered his DI to a chair.

'Good question. But we know the answer surely.' Darke frowned. 'She's his partner, but she's pretending not to be. Left alone together she'd make a mistake. There'd be some sort of intimate touch. There'd be talk about something she shouldn't know anything about. Yes, they are identical, and she wants everything the same, but in the one-to-one relationship there had to be things only they knew about, only they talked about. Like couples are, like Andy and me. All your little personal things you say to each other. Yes she's a cold bitch, but could that hold twenty four seven?'

Out at Saxilby, Jake Goodwin found Joaquima Chiquelho working away and immediately they went through the usual rigmarole of her pretending not to understand English.

It was an opportunity for Goodwin to be nosey. He had not been part of the two searches, and had only driven past the gated grounds that housed these two identical executive homes.

Five bedrooms were as everybody had said a large number for two people in one and just Eimear in the other. The kitchen was huge and a real throw back in style to how his parents' had looked when he was young, but bigger than his lounge. The lounge itself was very cream, with dark paisley patterned carpet and little furniture. A large television, a brown three piece suite that must have cost an arm and a leg and a coffee table. A bookcase and an old fashioned bureau. All dark wood all early last century to make the television look very much out of place. Big sturdy furniture you would now only find in second hand or antique shops. All very good quality but quality from another era.

Eventually young Joaquima understood and Goodwin was able to ascertain that on the morning Eilish's body was found as she approached the house, she was so frightened by what she saw with cars, an ambulance and police in numbers she had turned round and gone home. She admitted as her English improved quickly that she had phoned Eimear who said she would contact her when she was to return to work. This she had done, but only to clean for Eimear in her home.

32

Craig Darke had to be double sure about Eimear Kavanagh and made arrangements to have a chat and a practical lesson with his pal Home Office pathologist Dr Bronagh O'Carroll. He had to assume Eimear had all Eilish's documents, which meant she could be either twin anytime she liked. And she had complete control of TwinPrint, and that at the end of the day had probably been what it was all about.

Over coffee Craig and Dr Bronagh discussed the case and all its implications.

'We have a time of death of around seven or eight. Cyanide poisoning would take a matter of minutes, but your two suspects have alibis,' said Bronagh when they moved into the mortuary. The smell was always there. The disinfectant, the bleach and formaldehyde. No matter how many times he visited, it was always the same.

'Sebastian Quinn the partner was visiting a lady friend.'

'Regular or just a pick up?'

'One of those who uses divorce as a career move. Known each other a year, been lovers for about half of that. The sister Eimear Kavanagh is on CCTV arriving for work at that time.'

'We need time delay,' said Dr O'Carroll dressed in her green scrubs as her technician pushed a cadaver on a trolley past the pair of them. Clumping along in his bright blue plastic clogs. 'We know her sister or Eimear pretending to be her sister was on her second prescription. She has two choices. She can buy empty capsules. Problem there is, if Eilish has already been taking the medicine she will know what the capsules look like. What colour or in some cases what two colours. If buying matching capsules on the net isn't an option. She could have done this.'

From a small plastic box Bronagh produced two capsules she laid on the metal bench. She took a scalpel and carefully slid the blade between the two halves of the capsule, then pulled them apart and fawn coloured dusty contents spilled out. The doctor stood back and folded her arms.

206

'How's the little one?'

'She's fine,' in truth Bronagh thought young Niamh was better than that. She thought her six month old daughter was perfect.

'Sleeping?'

'Went through a bad spell, but we're fine now.'

'And Don. Happy playing at being dad?'

'New man. Your turn,' said Bronagh and handed him the scalpel. Carefully Craig repeated the process and he too had a capsule open. 'Now all you need to do is fill it with cyanide,' she said as she slipped the two halves together and using a small brush in the top of a bottle coated the join. 'Give it five minutes and it's watertight again. Swallow this now, and about nine or ten hours time your digestive system will have melted the capsule. You could be miles away by then. Happy?'

'What would I do without you? Didn't know you could get into capsules.' He looked at Bronagh. 'I even tried to get into a blister pack in my bathroom last night,' he admitted as his friend let her head shake.

Craig was more than just happy. He finished his coffee, patted Bronagh on the shoulder, pecked her on her cheek and he left her to open up another poor soul.

Left her to drive back to base racked in the torture of jealousy. Don O'Carroll had a delightful and successful wife in Bronagh and now they had little Niamh and life for them was probably perfect. What did he have apart from his career and a string of murders to solve?

Craig Darke and Brian Daniels just walked unannounced into Eimear Kavanagh's office and strode up to her desk with secretary Maureen traipsing after them.

'Eimear Keela Kavanagh,' said Brian. 'You are under arrest on suspicion of murder. I have to advise you that....'

'Stop it now!' she shouted.

'...you do not have to say anything...'

'I said stop!' she screamed and Brian did. 'We have people come into this office all the time who think they're dealing with soppy

than a bloody minute that shag took and I've been paying for the rest of my life.'

'Eimear…'

It happened in a flash. From somewhere Eimear produced a silver scalpel and in one swift movement it flashed across her neck.

Darke screamed 'No!' and launched himself as the instrument clattered down onto the desk, bounced off the edge and landed on the carpet as her eyes closed. Maureen screamed and Brian already had his phone out, as Darke grasped her shoulders, looked carefully at the tragic figure with tears strolling down her pale cheeks. Suddenly from somewhere deep inside came waves of sympathy for the woman, as he pulled her to him and held her tight. He had a need to understand.

Darke released his hold, moved his head away then sat on the desk, to look at her.

He glanced round. 'Make a cuppa,' he told the tall woman. 'Go on!' he had to shout to bring her to her senses. 'Fuckin' do it you stupid bitch!'

Darke allowed Eimear Kavanagh to just slump forward to rest her forehead on her hands on the desk and sob, as Darke slid off the desk and stooped to pick up the scalpel. It would never have done any damage, it was purely ornamental. As blunt as the butcher's dog's tail.

In front of her gawping staff Eimear Kavanagh was marched from the building and helped into a waiting police car.

Two hundred miles away tall dark-haired Niall Brian Barry finished his Olympic Breakfast in the Little Chef at Bangor, and considered making one last call from the pay-as-you-go his mother had bought in the name of his aunt. He decided against it.

He was loath to leave his mother on her own, but knew that his presence could very well jeopardize her freedom. It had all been her plan, her scheming just aided by a little early morning lifting he had been able to provide. He knew his mother simply hated being a twin, and in particular an identical twin. He also knew that had his mother and her sister not been twins, what they had achieved as a team

210

would never have been possible. They would never have been able to confuse the Police and leave them chasing rainbows.

He was also aware that had they done nothing. Simply packed up and headed back to Ireland they would be close to penniless. All his dear mother's efforts over the years would have been for nothing. Everything was owned by the company, even her home and her car. She would have given up everything for him.

Niall had been surprised at how streetwise his mother was. When she bought him a throw-away phone he was concerned where she had bought it and the address she had given. She told him so casually that it was from a motorway services and she'd given a blind address. He was staggered that she knew about such things. Find a street with a house pulled down and quote that as the address. Confuses the postman, but they usually stuff mail in the letterbox next door. Person next door then just dumps the mail in their bin. Easy peasy.

Over his coffee and toast he removed the sim card and once outside dropped it down a drain and drove his silver Suzuki Splash now with its real Irish number plates across to Holyhead and the ferry bound for Dublin. Ten miles out he'd toss the pay-as-you-go overboard down into the waves. Possibly just for fun, he'd make one last call to the cops in Lincoln to throw them a lifeline they could never grasp.

Niall had waited over twenty years to be reunited with his mother, and although the few months together had been a ridiculous clandestine relationship it had still been very special. Three years his mother said she had been secretly searching on line for him. He had her to thank and 'mum and dad' Peter and Deirdre Barry who were aware of his desire to make contact with his own flesh and blood and had offered assistance in his long search. They would of course remain part of his life.

All he had to do now was wait for the bewildered bumpkin cops to realise the evidence they had was no evidence, and he and his mother would be reunited permanently back in the home country that beckoned them both.

He could then become Niall Brian Kavanagh, the person he had always wanted to be.

33

Like us all, policemen also need somebody to talk to at times of great stress. As ever Craig Darke had nobody. Nothing to take his mind off it all. Brian would no doubt have left the sight of that poor distressed woman slumped in her chair at his front door. Mentioned the events very briefly to his wife, then sought out his son for a kick about in the garden.

A week down the line Craig Darke gathered his team together and with Eimear Kavanagh released on Police bail, explained it all to them, but not before Brian Daniels threw a reminder at him.

'Don't forget it's Sammy's wedding bash on Wednesday.' It wouldn't be as bad as a 'couples' event where he knew he would be like a fish out of water. Holding a little event in the local pub to celebrate her forthcoming wedding and give her a present was something he could handle. Knew he'd have to make a bit of a speech, but that was no problem and would make a change. Make a change from ravioli and another episode of *Brit Cops*.

'What did we get her in the end?'

'Quality saucepans.'

'Can she cook?'

'No idea.' Darke chuckled.

'Settle down everybody,' he called out and waited. 'Eimear Kavanagh the elder of the two like her sister had her name swapped. Why? We'd never have guessed, and even now we don't know for sure, but Eimear told me she thinks it was punishment for her pregnancy. By changing names, Fergus made her Eilish and made her by that, the younger daughter and lost all the advantages and ultimately control of TwinPrint. I'm convinced it was also to do with smuggling dope, but we'll never prove that. I reckon that's how he funded TwinPrint.'

'By now,' Daniels added. 'Eilish has become the younger sister and ends up with the minority shareholding.'

'I've spoken to people at the Border Agency and they reckon twenty years ago when things were less sophisticated than they are now, a man and a woman and a young girl with a backpack wouldn't get a second glance.'

'Could have gone back and forth,' added Daniels. 'Clocking up the pounds every week with a little trip back home.'

'Ten years ago her mother had become homesick and wanted to move back to Ireland. My guess is she didn't want to come here in the first place. They couldn't go back to Wexford because the father was still public enemy number one, so they handed the business over to the girls and went off to a place called Roscommon near Athlone. Fergus Kavanagh had a cardiac arrest four years ago and died. This left Mary Kavanagh alone with her religion. The reason contact with her daughter Eimear was to remain absolutely impossible. Being pregnant outside marriage for her is a mortal sin that will last a lifetime, even in this day and age.'

During interview Darke had discovered that other side to Eimear. The real person. A really lovely articulate, but sad woman. A million miles away from the bitch he had encountered in her office on more than one occasion. Truth was Eimear then Eilish and finally back to being Eimear had been acting her part, pretending to be her sister. Two identical twins but absolute poles apart in personality, as a result of totally different upbringings. The spoilt young thing doted on by her parents and in particular her mother had been turned into a nasty piece of work. Eimear on the other hand had suffered three years of manual labour almost behind bars with the nuns. Was obviously thankful for her new life compared with her sister who had regarded it as her right.

Both officers had to wait for the chatter to stop.

'And neither of them knew of course,' said a grinning Daniels. 'That Seb had got himself a woman and was himself getting ready to move out. Somehow it all comes to a head when Eilish wants to take a sabbatical and search out her kid. Her sister's having none of it, and as majority shareholder has all the power. Probably another fanatic who will never accept a child born out of wedlock, like their stupid mother.'

'When we say all the power, we mean all the power,' Darke emphasized.. 'Any time she liked, her sister could wipe her out of TwinPrint.'

'Stuff about family trees was all IT found on her PC. Dozens and dozens of websites she'd been on, we assume trying to track the kid she was forced to give up for adoption. Most of the sites she's made hits on are Irish ones of course like *Ancestry Ireland*. Plenty of their family history societies, but she's also delved into *Scotland's People* and others.'

'We're pretty certain Eilish put the cyanide in Eimear's capsules,' said Darke. 'Eilish had probably set this up ages ago. Took it upon herself to get the prescriptions. Had taken the capsules out of the blister packs and put them in one of those brown bottles. Her sister doesn't know any different. As far as she was aware her medicine always came in a little bottle. Eilish has got so much printing know-how she might even have printed new labels for the bottles. Then when the time came, simply changed the bottles over.'

'Next morning,' said Daniels. 'She did one of two things. Either moved the body from one house to the other, or somehow got her sister to pop next door before she fell ill and died. Then she puts the blister pack with the remaining real capsules in the bathroom cabinet and dumps the bad ones and both the bottles.'

'Then Eilish goes off to work,' Darke added. 'Cool as a cucumber turns up at TwinPrint as Eimear…'

'And starts laying down the law as she knew she'd have to.'

'Even has the nerve to phone poor old Seb to tell him his partner Eilish is dead. But of course his partner isn't dead.'

'So in effect,' said Rachel Pickard. 'Seb's dead partner phoned him to tell him she was dead.'

'If you put it like that. She phoned him from the grave.'

'Amazing what you can do with a smart phone!'

'It's all irrelevant now, but Forensics have got finger prints for Eimear in only one house. She forgot to put her own fingerprints on stuff in her sister's house she would have used if she was the person she was pretending to be.'

'Have to be honest with you.' Suddenly Darke had become very serious. 'Don't think CPS will see this through. How do we prove she did what we think she did? Can we really get a jury to believe she's guilty because there are none of her fingerprints, when she's got a cleaner who spring cleans daily? And four prints belonging to

214

who? They're not on the National Database. Don't belong to any of the staff we've checked, or one or two who've retired on bad terms. Only capsules we have are the real ones, legitimately obtained by prescription. No witnesses.' Darke hesitated. 'I think she'll go back to Ireland.'

'Seems in this case we're good with absences rather than presences,' Rachel offered. 'People who weren't there rather that those who were.'

'Think money will rule in the end,' said Darke. 'DNA of identical twins is more or less identical. Trouble is it would cost upwards of a million pounds to conduct an ultra-sophisticated genetic test to separate her DNA from her sister's.' He pulled a slip of paper from his pocket. 'Normal analysis compares four hundred base pairs of nucleotides. To separate those two they're talking about billions.'

'Has anybody heard anything about the kid?' d'Andrea queried, as the team took in what they'd been told.

'No,' said Rachel. 'Our man over in Ireland had just made contact with relatives. With Eilish dead and Eimear on bail, we've decided to back off. With it all being a delicate situation now, we handed it over to the Garda. But to be honest I don't think they give a toss.'

'Think the truth is, once her sister was dead; she simply reverted to who she really was.' Darke looked around the room. 'We thought she was up to goodness knows what, when all the time she was probably just being herself. She'll sell up, and go back home is my guess. Maybe carry on trying to find her son.'

'Bit like being the invisible man. We thought she was trying to be somebody who didn't exist.'

'Wake up in the morning and think. Who shall I be today?'

'Who we've got to be today, need I remind you' said Darke seriously. 'Is the team that finds who killed Gorich and Petchey. Back to it.'

215

34

Craig blew out a weary breath stood with the freezer door open trying to decide on the delight he would choose for his evening meal. Katherine Jenkins' *Serenade* playing loud enough on the system in his lounge for him to hear, and for the name to act as a reminder. It was the night of Sammy Lloyd's pre-wedding do in the pub. A buffet had been organised, but even so Craig felt he would need more than just a sausage roll and a vol au vent. A paper plate and a glass is always a balancing act one has to endure, so the less food you have to juggle the better. His front door bell rang.

'Yes,' was full of total disinterest as he pulled the big blue door open. Jillie. 'You're just in time for tea. Sorry, in your world it's probably dinner,' was an unnecessary jibe. 'You'll have to make do with Chicken and Herb Pasta or Chicken Tikka. Might be able to push the boat out and have a Lasagna.' He stood aside and she walked into his hall. The rivulets of hair ran to her shoulders in waves of reds, oranges and gingers. No words and lack of a kiss was very ominous. 'Coffee's on,' he said a little abruptly when they reached his kitchen, and pointed to the machine in the corner to the left of the window.

'You want one?' she asked.

'Got one,' he said and pointed to a blue mug on the table next to a dark maroon folder as he turned and disappeared to go to Katherine's aid and turn her off. Singing to nobody is such a pain, and the two women in his life were more than enough.

'Still working?' she asked when he returned.

'What else is there?' received no reply, as Jillie got on with pulling a matching mug off a hook, adding black coffee and then a little milk she found in the fridge.

'You sitting here?' she asked and pulled the chair out an inch or two more for him. Craig sat down, pushed the file to one side, rested his arms on the wooden table, and looked up at her. Loose alpaca cardigan, dark grey expensive looking woollen top and skinny jeans.

'This it then is it? Bit like coming back into court for the verdict. Would the foreman of the jury please stand'

She ignored him, rested back against the sink and splayed her arms left and right along the work surface. She looked left and right, up and down.

'Nice.'

'Thank you,' was bland.

'You're in serious trouble.'

'Is that right?' was no better.

'A dozen red roses every Friday was cheating.'

'Nobody told me there were rules.'

'Oh I'm sorry officer I didn't know I needed insurance for my car. Nobody told me there were rules,' triggered a smile. 'They were lovely.'

'My pleasure madam.'

'Shouldn't have put us through it, but I'm pleased I did,' she said as she crossed her lovely legs at the ankle, and cleared her throat. 'From time to time you read about these silly schoolgirls who have a crush on their teachers. Now and again they run off together, and they're all over the papers, and eventually he gets arrested and they're both in trouble. Usually a step father hovering in the background and you wonder what's been going on there. Teacher's married and she's underage. One or two stick it out, stay together through thick and thin, get married or live together and eventually.' She stopped to sip her coffee and went back to her stance. 'Goes tits up in the end usually. Well, to be honest nearly always. Been reading about it quite a bit recently on the net. What seems all sweetness and light. Loves young dream when you're a giggly schoolgirl is a whole different ball game when you're up the spout with your second kid and a pile of nappies in a rented one bedroom flat. He can't get a teaching job for love nor money, coz he's on the child offence register thingy.' She lifted the mug again and sipped. Craig watched her intently, desperate for her to get on with it, get to the big goodbye. 'Reckon I've found the answer.' She leant forward and placed her mug on the table. 'Best way is to subconsciously fall in love with this great teacher, but not realize it at the time and being with him is great fun and he's like your bestest mate. Absolutely love your time with him. But that's as far as it goes and you sort of put it on hold. Quite unaware he has left this indelible mark on your brain. Then you go off and do all the things you need to do like grow up and go to uni but not necessarily in that order, then one day you come back. I think you need to go through the experiences to see others for what they are. Something the pimply schoolgirl never does with her handsome teacher. And when you do return if you're really lucky…' It was as if suddenly she had a need to pluck up the courage to continue. She looked left and right.

'And…?'

'You realize you've been in love with him all the time, and you want to be with him if he'll have you. Now probably more than ever.' Craig wanted her to repeat what she had just said. 'We still on the honesty kick?' A nod was as much as he could manage. 'First time you kissed me, was that like…like no other kiss ever? As if it was the best ever yet at the same time very wrong, all illicit and very naughty but sweet and tender and don't tell my mum?'

'Yeh,' he admitted and confirmed it with a slow nod.

'Wasn't just me then.' Jillie pushed off from the sink took the few paces to clasp his face in her hands before their lips were together for another soft and tender kiss and the excitement had control of her.

'What about Germany?'

'You scuppered that. Before the Spring Fayre thing, going to Frankfurt was a strong possibility. Then you turn up, and then the roses. No way,' she smiled, then kissed him very gently. 'Bugger the Germans.'

'London it is then.'

'Not really.' The look she received told her to explain. 'I'm setting up a consultancy. Primarily to invest for me. I can play the markets at home and abroad. Talked to my old mentor and he's setting the wheels in motion. Offer a service to others who want to delve into the world of futures. Sort of financial consultancy with a difference.'

'Where d'you plan to do this?' Jillie bit her lip and looked up at the ceiling.

'Got a few questions,' she said in no more than a whisper. 'Can I have a look at your office? Can you bring my case in from the car?' she kissed him. 'We need to talk about something else after we've eaten, and any chance I can have the pasta?'

'What sort of day have you had then mister?' Jillie asked Craig the moment he walked in, as she poured coffee from the pot into two mugs. When she turned to look at him, she put her hands up. 'Explain the hair.' She said and smiled.

'Hair?'

'Yes. Why today have you combed your hair. Why does it look very smart and neat?' Craig half turned. 'No you don't. Come back here and explain.' He looked like a naughty schoolboy just found out by his mother.

'When I joined the force a mop of hair like I had back then was not acceptable. So I had it cut and it was always neat and tidy. Then I was out having a drink with a few lads back then and somebody asked why even when I was out I looked as though I was going to work.' He stopped to grimace. 'I just ruffled up my hair. Now I comb it neat and tidy for work, then when I'm home I ruffle it up and give it a bit of gel.' He looked at her adding milk to the mugs. 'Think it looks stupid?'

'No. Not at all. The ruffled looks good, but I can see you can't be a DCI with hair like that.' She slid a mug along towards him. 'Good day?'

'In life, nothing ever works out the way you think it will.' He said and leant back against the larder fridge. 'This morning was amazing. I've had a day of great news and real sadness, and coming home to you like this is very special.' She could see by the look on his face it meant so much to him, moved the few paces and they kissed..

'The good and bad?' she queried as she moved away.

'I was really nervous first thing,' he said. 'Silly really. Knew they'd all go on about you being at the pub last night. Me going to the pub was probably news in itself, but turning up with you. Wow! Bet that set the hares racing. Then when that calmed down a little, telling people you're pregnant was amazing.' Jillie moved to take

219

hold of his hand. 'One minute I'm flying high with my team taking the mickey and calling me daddy, next minute it's a real mixture.' Craig stopped to drink coffee as Jillie slid a chocolate biscuit in his direction. 'Truly a day of real contrasts. Talk about light and dark.'

'In what way?'

'Had a jumper,' he took a bite. 'Woman jumped off a car park.' He shrugged. 'It happens.' He blew out a breath. 'Suicide note in her pocket. So bloody sad. Taken us all day to piece some of it together.'

'You have to deal with suicides?'

'In this case, when they found the note they were straight onto us. Turns out this is a woman I've met. Apparently she was a foundling.' He sipped coffee. 'According to a neighbour, her mother abandoned her at about three days old. This couple eventually adopted her. The world being the way it is, as if being dumped is not enough bad luck, the bloke who had adopted her got killed in an industrial accident. The girl was only about seven at the time.'

'To he that hath shall be given...'

'And a poor bastard like her has everything taken away.'

'Life's a real shit at times.'

'Eventually she finished up working on family court proceedings at the county court.' He sipped. 'I've spoken to her a few times. She's articulate and very bright, or should I say was very bright, but really nerdy. Sort of Mummy's girl. Looks geeky.' He stopped and pondered. 'How shall I put this? Dentally challenged I suppose you'd say. Clothes were somehow all wrong, and I always got the feeling her hairdresser took the piss out of her when he cut her hair. Or her mother did it, or she did it herself. It's awful. Found out today, she's been the carer for her mother for years. Adopted mother that is.' He stopped for more biscuit and coffee. 'Mother's been getting gradually worse apparently, housebound and in the end almost bed bound, so we're told.' He banged his first down on the work surface. 'What had poor bloody Mavis done to deserve all that?'

'You seriously have to doubt the presence of a real God.'

'Whole thing must have got to her. No boyfriends, no proper friends at all as far as we can make out so far. Never seen her away from the court, but I guess you'd say she was socially awkward. People like that are often intense and very good at their work, which

I have to say she was. Then something gets to her seriously. Scrag arsed woman in court taking out a court order to stop the father of her kid seeing their child. Mavis it seems hears and reads more than she should have probably, and she works out she's doing it to spite her ex. Got no good reason, just feminine revenge. In her suicide letter she calls her jealous and controlling. Her own mother gave her away remember and she never knew her real dad. Or her mother come to that.'

'Don't tell me.' She gasped. 'Not one of these where the parent kills the kids?' Jillie pleaded.

'No. Our friend Mavis Chatterton killed this Gorich bitch.'

'You mean…?'

'Murder number one, last November. That's what this has all been about. These women using their kids as tools in their fight against the blokes they're shacked up with. Revenge of course is a female trait, often for its own sake. Mavis Chatterton never knew her father, and then when she had a substitute dad he got killed. My guess is this Mavis knew she was different. That she was a virgin nerd, never one of the girls. People sniggering and pointing. Probably had the piss taken out of her at school. Bullied all her life. Local yobs probably made her life a bloody misery.'

'Men won't give her the time of day.'

'Exactly. Or women come to that. No heels, handbags or botox so they're not interested. It's probably built up over the years. Seeing bad mothers being given custody over good fathers. In all the stuff she's written she refers to equality time and again. About women wanting equal rights, yet so often inequality in the treatment of children takes priority, through their lies.'

'How have we got to the state where we allow these feral women to use sex and the resulting unwanted children as a tool to beat a decent society with?' Jillie shook her head. 'Can you imagine how it must have got to this Mavis?'

'That's why she set out to stop it happening to other kids.' Craig took a good drink. 'The lad who's the father of Caron Gorich's kid is looking after him, with the help of his family. Good decent lad's got a job, looks like he's making a go of it.' He let out a sigh. 'That was our first murder. Knew she must have known whoever it was to let

221

her in. Something to do with seeing her in court possibly. Except we thought it was a bloke all along. Never gave thought to a woman doing it. Probably never know the full story now. Then along comes another one, and our Mavis is ready for this cow.'

'Another murder?' Craig nodded.

'Kirsty Petchey's out clubbing morning noon and night. We knew that much. Dumps the little girl on her mother, wont let the father anywhere near the kid, but is bedding some Rastafarian tosspot. According to Mavis's confession she told the court she's a perfect mother and the boyfriend's a total bastard and beat her up. My sergeant who interviewed him said he didn't appear to be that sort, and there's no record of violence at all. Mavis Chatterton described her as a slut and strangled her with one of those plastic ties.' Craig Darke looked up at the ceiling. 'Almost feel as if I want to say, carry on Mavis, here's a few more names you can have.'

'That number two?' Jillie checked and received a nod in return.

'This suicide note confession she's typed out on her PC tells us everything.' Craig stopped to think for a moment. 'Lads are still piecing it all together. Reckon she must have been checking up on her. Knew this Petchey is a spiteful vengeful bitch who went out all dressed up, or dressed down more like. Spending her benefit money on cheap booze rather than on her little kid. Strangling was easy. Our Mavis is not as stupid as she'd been painted. Think it all came to a head when her mother finally died. She was left with nothing. Probably only planned one, then realised her mother couldn't be embarrassed by her actions. Guess she knew somehow we'd catch up with her and had nothing to live for. Thought of prison and what they'd do to someone like her in there probably frightened her to death. What a waste.'

'Two murders you couldn't fathom' Craig nodded his head. 'Guess prison for her would only be an extension of what her life has been like, but only worse.'

'Talking to her line manager this afternoon. He confirmed how thorough she was. Considered she had a photographic memory that was never really put to good use. In her circumstance there was never a chance of her going to university.'

222

'If she was really meticulous she probably planned it all down to the finest detail.'

'That's now very obvious. Man in Imps red and white hat, man in black hat and black coat, man in yellow coat. All the same person. Our Mavis. She's a big woman, bit over six foot. Bloody coat was reversible. In the confession – and there's pages and pages of it, she even apologised for messing us about, said she thought about limping going over the level crossing on the spur of the moment. Burnt stuff, threw evidence in the river, buried other bits. Threw her shoes away. All sorts.'

Jillie chuckled. 'She had you beat.'

Craig sniggered at the suggestion. 'We were looking at doctors and nurses for the syringe murder. It was Mavis all along; she had to give her mother an injection sometimes three times a day. She could probably do it better than any Ward Sister I know. Pathologist even told me she thought it was done by a professional. She might as well have been the number of times she'd done it.' Jillie watched anger envelope his face. 'D'you know, according to the woman next door, the bloody district nurse who was supposed to deal with her mother persuaded poor Mavis to do it most of the time, when she wanted evenings off or just couldn't be bothered.'

'That's awful!' Jillie gasped, as Craig let his head rock from side to side. 'Bet she got paid though.'

Jillie looked at her man. 'In the house forensic boys found all her paperwork, things like gas bills, bank statements all perfectly filed. Found a letter too. From her …' He stopped and looked at the floor. 'Landlord telling her that as her mother had died and she wasn't a blood relative she'd have to vacate the property. I'm sorry but what sort of f...' Craig screwed his hands into fists in front of his face. 'Arseholes are these people?' and he blew out a breath of anguish. 'What had she got to live for? Parents both gone, about to get kicked out of her two up two down little home. Imagine what life in a crummy bed sit would be like for someone like her.'

'You all right?' Jillie asked but knew he wasn't.

'If she'd been a drain on society. If she'd been one of these feral youths on benefit with a fat sod in tow, society would have given her a decent home and a plasma tele. She'd have a bunch of over-paid diversity wasters in tie-dyed skirts and sandals offering her this that and the other. All paid for by the state' Craig took a big gulp of coffee. 'What did these useless bastards give her? Nothing. We spend too much time thinking about ourselves. Don't give enough of our time and of ourselves to others. To decent people not just scumbags.' He rested his arms on the work surface and peered through the kitchen window into the garden and trees beyond. 'If only I'd taken the time to stop and talk to her. It's not as if she was invisible. I knew she was an odd ball, on the outside looking in. Probably crying out for help.' Craig spun round and looked at Jillie. 'What did people do? They just took the piss out of her. It's not her fault those women are dead. It's ours. And she's had to pay the price.'

'You weren't to know,' she said, got to her feet and took his forearms in her hands. 'You can't stop and help every person you see who somehow doesn't fit the norm. I'm sorry, but there's so many odd bods these days, you can't help them all, and most of them wouldn't thank you for it anyway.' She smiled up at him. 'That's been a hellava day.'

'Think that's what you call a good day's work. I've got the answer to two murders and I've got my Sunday school pupil pregnant.' Craig Darke stood there smiling at her.

'You never have!' Jillie shot at him and stepped back hands to her open mouth in mock horror. 'You haven't got one of your Sunday school kids up the duff! That's terrible!' She patted her tummy and laughed out loud. 'You'll be in real trouble when the Police find out!'

EPILOGUE

For more than a century it was suggested that girls in Ireland who were promiscuous or worse became pregnant, were sent by their parents to workhouses run by the Catholic Church. These are now known as the Magdelene laundries.

These teenage girls so it is said were forced to work in laundries from dawn to dusk all year round in squalid conditions and fed little more than gruel. These workhouses were specifically built like prisons with high walls, locked gates and bars at the windows.

Some of the nuns who oversaw the girls so it appears, had at one time been inmates themselves and it is said they were the worst at handing out punishment.

The very existence of places renowned for their harsh regimes and industrial schools funded by the state and operated by religious orders were made known to most young women.

Just the thought of these asylums and 'stories' of what went on in them was used by parents as a form of discipline in an attempt to retain the rigid character of the Irish Catholic church.

There are those even to this day who deny their actuality, who say that due to the country's archaic attitude to sex, the suggestion of such brutal regimes in itself was enough to retain virginity amongst the young female population without them ever existing.

In 2013 the Irish Prime Minister, Enda Kenny, said he was sorry for what the women went through but issued no formal apology on behalf of the state.

***

By the same author:

A Shot of Snuff

ACKNOWLEDGEMENTS

My gratitude to all those who gave their time and of themselves to help me with research for *Dead Spit.*

Many of those who have done so will have contributed without any knowledge of having been involved. People I observed in a variety of coffee houses, restaurants and shops. On buses, planes and trains or just going about their business. Folk badly dressed or beautifully attired. Those with strong opinions, I agree with or with whom I beg to differ. The courteous and the rude constantly inspire me with their behaviour and attitudes. All providing information I am often able to use to build and develop the story and characterization.

To everyone, a big thanks for just being you.

Until the next time…

Printed in Great Britain
by Amazon

34431858R00128